Take Me to the Wedding

MIRANDA LIASSON

Published by Hawthorne House Press

Miranda Liasson, LLC

P.O. Box 13707

Fairlawn, OH 44334

www.mirandaliasson.com

Print ISBN 978-0-9986346-4-7

E-book ISBN 978-0-9986346-3-0

Cover by Kim Killion Designs

Author photo @2023 by M2Photos

Published in the United States of America

 Created with Vellum

Also by Miranda Liasson
(www.mirandaliasson.com/bookshelf):

The Doctors of Oak Bluff (Take Me Series)

Take Me Home for Christmas

Seashell Harbor Series

Sweetheart Series

Angel Falls Series

Mirror Lake Series

Kingston Family Series

For anyone who works in a children's hospital.
You are special!

Prologue

Caleb

If you're lucky, you'll know the exact moment that you meet the love of your life. A chance meeting, a glance, a quick lock of the gaze, and *wham*! Your life is changed forever. You've found your person, someone you'll be there for forever, and they'll be there for you, no matter what life throws at you.

I, Caleb D'Angelo, was eighteen when it happened to me. I never thought anything or anyone could ever come between us. Call me a romantic. Or just someone who believes in the power of true love.

But stuff happens—life happens—and Lilly and I didn't survive my move to med school. We were so young when we started dating. We had zero experience in the world. Med school turned into residency, and I moved on. At least, I tried. Outwardly, I'm sure it seemed like I was having a lot of fun. Yes, I dated around. I'm not bragging when I say that I was pretty popular, and finding someone to date was never hard.

But finding someone to love is.

The truth is, I've never stopped wondering *what if* with Lilly. And now she's free. Except someone I work with spread some gossip about me, and it got back to her.

As for that annoying colleague of mine who thought the worst of me and ruined my chances with the woman I love—well, she's impossible. As much as I'm easygoing and friendly, she's driven, outspoken, and never fails to give me a hard time. She's judgy and she hates my guts. We clash so much that I finally did something about it. I asked for another anesthesiologist for my case. *Anyone* besides her.

That made her dislike me even more. The problem is that I *have* to be nice to her because she's my sister's best friend. And we're both in the same wedding at the end of this summer. And, ironically, so is Lilly. All three of us. *Yay.*

But I'm not going to let Samantha Bashar ruin my chances with Lilly—again.

I have a plan. I'm going to find out if Lilly and I are meant to be together. And nothing—and no one—not even the she-devil herself—is going to stand in my way.

I'm going to hold my friends close... and my enemies even closer.

Chapter One

Samantha

I rolled back the curtain to the patient bay in the pre-surgical area of Children's Milwaukee and gave a thumbs-up to a nine-year-old boy lying on a gurney, looking small and stark against the white sheets. Flanked on either side by his worried parents, he lifted a skinny arm, now attached to an IV board, giving me a gap-toothed smile and a thumbs-up right back.

That smile melted me and made me want to live up to all that trust in his eyes. "Hey, my man, you ready?" I did a fist bump with his non-IV-boarded hand.

"Yep," he said with a big nod and a grin, full of positive energy despite being less than an hour away from a third surgery on his right femur, which had been badly fractured in a car accident a year ago.

"Let's do it then." I smiled at his parents, who didn't look nearly as calm, his dad anxiously tapping his foot and his mom holding her hands tightly in her lap.

I saw the fear in their eyes. Surgery was scary. But it was also life-changing. And this one would finally give Joseph a chance to be a normal kid again by evening out the length of his legs so he'd be able to run—not limp. It would give him wings.

"Hi, Dr. Bashar," Joseph's mom, Terry, said. "We're so relieved you'll be doing Joey's case today."

"I wouldn't miss it," I said.

"After this one, I'm gonna be GTG," Joseph said.

I shot Joseph and his parents a puzzled look. "Good to go," Terry said, smoothing her son's hair back from his forehead. "Dr. D'Angelo taught him that."

Dr. Caleb D'Angelo, the pediatric orthopedic fellow—meaning he'd finished his orthopedic residency and was doing a special fellowship year in pediatric orthopedics here at Children's—would be doing the case today. He was a good doctor, but we didn't get along at all. But because he was my best friend Mia's brother, I had to at least try.

"I'm going to play baseball and run track. Right, Dr. Sam? That's what Dr. Caleb said."

"That's the plan, Stan," I said as I prepared to do my routine pre-op assessment.

"My name's not Stan," he said with a giggle.

His hopeful and trusting demeanor tore me up inside. It roused all my protective instincts, as it did with all the kids I cared for as a pediatric anesthesiologist in my last few months of training. Then I'd be GTG, ready for a real job. And I couldn't wait.

Joseph's dad, Henry, squeezed his son's leg. "Last surgery, buddy. Let's get it done."

"Hey, everyone," my friend Ani, who was Joseph's pediatrician, called from behind me. She showcased a bright smile and two to-go cups of coffee that she passed to his grateful-looking parents. Funny what a good cup of coffee could do during a stressful time. "I just stopped to say hi and break a leg," she said. Joseph frowned. "Oh, sorry. That means good luck, but maybe that wasn't the best way to say it." She threaded her arm through mine. "Hey, y'all, I have to borrow Dr. Bashar for a minute, but we'll be right back!"

Ani was a human tornado, full of energy and endless optimism, all jam-packed into a five-foot-two frame. She was getting married in the middle of June, in just three weeks, and I was lucky enough to be one of her bridesmaids even if I personally didn't believe in love—at least for myself. But I tried to keep that opinion quiet.

Before I knew it, I was being pulled by the elbow down the bright central aisle of the surgical floor by a petite powerhouse of a woman with a halo of blond curls as a parade of people in scrubs all colors of the rainbow passed by, some dragging EKG and portable X-ray machines, others cradling their own early-morning Starbucks. Almost everyone smiled.

That's how it was in a children's hospital. No one was here for themselves. And everyone had one mission—the kids. I was so proud to work here.

"Sam, I'm so sorry," Ani whispered, stopping halfway down the hall, which filled me with sudden dread. "There's been a last-minute switch. Erin's been named anesthesiologist on this case, ortho fellow's orders. I tried to buy you some time—I told her to come back in ten minutes to do the pre-op interview."

My first reaction was confusion. Last-minute switches were unusual. "The ortho fellow took me off the case?" Suddenly the truth dawned. *"Caleb?"*

Ani didn't need to nod. The solemn look in her eyes confirmed everything. Hot indignation boiled my blood. *"He* did this." *He* being that awful splinter in my heel, the one person I tended to lock horns with personally and professionally.

Unbelievable—but predictable since there'd been no love lost between us from the very first time we'd met. I tapped my finger against my lips as I paced, trying to wrap my head around the fact that the person I despised the most was about to prevent me from doing my job on a case. Not any case: Joseph's case. I'd been in on both previous surgeries. I had a special place in my heart for this family. They knew and trusted me.

Some people thought that anesthesiologists were good at technology and procedures but had little bedside manner, but that was not true. One of the most important things we do daily is to help to calm and reassure patients and families on some of the scariest days of their lives.

Ani squeezed my arm. "I'm really sorry, Sam. Go talk with him." I immediately started to take off to do just that, but she held me back one last time. "More flies with honey," she warned.

"Thanks," I mumbled. She knew me too well. My tendency to jump into anything with both feet was good for tense situations in the OR but sometimes bad for conflict resolution. I often spoke my mind first and thought later. I guess that was why I wasn't a diplomat.

This time I had to be careful. I was in the last months of my pediatric anesthesia fellowship, and I'd applied to join the anesthesia group here at Children's. I couldn't afford to be unprofessional no matter how annoying Caleb was.

This was the first time any of our conflicts had escalated to this level. I'd make sure it would be the last. I couldn't allow anything to interfere with getting this job.

I strode at a fast clip across the massive pre-op area, my bright pink Danskos squeaking on the shiny tile floor. Around me, I heard the *screek* of curtains being pulled back on patient bays and gurneys being wheeled down the central aisle as the unit buzzed to life under the bright white lights like the floodlights of a movie set. *Lights, camera, action.*

I passed the giant whiteboard with all the day's cases. Sure enough, my name had been erased and replaced by my colleague Erin's.

I struggled to slow my breathing. A quick touch to my cheeks indicated that they were as fiery as my temper. This was sadly my normal reaction to Caleb. Nothing I did helped me to calm down. I was the emoji with the brains about to blow off its head.

One final turn and the object of my wrath came into plain sight. He stood at the central nursing station, his tall frame a little hunched over as he quietly examined an electronic tablet in his hands, prepping for his first surgery.

We'd miraculously managed to be civil to one another, especially at work. But this... this stunt meant war. I approached the desk where he was deep in thought, his thick, wavy hair tumbling forward as he read.

Before I could speak, Dr. Agarwal, one of the ortho attendings, walked up and slapped him on the back. "You ready, son? I'm just going to stand by and watch. The helm is yours, okay?"

Caleb saluted. "Aye, aye, Captain. As ready as I can be, sir."

Their interaction was friendly and harmless, a show of both how well Caleb was liked and his easygoing humor. It also showed —to me, a female physician—how male physicians spoke to each other. Would any attending, female or male, call me "daughter"?

I understood that I had built-in anger toward charismatic men: my mother had been briefly married to one, my father. After their divorce, he swept in and out of my childhood, promising the world and delivering only disappointment after disappointment, until finally he left for good. And my mother had ultimately done the same. So I saw through Caleb's charisma better than most. I tolerated him for Mia's sake and for the occasional times we had to share an OR.

My grandma, Oma, had warned me that a man could be a woman's downfall as had been my mother's. I prided myself on being the type of woman who didn't need that kind of man or, frankly, any man for that matter. Love was a fairy tale. Independence, strength, and self-sufficiency were what mattered. Men could be fun, but in general, they all sucked. I'd never had any reason to believe otherwise.

Dr. Agarwal left and I stepped up. A soapy smell filled the area surrounding Caleb that I immediately identified as Spring Fresh Dial, my own money-saving favorite that I bought in twelve-packs from the Dollar Store. Okay, so he smelled clean, and his looks might have been kissed by the angels, but I was not deterred. Looking around, I saw several people charting and making phone calls behind the massive nursing station. "Can I talk to you?" I asked while gesturing with my head toward a nearby door that led to the back transport hallway.

We walked through the double doors into the hallway, which was empty for now except for a lineup of clean gurneys along the sides. I waited for the doors to fully close behind us before I confronted him. "Why did you bump me from that case?" I struggled to keep my voice calm and even as Ani had advised.

He looked at me, his pale green eyes quietly assessing me, starting with my bright pink clogs, which caused him to lift a brow in disdain, up to my safari-print scrubs (hey, I work in a children's hospital) and my bouffant-cap-covered hair, ready for the OR. I ignored the unusual but intriguing color of his eyes and his calm, intelligent—if derisive—gaze. Women tended to fall at his surgical shoe-covered feet. His smiley, glass-always-full personality drew men and women like a magnet. But I found him childlike and entitled.

His thick, dark brows knit down in a frown as he seemed to carefully search for words. As if he could actually defuse the bomb that he'd already detonated. "Yes, that was me," he said, not really answering my question.

"At least you're not denying it."

He exhaled and then spoke carefully. "Look, Samantha, it wasn't a professional decision. You're good at what you do. But you're so—" His voice trailed off.

I crossed my arms and urged him to continue as I silently plotted his demise. "So...?"

"...argumentative," he said decisively, filling in the blank. "Headstrong. Obstinate."

"That's three adjectives telling me I'm determined. One would be plenty, thanks."

I *was* focused and goal-directed—and proud of it. I didn't allow people to trample on me. I stood up for myself. I'd had plenty of practice getting places on my own strength—my own stubborn will. Unlike him, who cruised by on his good looks and who played—a lot—instead of being serious. Who dated and discarded women faster than Kleenex. In fact, his latest victim had been my friend Nora, a nurse practitioner from the NICU, whom he'd recently reduced to an endless font of tears.

"I didn't want to deal with your, um—determination—in the OR during a tough case," he said. "It's unprofessional. Not to mention bad for patient care. And distracting."

"I *am* good at what I do." I enunciated every word slowly and carefully. "And I'm *never* unprofessional." I would never create drama, especially in the OR, that sanctum sanctorum where any careless error could mean the difference between life and death.

"You get along with everyone except me. You disagree with me on everything—publicly."

I frowned. "Like what?"

"You always give me grief when I ask you to turn up the pain control."

I tossed up my hands. "A surgeon has no conception of how much pain control the patient needs. I'm monitoring the patient while you surgerize, remember?" I tapped my chest a little too emphatically. "*My* job."

He did not appear convinced. "The table was too high, and whenever I ask you to lower it, you huff." He looked down his nose at me, which I had to say was his only imperfect feature. It was a little bit large, with the tiniest bit of a dorsal bump. Staring at that tiny imperfection gave me the courage to gather my thoughts.

Maybe I *had* fought him on some petty things. But if I was defensive, it was because he irritated me in a way that no one else did. "I know this family. I've done the anesthesia on both of Joseph's other surgeries. You know how much this means to me."

I had to shut down this entire issue fast. If the anesthesia chair, Dr. Benson, found out, I'd be crossed off the prospective employee list faster than the time it takes for the sedating effect of a Propofol drip to kick in.

"I'm sorry," Caleb said firmly, "but I can't have power struggles in my OR."

I shook my head, momentarily speechless. "*My* OR?" A voice in my head told me to put on the brakes. *Think of Mia.* His sister, my best friend. I would never do anything to put our friendship in jeopardy. Mia was wonderful, the dearest friend I'd ever had, and she was everything her dumb brother wasn't.

More urgently, all of us—Mia, Caleb, and I—were in Ani's wedding. She was marrying Tyler Banks, an invasive cardiologist who did things like place stents in clogged arteries, implant pacemakers, and open tiny coronary arteries with balloons. In truth, his personality was a bit invasive too, but that was another story.

The wedding was coming right up, and there was a bonding weekend for the wedding party next weekend at a farm in Waukasaw, about two hours away, which actually included the beautiful outdoor venue Ani and Tyler had selected. We *had* to at least pretend to get along for the sake of our friends.

Even more urgently, my car was in the shop, and Caleb and I were the only ones headed way out to the middle of nowhere from Milwaukee. My wheezing, chronically ill gas-guzzler, which was all I could afford after meeting all of my sister's college expenses, had undergone cardiac arrest, and the nice mechanic down the street from where I lived, Hal, was struggling to save it. He said that it would be a miracle for the car to be resuscitated in time for the farm weekend.

I was praying for one, because after this incident, I would never step into a vehicle with Caleb. I wouldn't trust myself not to commit a felony. It looked like I would be forking over the bucks on a rental because my pride would never allow me to ask him for a ride.

I balled and unballed my fists, thinking. He noticed. That was the trouble with him—he *always* noticed.

His mouth twitched. He was amused at my indignation, and that did it. I closed my eyes and shook my head and took a breath, but none of that stopped everything I was feeling from spilling out like a flood. "The fact that you think you can cancel me—publicly —on a whim simply because you don't like me, and that your attending actually allowed you to get away with that, says *everything*. You are a stereotypical meathead ortho guy. Handsome, but all muscle and no brains."

Okay, maybe I went too far.

Yep. I was met with complete, hulking, deadly silence. The pale green eyes glared.

Good. I'd made him feel my anger. Why hold back? Except now I'd be walking to Waukasaw next weekend.

"Wow," he said, staring at me. "Handsome, huh?"

I spun toward him. "What?"

There was that too-bright, mocking grin. "You said I was handsome."

I could. Not. Deal. With. Him. I took a step back and prepared to go.

"This isn't a joke," I said to his face.

I desperately needed this job. To stay close to Wynn, my nineteen-year-old sister, who was in college at UW. Also, I loved this hospital. I loved the complex and challenging cases. I loved teaching. All things I couldn't do in a smaller place.

Caleb crossed his arms and looked down at me. Way down, because oh man, was he tall. I would guess six-four to my five-nine. "No one will know about the switch unless you make it known. And I'm sorry about Joseph. But Erin stays."

The hydraulic double door swooshed open behind us. "Joseph's family is asking for Sam," Ani said in a pleasant tone. She walked over, handed me a clipboard, and turned to Caleb. "Maybe you'd like to go tell them why you don't want her in there?"

He shook his head and sighed heavily. Crossed his arms.

She dropped her voice. "This is ridiculous. You're both in my wedding. And I'm the *bride*. Get it together, both of you."

He had the decency to look chagrined. "Okay, fine," he said finally. His words came out heavy and flat, as if it nearly killed him to say them. I was a little shocked at the reversal. I don't know if it was Ani pulling the bride card that convinced him, or something else, but I didn't care. I was just relieved.

He narrowed his eyes at me. "This is a complicated case, and I don't want any distractions."

"You have my word, Dr. D'Angelo." I shot a grateful look at Ani, took the clipboard, and left.

For now, this was about our patient. I could wage the war with Caleb later. And make no mistake, there would be war.

Chapter Two

Samantha
One Week Later

It was nine p.m., and Caleb still wasn't back. I squinted through the peephole and peered into the second-floor hall of the hundred twenty-five-year-old Queen Anne Victorian that we both called home, but the door across the hall from my apartment remained closed and silent. I listened for the crunch of his tires on the gravel drive—nothing.

It had been a week since our little—um—confrontation, and we'd both managed to carefully avoid each other.

But I had a problem. That farm-bonding weekend was coming right up, and my car was still bone dead, waiting on a part that still wasn't in. I'd have to borrow a friend's or rent one, plain and simple. The third option, asking a favor from a person I considered despicable? Ugh. My pride hurt to ask the first and third favors, and I couldn't really afford option two after barely squeaking by— between loans and my savings—to meet my sister's tuition payment for a class she had to retake this summer.

Yes, retake. Take again. As in paying twice. *Ouch.*

I wrung my hands as I paced my apartment, talking to my little sister, Wynn. "Did you say you got a job in the *perfume* department?" I'd just learned that she'd definitely not been planning on spending the summer doing research in a lab like we'd planned. Working in the perfume department of a department store was not going to be a good cred to get her into medical school. Unless she was doing chemistry experiments there.

In between glances through the peephole, I paced the solid oak floor. It creaked in a few places, which ordinarily I barely noticed, but in my present state, every sound was like chalk on a blackboard.

"My job at Winterfield's starts next week," Wynn said. "So I'll have the restaurant job and this new one. Isn't that great?"

She'd mastered an enthusiastic tone, but it sounded fake to me. Which made me worry, worry, worry. Wynn was emotional, excitable, and young—the opposite of me, who was steady, even-keeled, and cautiously thrilled about only a few things. Plus she was just nineteen, a far cry from my own age of thirty-two. I didn't want her to have a truckload of worries, especially financial ones.

But it felt like I was going on fifty-two, because the trouble was that I found myself constantly straddling the gap between sister and parent, something that you'd think I should've mastered by now. While I wanted her to enjoy her time away at college, something I'd never truly been able to do, I wanted—make that *needed* —her to have a secure future. Basically, I needed her off the payroll ASAP. And that meant her passing her classes with flying colors, focusing, and declaring a major in the appropriate time frame to graduate in four years. Easier said than done.

The parent part of me couldn't let her off the hook. "I thought you were coming home to take calculus here in Milwaukee this summer." Summer housing was yet another expense I hadn't counted on. But the real truth was, I wanted her here. I yearned for our relationship to be what it used to be, before our grandmother died a year and a half ago.

"Home?" she asked in a deadpan tone that sent a chill through me.

Last year, after Oma died, I'd sold her house, and Wynn hadn't forgiven me for getting rid of the only home we'd ever had even if that money was now helping to fund her college. And even though Oma's neighborhood was becoming crime-ridden and scary—not the home-sweet-home fantasy anyone would dream about.

We were homeless, so to speak. A bit unmoored, but I'd vowed to be the glue. We'd always stuck together—except now there was a chasm between us. And I didn't know how to bridge it.

"Yes, home. Home with me." Not that this tiny apartment was so great, but I'd made the big bay window a sleeping alcove. I'd bought a cute futon with bright pillows and hung flowery curtains for privacy all around it. With the naturally quirky nature of this old house, that arrangement would work out great. Except that Wynn was throwing me a plot twist.

"To retake calculus," I added.

That was the elephant in the room: She'd failed calculus last fall. Not because, like a lot of us, her brain simply didn't *get* calculus, but because she'd met a boy first semester and had fallen madly in love with him—and had stopped going to class.

Ugh. A boy named Miles, whom I hadn't even met yet.

I was completely out of my wheelhouse here. The only reason I'd made it to college in the first place was my smarts, and without total focus, I wouldn't have survived. My future would have had as great a chance of being as chaotic as our mother's, who'd gone from bad job to bad job and worse man to worse man. Until one day she'd left us behind too, in Oma's care. Which was probably for the best for everyone.

"I want to *work* this summer." Wynn's tone was insistent. "That's more important."

More important than retaking calculus? "I admire that you want to work." So did my bank account. "But med school admissions committees aren't going to be excited about the perfume job."

I'd sent her the names of some doctors who were taking students to work in hospital labs for the summer and therefore take part in research—the typical med school application credential. If she could get into a prestigious lab and get her name on a cutting-edge scientific paper, it would be a great thing to put on her CV. I'd helped her fill out the applications—but she hadn't said anything about hearing back.

This was a different attitude from before... the boyfriend. Miles, who didn't seem to care about things like passing classes and planning for a good future. I looked down to find that I'd shredded a bunch of tissues into confetti on my kitchen counter as I talked.

I suppose that was better than nail biting or drinking, but still.

"I want to save up until I can pay for the class I have to retake," Wynn said. "And I want to stay here." There was a long pause. "With Miles."

Shred, shred, shred, shred, shred.

I supposed I should be glad she'd taken the perfume job. That one would be in addition to her job waitressing at a very chichi restaurant in downtown Madison. But would her grades suffer even more? When she first got the waitressing gig, I practically broke out in hives every night thinking of her walking out of the restaurant alone and taking public transportation home late at night.

So I'd bought her a used car, even as the dollar signs racked up. So many dollar signs that they appeared in my dreams at night. I'd been supporting both of us on a resident's salary, loans, plus all the moonlighting jobs I could find, including one spending weekend nights at a local psych hospital doing admission physicals on patients. Despite all that, the expenses felt endless.

That's okay, I told myself. It wouldn't last much longer. After one year of internship and three years of anesthesiology residency, I was now in a fifth year of training, a special year of pediatric anesthesiology fellowship—and I was finally applying for a real job. After years of sacrifice, real income was just around the corner.

"Don't worry about me," Wynn said. "I'm fine. Maybe I'm not as smart or as independent as you, but I'm finding balance. I'm learning how to study *and* have a social life."

That was a hit directed at me—the fact that I'd studied and worked my way through college. Even in med school, I worked as a phlebotomist from four a.m. to seven a.m. four mornings a week. My sister was now telling me I was one dimensional. Unbalanced. And too independent. She probably wasn't wrong, but I didn't have a choice. I chose to tamp down the insult even though it hurt a little. "You *are* smart. And I'm glad you're finding balance."

Not worry? Impossible. And her tone—so disdainful! I bit my tongue as I thought of more disasters. Was she using birth control, like I'd preached many times? But if I said that now, I was afraid she'd hang up.

I agonized. I shredded. I was wasting the whole fricking box of tissues. But it was better than losing my mind. No lab job, no calculus retake, no return home to be with me for the summer. *No, no, no.*

"You're using birth control, right?"

That was met with dead silence as I'd predicted. I *had* to ask. If I didn't and something happened, I'd never forgive myself.

"Yes," she finally answered, exasperation in her voice.

"Okay, just checking." I tried to strike a more positive tone. "Maybe I'll drive up for lunch or dinner next week," I said. "Would that be okay? We can go somewhere cute to eat." I paused. "Miles can come too." That last part cost me two more Kleenex, but I said it.

"Yeah, but I—uh—I've got exams. I'll text you when's a good time, okay?"

"Okay." I disguised a little more hurt. She'd been putting me off for the past month or two. When she was younger, she'd been filled with adoration for me, wanted to spend every moment with me. But she was an adult now. And now our relationship was fraught with all these other things. "You sure everything's okay?" Actually, she sounded fine. I was the one who was not okay. "Sam, I'm doing great. Don't worry so much, okay?"

The floor creaked again under my pacing. *Thump thump thump* sounded from below my feet.

That would be Mrs. Von Gulag, my elderly landlady, who lived below me. To be clear, that noise was her broom handle—and her temper—hitting the ceiling.

I glanced at my watch. Nine on the nose. Her way of signaling me to stop pacing, walking, talking, and also breathing, since it was her bedtime.

"Okay," I conceded. "I just— I love you. Make good choices," I snuck in at the last minute.

The line went silent. Wynn took a breath, gathering patience, no doubt. I should've left out the Jamie Lee Curtis line.

Oh, but I had so much more I wanted to say. *Make other friends. Don't let anyone distract you from your goals. Work hard* and then *play hard.*

I knew that sometimes I sounded pushy, and I tried to keep my mouth shut. But sometimes I just couldn't.

You know why? Because I was frightened. I didn't want her dreams to get derailed. I wanted her to have every chance, every opportunity. I wanted her to have an easier way than I did. And I wanted my hard times to be worth something. Like, I'd put in the suffering for both of us, and now it was over, and she'd never have to experience it.

"Love you too," she said in a cautious tone. "Talk soon." Then the call ended.

I sat down on the cute futon, totally distressed. If only Oma were around, she'd manage to laugh this off somehow. Make me tea. Sit down beside me and put her arm around me and surround me with her love. But there was no Oma. There was just me, alone in the cheapest (but safest) apartment I could find.

Oh, I had good friends. But trying to talk to them about parenting matters was... difficult. They were always supportive, but it was like asking a Burger King employee to create for you a James Beard recipe. No experience.

In some ways, I perpetually felt that my sister was one misstep away from disaster. From flunking important classes to getting involved with the wrong boys to spending money that I couldn't replenish fast enough. I was always torn between pretending that everything was normal so that she could enjoy a college life relatively free from worry to coming down on her hard and demanding that she get it together *or else*, whatever that meant. And so I said nothing, afraid to drive her away for good.

I would never do anything to drive a stake between us. It was bad enough we'd grown up without a father—at least, by the time she'd come around, he was long gone—and that our mother had been capricious, floating in and out of our lives as randomly as a bubble in the wind, bringing the promise of excitement and fun and raising our hopes, only to have them all dashed.

After a while, that kind of hurt makes you want to give up on people. You don't trust anyone except yourself. And you end up alone.

I didn't even have a pet. I wasn't sure that I could manage one more responsibility.

But at least I could depend on myself, right?

I just had to figure out how to handle my sister. How to be a good big sister. How to help her reach her full potential. Be a mentor. And love her. But how?

I had no clue what I was doing. As I lay back on the pillows, my phone fell from my pocket and clattered on the floor.

The broomstick banged again.

Caleb never got the broomstick.

He got leftovers and pieces of homemade pie and cookies while I got... the broomstick.

But then I was a woman. I was used to working hard in what was very subtly still a man's world without perks or privileges. I didn't expect cookies or leftovers or a friendly landlady. I didn't expect the world to give me anything. I'd come a long way on my own willpower. And I would be just fine.

Chapter Three

Caleb

I was trying to be as silent as possible as I crept down the hall to my apartment, not only because of my landlord's excessively early bedtime and insistence for us to basically play dead any time after it but also because I had a feeling that my nosy across-the-hall neighbor wanted to talk to me.

"The wedding bonding experience" that my friend Ani had come up with—a weekend experience that was meant to replace the bachelor and bachelorette parties—was taking place in just a few days. Being trapped at a farm in rural Wisconsin would require Samantha and me to bury the hatchet, at least temporarily. She'd been lying in wait for me the past few nights, and I'd barely escaped, her door opening just as mine shut—but she never knocked, and I didn't answer. I was waiting for my temper to cool.

I usually didn't require that—I was a fairly easygoing guy, and I didn't typically harbor anger. But through a strange twist of fate, Samantha had unknowingly thrown another complication into my life that had messed with my relationship with Lilly, my first and potentially only love, who was Ani's oldest friend and in the wedding too.

Call me romantic, call me an optimist who doesn't know when to quit, but I couldn't stop wondering if Lilly was the One. Things hadn't ended well between us, but there were circumstances. This wedding weekend was my chance to set things right and start us off on a better foot, in a brand-new direction. I didn't want to live with *what-ifs* and *what-might-have-beens,* and being in this wedding together would be the perfect opportunity to resolve things.

I'd grown up understanding that love was a rare and precious gift and the only thing that truly mattered. I learned this because I'd lost a sibling—my younger sister Mia's twin—when I was eleven. So nothing Samantha said or did could stop me from taking my last chance with Lilly.

I dreamed of being an orthopedic doctor in our quaint little hometown, where Lilly worked as a florist. We'd have a cute house near my parents' farm, and our kids would grow up roaming the fields and forests and having a great time being surrounded by family just like I did. The dream was there, within reach—I just had to actualize it, starting this weekend.

Tonight I was tired after a long day and definitely not in the mood to hash anything out. I was okay with pretending that Samantha and I liked each other for the weekend, but I had no desire to talk with her about anything. Silent as a cockroach—or any one of the random critters living in this old place—I turned my key but accidentally dropped my keys. They hit the wood floor with a metallic *chink.* Behind me, Samantha's door opened with a loud creeeaaaak.

I spun around to find my annoying neighbor standing there in shorts, a Brewers T-shirt, and pink fuzzy slippers, her long black hair wet from a shower. I'm not even going to mention catching a glimpse of her nicely tanned legs, which made me do a double take that I instantly regretted.

Samantha looked fun, attractive, and not at all like someone impossible to be friends with—but looks are deceiving. She didn't have a stitch of makeup on, but she had long, thick lashes and pretty, full lips and didn't need it one bit. Looking at Samantha sure wasn't painful, but talking to her definitely was.

I reminded myself to be cordial for my sister's sake. But I was still so damn angry.

"Why, if it isn't the notorious Dr. Gas," I said in a false-pleasant tone, using the common nickname for anesthesiologists as I slowly straightened up in the dim hallway. "Awake past curfew, I see." My gaze flicked up and down, until I realized that I was staring at her legs again. I diverted my gaze directly up to her face and forced it to stay there.

"Dr. Bone Cracker," she shot back, glancing at her watch. "You barely squeaked by, I see."

"Mrs. Von Gulag thinks I'm charming. *She* always cuts me some slack."

"Men always get cut slack. But we women don't need any slack. We make our own destinies."

I usually got this type of diatribe about women vs. men, which for some reason she felt I needed to hear. I tried to remember that Mia loved her—they were the very best of friends. I honestly didn't have a clue why.

Small talk was over. I was ready to call it a day. So I turned back to my door and jiggled the key—or rather, tried to. But it was now stuck. I silently cursed.

"I need to talk to you about something," she said.

Dammit. Reluctantly I faced her again. The light above our heads was shining on her hair. Black, shiny hair and so much of it, thick and lustrous. I pushed the distraction out of my mind. Sooner or later I was going to have to confront our troubles.

"Funny you should say that," I said. "I've got something to get off my chest too."

"I hope it involves an apology for trying to boot me off that case last week."

I bristled. "You make being nice so hard, Gas." I pinched my nose for patience. If only my key wouldn't have stuck.

"This is no joke," she said. "What you did could have cost me my job application. I was lucky no one told Dr. Benson about it."

I crossed my arms and looked down at her. Not that far down, because the woman was tall—not the usual dynamic I had with women. I disliked Samantha, but she was a conscientious doctor. What I'd done about trying to replace her on my case was a little reckless, not my usual behavior, but nothing bad had come of it. Just this painful conversation.

"You're right, our dislike of each other isn't a joke. I admit that what I did wasn't the greatest way to handle things. And I am sorry about that. But this time *you* went too far, and it cost *me* something too."

∾

Samantha

"*I* went too far?" I couldn't wait to hear this.

Caleb tipped his tall, lean frame against the scarred doorjamb. "For your information, you cost me something with someone I care about."

"I'm confused. You actually *care* about someone? With human emotions?" I instantly regretted being snarky. The hospital grapevine said that he dated around a lot. I wasn't sure if he ever went out with anyone more than a couple of times. But then I didn't pay much attention to the daily dish.

"Judge much?"

"I can't help it if I find you reprehensible." Okay, so subtlety wasn't my strength. At least with me, people got what they got. I wouldn't apologize for that even if his frown lines were distractingly cute. Who has cute frown lines?

"I can't help it if you've got a tree trunk up your—"

"Just tell me what happened, okay?" Somebody had to be mature here, so it might as well have been me.

"Something you said last week got back to someone I care about."

"I don't gossip," I said firmly. I couldn't fathom what he was talking about. But I *had* been royally upset after he'd nearly booted me from that case. Had I vented to a couple of my girlfriends? I had. But I don't have the kind of friends who break confidences. "Who?" I asked, straining to remember what I said and whom I said it to. "Got back to whom?"

"Lillian Hardy."

Lillian Hardy? Never heard of her. Wait a minute—yes, I had. *Lilly.* She was Ani's oldest friend from childhood, and she was one of her bridesmaids, along with me and Caleb's sister Mia. "From Oak Bluff?" That was Caleb and Ani's hometown, a quaint little place in the middle of a lot of farmland, about two hours from Milwaukee.

The look in his eyes confirmed a yes. "Lilly happens to be very special to me, and she'll be at the farm this weekend."

"I'm still not following."

"She's my ex. My first love. I hope you understand about love."

He got an eye roll for that. "Your first love?"

Caleb sighed heavily. "I don't want to talk about this. But yes. Things didn't end well, but I have a chance to make them right. Except someone at the hospital spread some rumor—that I don't treat women well."

First love—didn't end well—make it right. That sounded to me like strikes one, two, and three. I would've never pegged him as a full-blown romantic. *Good luck with that, buddy*, was my first thought.

"I have no idea how you treat women. I only know how you treated me, which wasn't nice. Or collegial. Or fair." And I was still pretty steaming mad about that.

"Lilly is good friends with Stacey from 5 North," he continued, "and Lilly apparently... heard things from her." He cleared his throat. "Things 'the anesthesiologist on the case with the child with a broken leg,' said about me."

A dull sense of dread seeped into my veins, like anesthesia before a surgery. That happened in the OR all the time. Patients felt a cool sensation and started counting backward from ten, and by eight they were out. Stacey was a nice work friend. I knew she was chatty, but I guess I'd been angry enough to be careless with my words.

Nora, our friend from NICU, had been beside herself that week. She'd gone out with Caleb a few times, but then the very next week, he dumped her for a respiratory therapist who *also* worked in the NICU—whom Nora said he'd been dating at the same time.

I'd vented to Stacey about what a terrible person Caleb was. How he indiscriminately dumped women, how he'd screwed me over and nearly got me called in by my department chair. And Stacey must have told Lilly.

"And now Lilly doesn't trust me," Caleb said. "She broke off with her boyfriend a few months ago. I finally have another chance with her, and now it's blown—because of you."

All the blood left my head. I got so weak-kneed I had to back up and lean on my grandma's little book stand for support.

I'd been so upset. So appalled at what he'd done to me. When I'd heard what he'd done to Nora, I guess I'd just lost it—I'd told Stacey everything.

I felt terrible. Also, how was I going to tell Mia what I'd done? Because this would upset her too.

Anger had disconnected my stupid mouth from my brain.

Stacey knew Lilly? How was that even possible?

And Lilly was the love of his fricking *life*?

Ugh. No matter how terrible Caleb was, Oma didn't raise me to be a vengeful person. And I wasn't a gossip. And I especially wasn't one of those people who ruined someone's chances at love.

In my family, that was a mortal sin.

My last name, *Bashar*, means bringer of glad tidings, of love. Oma was a matchmaker. She'd proudly matched over one hundred couples in her lifetime.

I thought that maybe I'd inherited her gift too. Which sounds strange, but I had a special sense about couples who were meant to be together. So far, I'd predicted five marriages among my friends. Five, including Mia, who'd been dating our colleague Brax since last Christmas and wasn't engaged yet, but honestly, those two were a perfect match.

"I don't care what you think of me." Caleb leaned in very close, his eyes glinting with anger, "Just know this: I. Am. Not. A. Cheater."

He looked so determined, his distinct-looking brows turned down in a formidable frown. I'd never seen him that way before. He spoke forcefully, vehemently. Like someone telling the truth.

"I don't owe you any explanations about my personal life," he continued, stabbing a finger at me. "But since you're my sister's best friend, I'll tell you that I never date anyone who wants to get serious. Nora happened to want more, and when I broke it off, she got angry. End of story."

"You're saying she lied?"

"To start a rumor, yes. Maybe to hurt me as she felt she'd been hurt."

I had to admit, it sounded plausible. He certainly looked and sounded adamant.

"Fair enough." I stood up straight. "Regardless of what I think about you, I owe you an apology. I'll make it right—with your friend." There. I wasn't beyond apologizing. And I *would* make it right. That was who I was.

"No, you won't," he said quickly.

What? "I insist," I said carefully, standing my ground.

"You've done enough. All I want now is for you to stay out of this."

My head was spinning. I thought of Oma. She would be so ashamed that I'd stood in the way of someone's chance at love. Even someone like him.

"Really, I feel terrible," I said. "I may not like you, but I-I would never... I'll do whatever it takes to keep the peace this weekend." With a brief nod, he turned to place his key back in the lock. This time, I heard a successful *click* before the door swung open. I figured the discussion over, so I opened my door and started to walk into my apartment.

Then I heard, "Just be ready by eight on Thursday."

I spun around. Did I hear that right? He wouldn't be... could he be? "You're offering me a ride? After all this?" I was incredulous.

We disliked each other. He was furious with me. I was still furious with him, despite feeling bad about Lilly. When he turned to face me, he looked... normal. Not fuming, not pissed. "Is this a trick?"

He scowled. "No."

This had to be a trick. "Like, are you offering me a ride, only to leave me dead in those woods that line the highway all the way to Waukasaw?"

He rolled his eyes. "Mia told me about your car."

Oh great. *Thanks, Mia.* She was a wonderful friend—well, except in this case. I, however, sucked, because look what I'd done. I narrowed my eyes. "What exactly did she tell you?" I didn't want any pity about sacrifices I'd made for my sister.

"That it's in the shop." He paused. "I don't mind giving you a ride, but I have a few conditions."

Conditions? The nerve. "I *was* going to say that was incredibly nice of you, but now I changed my mind."

He ignored that. Instead, he simply counted them out on his long, elegant fingers. "First of all, I'm spending Thursday at home with my family, so hope that's not a problem. Number two, I don't want to discuss Lilly anymore. Three, I'd prefer you not mention any of this to my family—especially to Mia. And four, most importantly, I need you to stay out of my way. Please," he added, sounding vehement. "Absolutely no interference."

I narrowed my eyes. "You don't want Mia to know that you're planning to get back with your ex?"

He shrugged. "I don't know if I'm getting back with her. But I need to resolve some things. And I like to keep my business private." He got up close. So close I could see the pure, unusual green of his eyes. I'd never seen eyes like that before. They might be beautiful, if he wasn't someone I wanted to run from screaming, as far away in the opposite direction as I could. His expression was dead serious. "Okay, Dr. Bashar?"

"Yes. Fine. I'll be ready." I hesitated, knowing what I had to do. I opened my mouth. Cleared my throat. Forced out the words. "Th-Thanks." The word stuck like dry, sticky rice to the roof of my mouth. "Thank you."

As painful as a shot in the butt, but I'd done it.

He gave me a nod and a self-satisfied smile. Then he disappeared into his apartment.

Behind his back, I flipped him the bird. *No discussing, no mentioning, no interfering*, I mimicked to myself. What a sanctimonious jerk.

But at least he was a sanctimonious jerk with a vehicle. And he'd been nice to save me the humiliation of asking.

So, fine. I'd follow the rules.

Except for that last one.

I lived my life like I lived our Hippocratic Oath; above all, I tried my best to do no harm.

Plus Dr. Annoying was Mia's brother. Granted, he annoyed the hell out of her too, but she loved him. I had to fix the damage I'd done—fast. I wouldn't be responsible for someone losing their true love. I committed to do everything I could to help.

I was almost inside my apartment when I heard his voice. "By the way, I saw that," he called over his shoulder.

Chapter Four

Caleb

I'd told Samantha that we were leaving at eight on the dot, and I meant it, I thought as I checked my watch that Saturday morning. She might've sounded apologetic for what had happened, but I trusted her about as much as I'd trust any fresh-faced, brand-new ortho intern to reduce my compound fracture on July 1 of any given year.

And so, on that bright May morning, the birds rioted loudly in the trees, and the clear blue sky promised a sun-kissed day. My great mood was on the brink of teetering when eight a.m. came and went, Samantha nowhere in sight.

Figures she'd be late, I thought as I sat in the driveway, drumming my fingers on the wheel of my voodoo-blue Toyota Tacoma truck. I ran my hand over my few-days stubble—I hadn't bothered to shave, but I would for sure before I saw Lilly, who'd agreed to meet me for coffee later today. I was just texting Sam *The bus is leaving* when suddenly my passenger door opened and there she was, waving and smiling a startlingly white smile that contrasted with her dark-as-midnight hair, which she wore up in a high, thick ponytail that reminded me of a thick rope of silk.

"Hi," she said like we were old friends, tossing a brown lunch-sized bag onto the seat.

For a moment, my brain took a detour. I momentarily forgot that we were going to have to sit together in my truck for two hours breathing the same air. She handed me a cardboard drink holder with two steaming coffees as she climbed in.

"Sorry I'm late. I got us some breakfast." I was confronted by a pair of big brown, worried eyes. Doe eyes that could cause the snarliest grouch to melt. "Peace offering."

I glanced at the iconic brown bag with a red stripe. "You went to Donut World." That was the local donut shop around the corner. There was no bad donut there. I should know; I've tried every single one.

She clicked on her seat belt, opened the bag, and held it out to me.

"Thanks," I said, suppressing a groan of ecstasy. First choice? I definitely wasn't going to let on that cream sticks were my favorite, and one was sitting right there, calling my name.

So Sam was pretty, *and* she'd brought donuts—that didn't mean she wasn't the devil.

I helped myself to the cream stick, not feeling a stitch of guilt.

"They're my favorite too." For a minute we devoured our donuts. Then I sat back and placed an earbud in my ear. "You don't mind if I listen to my book with one of these while I drive, do you?" I was going to set the precedent early. Low expectations on conversations meant less getting in trouble.

"No, of course not." She reached into a canvas bag and pulled out a giant library book.

Guess my mouth dropped open because she turned and stared at me. "You okay?"

I quickly closed it and wiped my expression clean. "Yeah, of course. Ready to go?" I started the truck and pretended that I wasn't listening to the same exact book, a popular fantasy novel that was hitting the charts.

About ten minutes in, I started to feel guilty for ignoring her. Not because I wanted to talk with her but because my mom had taught me good manners. I guess I'd half expected her to try to get *me* to talk, which she didn't. Which oddly disappointed me. I guess part of me was looking forward to the sparring.

She was sipping coffee and looking out the window when I said, "Whatcha looking at out there?" The entire way to Waukasaw, the highway would be rimmed with tree upon tree. Wisconsin was a beautiful state, and large swaths of it were natural and wild, but I couldn't understand the fascination—after a while, the landscape tended to look the same to me. Maybe she was staring out the window, secretly plotting my demise.

She started at the sound of my voice, which made me bite down on the insides of my cheeks to suppress my smile. "There's so much wildlife," she said. A field with cows grazing flew past the window. More trees. A little lake. "I swear, Wisconsin is the prettiest state."

"Wisconsin *is* the land of 10,000 lakes. Didn't you grow up in Milwaukee?"

"My grandma raised us in an apartment downtown near the hospital. She worked as a nurse, and we didn't have a car, so we walked everywhere, but our neighborhood was mostly concrete. We didn't have a patio or a balcony, and it always seemed that outside was so far away, if that makes any sense. Going outside meant walking to the park down the street. And it always meant waiting to go with someone, because Oma didn't allow us to go by ourselves."

Maybe I shouldn't have started this. Because there was more info to unpack about Samantha in those few sentences than I'd learned from my sister in the past three years. "I grew up on a farm in Oak Bluff. I can't imagine not being outdoors a lot."

She was still staring out that window, and I was still glomming on to every word she said. "We had a membership to the Y, and I used to swim every day, so we made the most of it. I still remember the first time I saw a cow. It was on a field trip in kindergarten. My grandma had given me a little camera, and I took like, twenty photos of that cow. I'd never seen farm animals up close like that, let alone such wide-open spaces. I'm excited to see them this weekend—cows and pigs and horses. And I love hiking. I can't wait."

"You sound *super* excited." For some reason, I thought of Lilly, who always carried a sample-sized bug spray hooked to her backpack, and who would only hike if it was less than eighty degrees.

Sam frowned at me. "I *am* excited. And I've actually been to your farm—with Mia. It's pretty." Mia had said something about her having a tough childhood, that her grandmother raised her, and that she had a younger sister. That was about all I knew.

It occurred to me that the *excited* comment might've sounded sarcastic. "I didn't mean the excited thing in a snarky way. When we talk, we tend to argue, but I was just making a statement."

She shrugged. Like she couldn't care less whether I was trying to insult her or not. That was the thing about Sam. She didn't care what anyone thought of her. I knew this because she often spoke her mind, like when the hospital administration told us we'd have to take more call for the same salary. She rose her hand in the meeting and politely yet confidently expressed her opinion. Then she wrote letters and got everyone else to write them too. And you know what happened? We still had to take the extra call. But we got paid for it. Brava, Sam.

I should have just shut up and drove, but something made me want to smooth things over. I blame it on the donut. "So, I know all these obscure facts about our state. Do you?"

She turned and gave me a peculiar look. "I thought you didn't want to talk to me."

I rubbed my neck and confessed. "My mom would have my hide if I tried to ignore a guest for two hours." The truth was, I had no idea why I was making conversation with her. Something about her story got to me, I guess.

"I'm a guest?"

"Well, you're staying over at my house tonight, so yes, that makes you a guest." I glanced over at her. "You just said you've been there, right?"

"Enough to know your family is much nicer than you." She shot me a mischievous grin.

"Can't argue with that." I couldn't help smiling. "Then you know what you're in for."

"I love your mom," she said sincerely.

She already knew what I'd been about to say. "Make no mistake. My mom works full time on our farm, but she loves to mother people. Oh, and to cook. You've been warned."

"Once your mom made us lunch." She opened her arms wide. "It looked sort of like Thanksgiving dinner."

"Well, I know she misses us kids. Of course, she still has our little dachshund, Cooper." Sam stiffened just a little, which made me remember something else Mia had told me—that Sam had a fear of dogs. "Cooper's a love hog, but if you pass, he moves onto the next sucker—I mean *person*."

She was strangely silent.

"You okay?" I asked.

"Oh yes, I'm fine. I-I had a run-in with a stray dog when I was a kid. I'm not very comfortable around them."

"No worries. We'll keep him in check. Besides, he's about the size of my foot, so nothing to fear." I felt like there was a lot more to that "run-in," but she wasn't about to share, so I changed the subject. "So do you want to hear my Wisconsin facts or not?" I counted them off on my fingers. "The first ice-cream sundae was made here. We're the largest producer of cranberries in the US. The largest woolly mammoth was found in Kenosha County. And supposedly, we hate margarine—it was banned until 1967."

I checked to see if she was bowled over by my vast display of knowledge.

"Is that how you impress women?" she asked. "Because I don't recommend trying that with Lilly."

Okay, definitely not bowled over. "Why not?"

"Because it's show-offy." I was offended until I saw her mouth turning up. "I have one. Barbie's hometown is Willows."

"Which doesn't exist."

She pointed a finger at me. "See? Totally show-offy."

I couldn't volley back, because her phone rang, and she began talking to someone named Wynn, whom I eventually figured out must be her sister.

I was thinking that I should probably stop talking with her because if circumstances were different, I might actually *like* her.

"Hey, I'm driving with Mia's brother," she said in a low voice. "Is everything okay?"

Then, "You sure? I can call you back once I get to Mia's house."

I heard a female voice on the other line. "I-I just wanted to tell you that I'm going to be all right. And I'm going to make you proud, you'll see. Talk soon, okay?"

Sam dropped her voice, but I still heard. "I love you. You know that, right?"

I didn't catch the response. But Sam ended the call and slipped her phone back into her purse.

"Everything good?" I asked.

Her joking demeanor had vanished. "My sister's had a tough freshman year at UW in Madison. She's determined to stay there this summer and work. But I wish she'd come home and retake a class she needs instead."

"Where's home?" I asked.

She shook her head. "I hate to say it, but my apartment for now." Her crappy apartment? I didn't know what to say to that.

"Wynn's my only family, and I'm responsible for her. I love her a lot." She paused. Wait. Was she getting teary-eyed?

Okay, so I guess Protective is my middle name. After we lost Grace, I guess I worried a lot about Mia. And I've always tried to look out for her. I touched Sam's arm without thinking. "I could *tell* you love her a lot. Want me to take you back? It's not a problem." I couldn't believe it. Less than a half hour in, and I was not only tolerating her but actually talking to her *and* being nice to her.

She shook her head. "Thanks, but she's at college. There's literally nothing I can do but worry." She swiped at her eyes in that way women do when they don't want their tears to ruin their makeup. "I had to sell our grandmother's house last fall to help pay for her college expenses. I think she prefers to stay at college because coming home won't be the same." She paused a long time. "Wynn blames me for getting rid of the only home she's known." Another swipe at her eyes. "And... I have no idea why I just told you all that."

I felt helpless. Being a surgeon, usually I solve that problem by taking action. So I exited the highway and drove a half mile down a country road to a lake with a dock, parking in a little gravel lot right in front.

"Where are we?" she asked, glancing around.

"I'm not exactly sure, but it says Priceless View. Let's get out for a minute."

She whipped her head from the window to give me an incredulous look. "It did not."

"It actually said Scenic View but same thing, right?"

"Look, I'm really fine." She motioned to the steering wheel, as if that would start the truck again. "Just keep driving."

"Too late." Out my window, I saw vast, blue water, sparkling in the midmorning sun. The lake was long, with a meandering shoreline, surrounded by forest. And a dock to walk out on. "Look, this is number one of those ten thousand lakes I told you about. We might as well see it." I'd been here a lot with my family. It was a fun place to bring picnics and kayaks, and it had a quiet, peaceful vibe.

"This is just way too much friendliness for me," Sam said under her breath as she put a hand on the door.

I gave her my most winning smile. Everything seemed to be making me see her in a different light. Sure, I'd considered her pushy, but she'd probably had to be to get to where she was. "I told you, I'm only trying to get you to stop being upset before we get to my parents' house, or else my mom'll blame me." My mom always told me that even as a young kid, I could never stand to see anyone cry.

She kept a poker face. "Does that mean you're going to turn back into an asshole after that?"

I burst out in a laugh.

"You're afraid of your mom? She's the sweetest mom on the planet."

"I'm not afraid of my mom," I said defensively. This woman certainly knew how to push my buttons. Actually, my mom already knew that Sam and I didn't care much for each other. But she'd still expect me to treat her nicely.

I got out and grabbed my thermos and then ran around to her side to open her door, but she was already walking over to the dock.

At ten a.m., the May sun was bright and strong. The breeze brought riots of birdsong. And the water was a bright, deep blue. I walked out to the end of the dock, gestured for her to sit, and opened the thermos. "Everything looks better with caffeine."

"I didn't know you made coffee."

"Well, you brought some, so I wasn't going to tell you."

I poured some out and offered it, and she took a sip. "This isn't regular coffee." She tasted it again. "You made cappuccino *and* packed it up in a thermos? Who are you?"

"A barista," I said with a straight face. "You like it?"

Her turn to laugh at my joke. As she nodded and handed me back the cup, our hands barely grazed. But I felt an odd flash of heat travel straight through me, a weird awareness that made me so uncomfortable I had to look away, focusing on the opposite shore.

What was *that*?

I managed to take a sip, but I was so thrown I couldn't really appreciate the taste anymore.

"So how did you manage to make a cappuccino?"

I was strangely pleased that my coffee was such a hit. "Well, I cheated." When she gave a little frown, I said, "The first thing I bought after I was able to make my rent was a restaurant-grade espresso machine. Makes my day every day." Then I kicked myself. "Sorry. Here I am talking about extravagances."

"No. This was just what I needed. Your coffee made me forget that it's hard, trying to parent your sister. I have no idea what I'm doing."

I thought about my relationship with Mia. "I show love for my sister by tormenting her as much as possible." I chuckled. "I've never been responsible for her, although I did my best to look out for her when she was younger. Especially after our sister Grace died." I instantly regretted mentioning that. "Now we look out for each other."

"Mia's told me about Gracie. I'm sorry." She paused. "I envy your family. You're all so close."

I shrugged. "We had no choice." I grinned. "My mom and dad were relentless about us loving each other. But it wasn't easy. All of us had our moments." I tossed a small stone from the dock into the water. "As for your sister, she made it to college. You must be doing something right."

"I just want her to have a great life." She braced, ready to get up, as if conscious her time for having problems was over. "She's why the hospital job is important to me. It keeps me in close range."

He nodded. "Nothing like family. I want to work in Oak Bluff one day. Actually, I already interviewed with an ortho there. I'm waiting to hear if I got the job."

"Well, good luck. Thanks for the detour. And for listening."

"Hey, no problem." I noticed that her brown eyes had flecks gold around the rims—I could see them in the bright sunlight. I realized I was staring too intensely and broke off my gaze, busying myself with putting the lid on my thermos.

It had been easy to listen. I sensed something else besides stress... loneliness. She appeared to be going it all on her own, selling houses and supporting her sister. I had this crazy impulse to hug her. But just then, she stood and dusted herself off and we made our way back to my truck. Good thing I didn't.

"So," she said, "I just told you about my sister, and that wasn't completely awful. You want to tell me a little about Lilly?"

I gave her a warning look.

"I mean, we're going to be spending the weekend together. And I know you don't want interference, but if I know just a teeny-tiny bit about her"—here she made a teeny-tiny sign with her fingers—"I can talk you up or something."

"I don't need you to do that." I used my most definitive tone. "Actually, that's why I'm going home a day early—so I can spend some time with her."

"Okay, I get it. But help me to understand your history. You broke up a while ago, but you think now's a good time to try to get her back?"

We had an hour left of making nice, but I felt it was prudent to tell her the least amount possible. "You aren't going to let this go, are you?"

"I could ask your sister." She reached for her phone. "She'll give me answers pronto."

Sisters' best friends were *the worst*. "Okay, fine. When we were growing up, I had a crush on her for the longest time. We started dating in college."

I crossed my arms. "College sweethearts?"

"Yep. Then I got into med school in Milwaukee, and she got a job, and we moved in together."

"Oh. That's serious."

I nodded. "But then med school got tough, and I wasn't there for her." Sam lifted a skeptical brow but didn't say anything. "I know what you're thinking. Med school *is* tough. But I was always either in class or studying. Lilly was... lonely. I mean, she gave up everything that she wanted to do for me. I took her away from her family and friends and the job she loved. Her dream was to own the floral shop her family started downtown, and she did—that's what she does now. A few years have passed, we've both grown up, and she recently broke up with her boyfriend, so now's my chance to see if the magic's still there."

Sam went quiet. Which made me really nervous. Not that I needed her approval or anything, but I found myself asking, "Are you processing that or judging me?"

"I'm trying not to judge you. Love is love."

"I hear a giant 'but' in there."

She gave a casual shrug. "It's not my place to say."

"It is if I ask you."

"Well, okay. It's just that past relationships are tough, in my opinion, because people have to change so that the reason you broke up doesn't repeat itself. As time passes, people tend to look back with rose-colored glasses." She paused. "It takes hard work to understand what really happened and move forward."

I thought about that. "Med school broke us up, and that stress certainly doesn't exist anymore."

"I don't mean just external factors. I mean internal ones. You have to dig deep and figure out what made you both so unhappy during that time of extreme external stress."

That was interesting, and I got all of it, but to me there was more. "I feel that Lilly and I didn't get a fair shot. It's always been an unresolved issue for me. I want a chance to see if things might be different now that we're older and more settled." Then something occurred to me. "Wait a minute. I thought you didn't believe in love." Mia had lamented this fact to our mother multiple times. *Sam's such a wonderful person, but she won't date anyone seriously.*

Also, why was I telling her everything, as if she was some kind of love expert or something?

"Not for myself. But my grandmother knew all about it."

That made me chuckle. "Your *grandmother*?"

"Uh-huh. She was a matchmaker."

"I thought you said she was a nurse."

"That too. In the newborn nursery. She got over a hundred couples together—for life." She snapped her fingers. "She could tell in an instant if they were meant to be or not."

"You're joking."

She bristled. "I'm not joking."

I had so many questions. Like, what was this woman's batting average? Did the couples really stay together? Was this voodoo a family thing? If it was, I could ask Sam to help me out and reverse the damage with Lilly.

Sam studied me, her expression defensive. It was time to change the subject.

"Anyway," I continued, "I want to put my best foot forward this weekend—not just with Lilly. Most people like me. I mean, besides you." She rolled her eyes. "I hope that with the wedding you and I can be mature adults and get along—for Ani and Tyler's sake." I held out my hand for a potential fist bump.

She bumped it with her fist, then slapped it with both sides of her hand, like some fancy funky handshake. But I was right with her on that, and I couldn't help chuckling.

She was interesting, that was for sure. For the first time, I was starting to see a peek of the Sam whom my sister loved. It was a relief, a little bit, but also like a red flashing danger sign. I couldn't afford any distractions on my way to figure things out with Lilly.

Chapter Five

Samantha

At the two-hour mark, we finally pulled up to a postcard-perfect white Victorian farmhouse surrounded by rolling fields plowed into tidy rows. As we got out of the truck, even the air smelled fresher this far out in the country. The D'Angelos weren't a perfect family, but they were close-knit. Beth and Steven always treated me like one of their own kids, and I loved spending time with them. I'd never been here without Mia though. And while Caleb might have been tolerable on the drive, I had no desire to hang out with him.

As I followed Caleb through the front door, a little wiener dog dashed out to greet

him. I reflexively recoiled, clinging to the door in case I needed to bolt.

Caleb bent down to pet the dog, who immediately rolled over for a tummy rub. "Hey, Coop, how are you, buddy? How's my little brother doing? I missed you, buddy, yes I did."

Hearing a giant grown man talk baby talk to a little dog made me relax a—but just a little.

"You can shut the door," he said. "I promise the only thing he might do is lick you to death."

Dog saliva. Ew. "Does he jump?"

"The only thing he does is try to cuddle up with you. I swear." He watched me close the door as if I wished I didn't have to. "Are you okay with him being loose?"

"Um, yeah. No problem." I wasn't okay, not really. But I braced myself for impact.

"Okay, then. Here goes." He stopped petting the dog. Cooper immediately rolled over, stood up, and bolted right over to me, sniffing my legs and looking up at me with big brown doggy eyes.

"You don't have to pet him," Caleb said. "But maybe just say hi."

"Hi, Cooper," I said. "You're—you're a good dog." Could this be over now?

The dog gave a little whine and then lay down, resting his head on my tennis shoe.

Caleb burst out laughing.

"What? What's he doing?" I glanced apprehensively from the dog to Caleb. Neither seemed especially concerned.

"I think he's telling you that everything's going to be okay." Then he grabbed my hand. "Come on. Come see Mom. She's making us lunch."

As he tugged me away, the dog bolted off my foot and ran ahead of us. We walked through the foyer, past a grand oak staircase, and into a big bright kitchen. Mrs. D'Angelo was chopping something green on the large island. Caleb greeted her with "Hi, Ma!" and swept her up in a huge hug.

I had time to process something—did Caleb just hold my hand? He'd just reached over and pulled me away, his grip strong and warm and decisive. I decided that no, he did not. He was only trying to help me to get away from the dog.

Laughing, Mrs. D. wiped her hands on her apron and gave him —and then me—the biggest hug I'd had in a long time. Well, since Oma. That hug triggered all my feelings about missing her, but I quickly banished them before any tears could sneak in.

I didn't know why I still felt so emotional. I guess being with this family made me miss the tiny family I did have. And I was seriously hug deprived.

"Oh, Samantha, honey, so wonderful to see you." Mrs. D. held me at arm's length. "And you're so thin. Good thing lunch is ready."

I grinned. "You're the only person who ever tells me that." Actually, Oma used to as well, usually right before she served me a plateful of her sweet, sticky baklava.

"Where's Dad?" Caleb asked, scanning the kitchen in that predatory way young males do for any freestanding food but only finding lettuce on the cutting board.

"He's working the south field," Mrs. D. said. "He'll be back soon. I made strawberry pie, so you'd better be hungry." As she finished chopping, she nodded toward the door. "I set up everything on the patio." The patio was actually a raised deck that overlooked a long, deep blue lake just fifty feet from the house. A little pontoon boat sat docked near shore that seemed to be begging to be taken for a ride packed with family, whom I knew included Caleb and Mia's oldest brother Liam, his wife Dina, and their little daughter Emma. I wondered if Ani would notice if I skipped the farm weekend and just stayed here.

"Caleb Michael, what is with that beard?" Mrs. D. asked as she gestured to his scruffy cheek. "You look like a woodsman."

"That's the look I was going for, Ma." He grinned and flexed, making a big show for his mom, then rubbed his three-day beard against her face. She laughed and shooed him away.

Caleb was one of those men who could be clean-shaven or scruffy and still look handsome as the devil in a natural, unforced way. But what really got me was the easy, fun way he interacted with his mom.

Lucky. He and Mia were so lucky. Both of them referred to their parents as Beth and Steven when they talked about them to us and often joked about the funny or quirky things they did or said. Maybe it was that they'd lost Grace or that Beth had beat breast cancer last year that had given them a special appreciation for each other that seemed to surpass any petty annoyances. All I knew was that I was fortunate to be in their orbit.

That was the thing though. I'd always be a little on the outside looking in no matter how wonderful they were about including me.

"Isn't that beard a little hot for June?" Mrs. D. asked, now chopping spinach.

"Keeps the bugs away," he retorted.

"Okay, whatever. I just love seeing your face, and with all that hair... well, never mind."

Without warning, she took his hand and then, horrifyingly, mine as well, and led us out together through a sliding door to the deck. "I am so thrilled you two rode together. I always knew you'd find common ground."

Ugh. Mrs. D. and Oma would've gotten along great together. I decided to punt on that comment though. As I met Caleb's gaze, he looked determined to shut that right down as well.

I took in in the picnic table with a bright green umbrella stationed over the reddish-stained deck. As I was checking out the breathtaking view, Caleb reached over and grabbed a carrot out of a bowl. "We don't get along any better than before, so don't get too excited. You know I'm meeting Lilly later on today."

She cleared her throat. "Oh yes, of course," she said in what might have been a faux-perky tone. "Well then, I'm glad you two have agreed to disagree then." Then she wisely changed the subject. "I thought Quinn was supposed to drive with you to Waukasaw."

"He had to take call tonight, so he'll get here tomorrow

morning in time to drive out to the farm with us." He grabbed another carrot and addressed me. "Quinn is Tyler's friend from med school, and he's doing a gastroenterology fellowship in Chicago. You'll like him. He's a great guy. And he's single." He made sure to emphasize that last word.

"I'm sure he is, but I'm not interested." Was he seriously trying to fix me up?

"In nice guys?" he asked in a saucy tone.

"In *any* guys," I said.

"Oh dear," said Mrs. D. with a look of concern, "I mean, whatever your preferences, we're fine with it."

I laughed. "What I meant was, I *do* like guys, except I'm not interested in being fixed up with anyone." I turned to Caleb, who was standing in front of me, staring down at me, too close for comfort.

"Okay, I get it." He raised his hands in defense. "I was just trying to be helpful."

I dropped my voice. "Maybe you were just trying to get your mom off your case." I wanted to ask him if there was a problem with his family liking Lilly, but it wasn't my place.

"Are you always so cynical about everything?"

I shot him a look of annoyance, but inside, that blow hit a little too close to home. I often felt that life had hardened me. Beat all the fairy-tale hopefulness right out of me. "No," I said with a sweet smile. "But there's just something in you that drives me to it."

"Okay, you two, cut it out," Mrs. D. said, holding a pile of plates as she went around setting the table. I grabbed some napkins to help. "Caleb, since when do you try so hard to fix people up?"

"That was Mia's suggestion, but I fixed up my friends Gerry and Christian, and they just got engaged." He turned to me. "I think I've got a little knack for matchmaking too."

I tried not to roll my eyes at his cockiness. "Not so fast. They broke up last month." Also, it had been Mia's suggestion to fix me up with this guy Quinn? I'd for sure be speaking to her about that.

"What?" he exclaimed. "That's a shame. They were perfect for each other."

I shrugged. "Maybe you should leave the matchmaking to the professionals."

"Maybe you should kiss my—"

"Too?" Mrs. D. interjected before I could hear the end of that. "Did you say 'I've got a knack for matchmaking *too*?'"

"Sam comes from a family of matchmakers," Caleb said. "Right?"

"Well, my—my grandmother was very good at it. She had —methods."

Caleb looked very interested. "What kinds of methods?"

I sensed that his next question was going to be if I'd use them on him and Lilly, which I absolutely was not going to do. "Like, she'd put one hand on each person's shoulders and close her eyes and then somehow be able to sense if they were a match or not. She was really good at it."

Caleb scrunched up his face. "Like, magic or something?"

I shrugged, because it was often something I wondered myself. "It was just something I grew up with and didn't question much." I should have questioned Oma a lot more, because I didn't understand enough about what she actually did during the matchmaker test, how she felt, if she'd simply trusted her instincts, or was there more? I mean, I didn't want to say magic, because I didn't believe in that, but there was so much I didn't know.

Caleb still looked way too interested. "Can you do that?" He wiggled his fingers as if he were casting a spell.

"No," I said in an abrupt tone meant to stop his questions.

The truth was, the closest I'd come was once when I was sitting in a restaurant in between Mia and Brax, and I did happen to touch each of their arms at the same time. And I swear I felt... something. A current, an energy, an excitement. It could've been simply being in the presence of two people in love. Or... absolutely nothing but wishful thinking. "I've never really tried."

As for the five couples I'd predicted would head to the altar, I didn't know if there was anything special about that. I tended to think of it as instinct—sort of like a predictive empathy. Of course, that instinct didn't tend to work with myself or with any other problems in my life, like how to handle Wynn.

Both of them, mother and son, stared at me with the same fascinated expression. I realized that they both had the same identically shaped eyes, but Mrs. D.'s were blue, not pale green like Caleb's. The green looked pretty against the backdrop of trees lining the lake. A man with pretty eyes.

Ugh. I should've kept quiet about my family quirk. And I needed to stop analyzing his eyes.

"Maybe you can try out some of your skills with me and Lilly," he said, returning himself to total annoyance level.

"That's not a good idea," I said, shutting that idea down quick. "I'm not my grandmother. I can only help you using my brains like normal people."

But I could tell the wheels of his mind were turning. Stubborn man that he was, he wasn't going to let this go.

"And I suppose it's bad luck to match yourself?" Mrs. D. asked.

"No, it's *impossible* to match yourself."

Caleb tossed me a puzzled expression.

"It just doesn't work. Matchmakers are as blind to their gift as everyone else."

I was talking about myself as if I believed in my grandmother's abilities. As if I believed that I possessed them too.

In truth, I'd scoffed at the process. Evaded Oma's attempts to teach me. And while I still didn't believe it was a thing, I regretted not learning what she was trying to pass along to me. For the family folklore part of it at least.

"Tell you what," Caleb said. "You help me and Lilly, and I'll fix you up with Quinn. How's that?"

I held up my thumb and index finger and pinched them

together. "With you, there's such a teeny-tiny line between help and torture."

"I think it would be fun to give you a dose of your own match-making medicine. You never know. It could be fun."

"I feel right at home," I said to Mrs. D., still looking at Caleb. "Caleb endlessly tortures Mia, and since she's not here, me."

Caleb looked surprised. Taken aback. "Well, I've got to keep my skills up for her, right?" He glanced at his phone. "Looks like Quinn's decided to drive right to the farm. So no worries about getting to know him during the long drive to Waukasaw."

"Great. I'll just focus on sitting in the back seat and doing my hocus-pocus on you and Lilly." I wiggled my fingers in the same way he had.

Mrs. D. burst out laughing. "You two are the cutest."

Mr. D'Angelo appeared at the door. He walked over and smooched his wife on the cheek. "Hey, Beth, sorry I'm late. Tractor stalled on me. I've still got to wash up." He saw me and broke out into a big smile. "Hey there, Sammy. I owe you a big hug. Except I'm covered in tractor grease."

I made air hug motions, and he made them back, chuckling. He was the only person who called me Sammy, but I didn't mind. I liked how he said it in an endearing way.

"I'll come with you." Caleb hightailed it after his dad, his enthusiasm to leave apparent.

"Hurry back," Mrs. D. called. "I'm about to take the frittata out of the oven." She linked her arm with mine as we stood there. Then she patted my arm. It felt awkward and sweet at the same time. "I can't really see you and Quinn together," she said in a conspiratorial tone.

"I don't think it's a good idea to date anyone you're in a wedding with." That seemed like a safe thing to say. Mrs. D. had this way of making you talk, and I really didn't want to open myself up to any questions. So far, I'd been immune to her attempts to get Caleb and me together. I was hoping she'd give up, now that Lilly was back in the picture. And she was so nice—but did she not like Lilly? If that was the case... why? I mean, sometimes Mia referred to her mom as Saint Beth. If *she* didn't like someone, then we were all in trouble.

"I don't usually weigh in on these things, but I'm not sure you want to be fixed up with him," she said.

I took a seat at the island. "I can't wait to hear this."

"Oh, he's nice enough." She put on mitts and peeked in the oven. "Needs a few more minutes." She closed the door and pulled off her mitts. "I'd wager to say he's *too* nice."

I lifted a brow. Did she think I didn't deserve nice men?

"What I mean is, he's—well, he's quite agreeable. Like, extremely agreeable."

I couldn't repress a giggle. "That's a bad thing?" I envisioned a man who didn't buck me at every turn, like her son. A peaceful coexistence would be delightful.

She sat down and took a sip of coffee, which was in a mug that said KISSIN' DON'T LAST—COOKIN' DOES. "Honestly, I wouldn't be able to survive with a spouse who agreed with me all the time. I think disagreeing leads to more passion." She gave me a wink. "Poor Quinn recently had a bad breakup. I think he feels a little desperate for love right now."

"Good to know," I said. "How do you... know all this?"

She shrugged. "Mia tells me."

"Mia usually tells *me*." Also, she wanted to fix me up with a desperate man? She was definitely going to hear about this.

"Well, I think she didn't want you to judge him. I mean, he really is a nice guy. I probably just said too much, didn't I?"

"I'm personally grateful that you did."

"Well, I'm not a matchmaker, but I do know that you should never say never. When you least expect it—*wham*." She clapped her hands together. "That's when it hits."

"I really don't want anything to hit."

She flicked her gaze up at me. "Why, Sam, how do you know?"

I was taken aback. Before I could think about it, she said, "I have another confession. Something I haven't told Mia. But you have to promise not to tell her."

My imagination whirled—and not in a good way. More matchmaking shenanigans? "What is it?" I asked carefully.

"I don't have a dress for Ani's wedding. Everything I have is from before the cancer. You're such a stylish dresser. Maybe you'd help me look online later?"

"Of course. But why don't you want to tell Mia?"

"Oh, Mia's always trying to get me to dress outside my comfort zone, be more fashionable, that kind of thing. She keeps saying that I should spend more money on myself. But for me the thrill is in the hunt. The bargain hunt, that is."

A woman after my own heart. "We can fix this," I said. Caleb planned to meet Lilly this afternoon, so maybe Mrs. D. could sneak away for a while? "Isn't there a cute dress shop downtown?"

"I haven't gone in. I'm afraid I'll be pressured to buy if I'm by myself. You know how some of those places are."

I reached over and patted her hand. "When would you want to go?"

She glanced at the kitchen clock. "How about right after lunch?"

"You got it." If it got me away from discussing my love life—and from Caleb—that would be fine with me.

Chapter Six

Samantha

The downtown dress shop, *Ms. JESSICA'S*, as the over-the-door sign in scrolly font announced, was high-end, judging by the designer names and the price tags I secretly checked as we browsed. I got the feeling that Mrs. D. was not going to go for this level of luxury. The hovering salesperson, Ms. Jessica herself, wasn't helping her feel any more comfortable. She was a stunning-looking woman with dark hair and a lot of makeup who could have been forty-six or sixty-four, I couldn't say.

"This is simply stunning and elegant." She held up a navy-blue one-shouldered dress with a cute tulle ruffle going across the top of the bodice and then trailing down the front.

"Oh, that's really pretty," Mrs. D. said. As Ms. Jessica went back to the racks to look for more, Mrs. D. rummaged for the tags. She took one look at the price and blanched. "It's eight hundred dollars," she said in a horrified whisper. "This was a mistake." She looked a little panicked.

"We can leave," I said. "Or maybe just try it on for fun? It will give us an idea of what looks good."

When I told Caleb that I was going shopping with his mother, he'd actually smiled. And I must admit, it was quite an experience being on the receiving end of that head-on smile. It was spontaneous and open, his teeth white and straight but with just enough imperfection to look boyishly attractive. "She never spends money on herself," he said. And then he insisted on handing me his credit card.

"Are you sure you want to give me this?" I asked. "If you see a charge for a Caribbean vacation, it totally wasn't me."

"Ha ha," he said. "Sneak pay for the dress, okay? Have her get a really nice one."

"Can I get a really nice one too?" I looked up at him with feigned innocence. "If you see a duplicate charge, that was purely accidental. Also, I have no idea how I'm supposed to sneak pay for something. Maybe I can sneak pay my credit card balance, what do you think?"

He made a strange face.

I squinted and examined him closely. "Did you almost laugh or is that your constipated face?" I asked.

He didn't answer, just shook his head and walked away. I didn't know if I could pull one over on Mrs. D., but I did like that Caleb wanted her to have something that she didn't feel comfortable buying for herself.

And also, I was definitely buying us ice cream on his tab.

We walked past a wall of greenery into a sitting space with white couches, rubber tree plants, and gauzy draperies where people could try on expensive dresses accompanied by any number of female friends and relatives. It was a lovely shop, but I had a feeling it was as far out of her comfort zone as it was mine.

"Look what I have." Ms. Jessica suddenly appeared in the fitting room doorway. Mrs. D. and I simultaneously turned to find her carrying a mountain of tulle, satin, and crepe in a rainbow of colors, some sparkly, which I couldn't help noticing. "I hope you don't mind, but I found a few more you might like." Mrs. D. gave an "Oh well, guess it's too late now" shrug and pulled a comical face as she closed the curtain.

I shook my head and laughed. She had a fun sense of humor. Again, I noticed the resemblance to her son. If he ever laughed, would he pull funny faces too? I'd usually seen him when he was annoyed.

As I waited outside the fitting room, I texted Mia.

Your mom is trying on dresses at Ms. Jessica's. Wish you were here.

How on earth did you get her in there?! came the reply.

A few minutes later, Mrs. D. stood on a carpeted platform, and I was taking pics of her from all sides.

"It's very slimming," she said. A rather large ornamental silk flower was sewn at the shoulder, and she instinctively pushed it away from her face. "The silk flower is pretty, but can it be removed? It's choking me a little." She fake-choked and bit back a laugh. Then so did I.

"Oh no no, you must not touch the flower," Ms. Jessica said, spreading it out so that it flared out over Mrs. D.'s neck and avoided her face. As soon as she let go, the flower sprang up and hit her in the neck all over again.

"I've never had a dress like this," Mrs. D. said, "but I like it. Except it looks more like a mother-of-the-bride dress than a dress to wear to a wedding."

"Well, Mia and Brax are headed to the altar eventually," I said. "So try out the fit by pretending to do mother-of-the-bride things." I had no idea why I was acting so impulsively silly, but I just went with it. "Let me fix your train, my dear," I said in a quasi-British matron voice, bending over, pretending to fix an imaginary bride's train. Mrs. D. bent over too.

"It feels pretty comfortable," she said. "Now what?"

"Now you greet all the relatives. 'Hi, Uncle Martin,'" I said to the air in front of us. "'How was your trip from California?'"

"Martin," Mrs. D. said, talking to the same invisible person I was, "I'm so sorry about your divorce. How's your twenty-five-year-old girlfriend that you left Mildred for, who happens to be a year younger than your oldest daughter?"

We both laughed hysterically. I glanced around to make sure Ms. Jessica wasn't watching. I didn't want us to get kicked out of here like two teenage girls at the mall. "You look very elegant," I said in my own voice, putting my fingertips together as if I were holding the stem of a wineglass and pretending to hold it out to her.

She gave me a questioning look. "What's this?"

"Your drink. You deserve it. You just married off your daughter."

She laughed. But I wasn't through yet. "See how it feels when you sit." I directed her to a velvet bench nearby.

"Pretty good," Mrs. D. said as she sat. "But the eight hundred dollars feels like a giant pain in my butt." And then she giggled.

Which made me giggle. But then suddenly we heard the telltale click-clack of Ms. Jessica's heels on the polished wood floor. "Hurry," I whispered, guiding Mrs. D. into the fitting room. "Get in there and change before we get kicked out of here." As I helped unzip her, I had an idea. "Would that thrift shop we passed have any dresses?"

I could only describe her look as one of pure relief. I knew that look well, because I was a thrift shop gal myself, through and through. "I don't know," she said. "But let's go."

～

Caleb

. . .

"So, Lilly." I smiled at her over coffee and a cinnamon bun, which we were sharing at our former favorite coffee shop, *Bean There, Done That*, on Main Street. "Thanks for coming out to meet me." I was trying to be nonchalant and look cheerful in a carefree way, but I could feel my neck sweating against my shirt. At least I was clean-shaven now, putting my best foot forward, so to speak.

"Of course. It's good to see you, Caleb." She gave me a genuine smile, which made me remember the many other times she'd smiled at me like that. She was still so pretty, with blue eyes and blond hair. Except now she wore her hair sleek and straightened.

Her pleasant greeting gave me the confidence to continue. "Listen, I wanted to meet you face-to-face to clear up a misunderstanding."

"We talked about this a few weeks ago." She sat back, her tone cautious. Yes, we had, but it hadn't gone well. I'd called her to discuss the fact that we were in the wedding together and wanted us to start off on the right foot. But the conversation had devolved into a tawdry episode of Grey's Anatomy. I'd made my case and told her it was all hospital gossip, that I wasn't a faithless dirtball who disregarded the feelings of women, but the damage had been done.

"I wanted you to know the truth," I said, persevering. "Especially since we're going to be spending some time together over the next few weeks."

"Look, you can date whomever you want. It's not my business."

"Fair enough." What I really wanted to tell her, hospital gossip aside, was that I was here to find out for myself if she might be the One. If we might have missed our golden opportunity together because of all the stress we were under. That I had all these unresolved questions that had been eating away at me. That I had to separate out the *what-ifs* from reality, and I didn't want to look back with regret.

But I knew that if I said any of that, she'd flee as fast as she could though the streets of Oak Bluff. So I started with the issue at hand. "What you heard about me was gossip, not the truth."

She sighed. "Stacey is always over the top."

"I didn't want you to think that I'm dishonest or a cheater," I said. "I'm the same person I've always been." I felt a sense of relief. This was what I wanted her to know.

"Well," she said, "I believe that we can't help but be different people now. I'm in a good place, Cay. I love my job. I'm proud of what I've accomplished. You were right when you called me out on being unhappy in Milwaukee. I was miserable. My dream was always to stay here and do this."

I admired her honesty. "Lilly, we've both matured," I said. "We've found ourselves. I'm really glad this wedding made our paths cross again." I stopped an inch short of "Sometimes I wonder what it would be like to try again," but I was afraid to say it. So I let the words hang.

Too soon. It was too soon for me to play my hand. My palms got suddenly clammy, and sweat ran down my back. Did she believe that I wasn't a cheater and a player?

She set down her cup.

What I'd said was the most nonthreatening language I could come up with. So much better than *I totally stalk you online, and I think that maybe I might still be in love with you. Or something that I can't define.*

She smiled a little. "I'm glad we were able to talk today. We were friends for so long. I didn't like the way we left things."

I didn't want her to know that I'd been thinking about this ever since Ani had told me Lilly was going to be one of her brides-maids. Would she be open to us trying again? Before I could over-think what she was saying, more words spilled out. "I had a job interview at the clinic," I blurted.

Her fine brows lifted. "Oak Bluff Medical?"

"I met with Dr. Blumenthal a few weeks ago about a job in his practice. I should know whether or not I got it any time now."

"Oh."

I interpreted that as an interested *oh*. As opposed to a disappointed or a shocked one.

"That's exciting, Cay. I'm happy for you. I never imagined you'd come back to practice in a small town like Oak Bluff." She took off the lid of her coffee and swirled it around. "Oh no. They put soy milk in my coffee again instead of oat milk." She rose from her seat. "I'm going to get it fixed." She looked up at me. "Will you wait?"

"Yeah, sure. Of course." She left. The air surrounding her had a soft, feminine scent. She was still so beautiful. Since when did she start drinking something other than plain coffee with lots of cream and sugar? I smiled. What else would I discover about her that was different? I couldn't wait to find out.

My phone chimed with a text. It was a video of my mom, dressed in a light purple satiny gown... with her arms flung out, dancing.

Wait. *Dancing?* My mother was doing the electric slide in a store?

Three dots were also dancing under the photo. *"Your mom looks AH-MAZING in this dress, right??? If you're nearby the thrift shop, plz stop by and tell her that! I think she should buy it! She needs some encouragement."*

I texted her back. *"Reclaim?"*

"YES!"

I rubbed my forehead and chuckled. My mom was the most ferocious bargain hunter this side of the Rockies. She called the Dollar Store the Treasure Trove. She didn't ever pay full cost for, well... anything. Taking her to the thrift store was a stroke of genius.

Surviving cancer last year had been an ordeal for my mom—for all of us—but she'd come out of it more grateful and joyous about life than ever. She'd often said she wanted to refresh her wardrobe to reflect her new attitude, but she hated shopping alone.

But this took the joy thing to new heights. She'd trusted Sam to go with her. But enough to do *this*?

Lilly returned and sat down again across from me. "The barista's working on my drink. She said someone would bring it over."

I took a bite of cinnamon roll and gestured for her to do the same. But she held up a hand and deferred.

"You go ahead." She pushed her fork away. "I can't eat like when I was a teenager." That made me a little sad. The giant, gooey, sweet-smelling cinnamon roll we always used to share was a happy tradition. But maybe I was wrong to try to remind her of the past. Maybe I should focus on making new memories instead of reliving old ones. "I'm excited to go to the farm with everyone this weekend," she said. "I hope we can catch up." She reached her hand out across the table.

I took it, as I had many times before. Surveyed her smiling face. Did I hear birds singing along with a heavenly chorus of angels when she touched me? Not exactly. But I did feel good. Hopeful. She was sort of maybe giving me a chance. And she was smiling. Those were positive things, right?

"Hey," I said. "My mom's at Reclaim with Samantha. Have you met her yet?"

"No, but I'd love to. Mind if I go with you?"

I wasn't expecting that, but I said sure. As I sat down and took a couple more bites of the cinnamon roll (why waste a good thing?), a flustered barista ran over to our table with Lilly's drink. "Here you go," she said. "Sorry for the error. We're training someone new today and she's a little nervous."

"Thanks," Lilly said with a wide smile, standing up as she spoke, "but it's a little late. Sorry you're too busy to properly supervise your trainees."

The barista looked a little surprised. Frankly, so was I.

Lilly's words certainly didn't come out right. I was sure she didn't mean them in a stinging fashion. Did she?

"It's all hands on deck when the new interns come every July too," I said with a sympathetic glance at our harried barista.

Lilly gave me an unreadable look, then pulled a bill out of her purse and traded the drink for the bill. "I'm sorry if that came out harsh. Thanks for fixing it."

"No problem," the woman said with a smile.

I wanted to add about nine more dollars to the buck tip. But to be fair, she'd apologized.

As the employee walked away, Lilly said, "Caleb, you've always been such a softie. Always trying to smooth out conflict."

I shrugged. "Comes with the middle-child territory."

"I just think people need feedback when new employees aren't being carefully supervised. As a business manager myself, customer service is really important. It impacts people's perception of the business."

"I get it," I said, but all I wanted was to let this go. Also, was she mansplaining to me? I wanted to tell her to chill out a little. I mean, give people the benefit of the doubt when they're new, you know?

We started the two-block walk. I hadn't been back to town since Christmas, and believe me, the holidays here are beautiful, but there is nothing like a stroll on a beautiful June day with pots of colorful flowers bursting everywhere in front of all the store-fronts. And the smell of homemade fudge from the ice-cream shop carrying on the breeze. And everyone saying hey instead of huddling inside their winter coats. I must've seen about six people I knew from growing up.

It felt great to be home. It reaffirmed my desire to come back and settle down here. Of course, I hadn't told my family yet—I knew they loved me so much they'd be all over that news, and I wanted to make sure I had the job first. And I'm kidding. They do love me, but what my folks really wanted from me now were grandchildren, preferably as near as next door.

It felt good also walking beside Lilly just as we had so many times before. But I didn't try to hold her hand. I just let it sink in that I was with her and that I wanted to get to know the person she was now. Things were feeling pretty good so far.

The shop bell of Reclaim chimed as we walked in. Chipped chandeliers—my sister would call that shabby chic—hung from the ceiling, and the place was surrounded by racks of—well, any kind of clothing imaginable. The owners had bought the space next door, and that part contained household items of all types—china, books, glassware, furniture, the walls covered with framed paintings of all sizes and types. I'd only been here once before—years ago when Mia was looking for a prom dress—but I didn't think that any of the decor had changed.

At first I thought that no one was around except for a few senior volunteers sifting through several long tables piled high with clothing. But then I heard laughter. Which I would describe as completely raucous. As I turned toward the voices, I saw, in the center of the room, in front of a massive mirror, two women... dancing. To be fair, Earth Wind and Fire's "September" was playing over a speaker, and who could resist dancing to that? But still.

"My God, Caleb," Lilly said, tugging on my shirtsleeve, "is that your *mother*? And who is that with her?"

I didn't know what disconcerted me more—the sight of my mother shimmying around, shaking it with her arms above her head in that fancy purple dress, or Sam, in a bright shimmery orange dress, letting loose right next to her.

Probably the latter. My mom used to act spontaneous like this when we were kids. "Come on, we're pirates," she'd say, grabbing a paper towel roll. "Now get your swords ready and prepare for battle!" Or waltzing into the kitchen after school with a giant Snickers bar on a cutting board and cutting it into slices we all shared, each piece a tiny prize. She was a fun mom, full of imagination. But I didn't think she'd done a lot of anything like that since the cancer.

Sam was laughing with my mother, her hair spilling out of her ponytail, her laughter boisterous and even a little loud. *Who knew she had that in her?* And she looked amazing in that dress, free and unrestrained, letting loose. I felt confused. A little stunned. But also weirdly happy. Like, a big part of me wanted to join right in with them.

Oh, and it appeared champagne was involved, judging by the two plastic half-empty glasses nearby.

What kind of thrift store was this?

Lilly leaned over me to see. "Oh my gosh, your mom's got some moves."

Yeah. And you know who else had them? My nemesis. Sam was dancing with abandon, jumping up and down with enthusiasm, hip-bumping my mom.

It was quite the spectacle.

Confused and half embarrassed, I turned to leave.

Lilly had other ideas. "Hi, Mrs. D'Angelo," she called over the music, already heading over there.

Both women halted. My mom turned around. She blew back some hair that had fallen over her face.

My mother was absolutely not the type to appear disheveled. Or to be wearing a colorful purple dress with some kind of sparkly overskirt.

Even more baffling was that this woman that I sincerely disliked was bonding with my mother. Helping her to get a dress not in the *chichi* dress shop but in a thrift shop. And acting wildly fun in a way that I'd never seen.

The music ended, and my mom, still laughing, pulled Sam into a big hug. She said something to her that I couldn't hear, but Sam nodded and looked sincerely touched. Then my mom's gaze drifted over to me, and she smiled.

That smile could've meant anything from *I'm so happy* to *This woman is wonderful*. I wasn't sure which, but I didn't have to figure it out, because just then, Lilly clapped and said, "Mrs. D'Angelo!" and went running over to them.

"Oh my goodness. Hi, Lilly," my mom said in her usual genuine manner and opened her arms to hug her.

I can't tell you how I appreciated that because... well, our breakup had been rough. At least on me. Now, I have to hand it to my mom. She'd greeted Lilly unconditionally and warmly, not coldly or judgmentally, which she well could have done.

Sam stopped laughing, smoothed down her flyaway hair, and extended her hand. "Hi, Lilly, I'm Samantha. Sam."

"Oh, of course," Lilly said. "Ani's told me all about you. It's so nice to finally meet you. We were at the coffee shop—I hope you don't mind that I stopped in too."

"Oh, of course not." My mom flapped a dismissive hand. "It's nice to see you, Lilly."

"Mom," I said, smiling and holding out my hands. "You look terrific."

She looked pleased. "Sam helped me," she said a little out of breath. She dropped her voice and swatted at a giant flower that appeared to be resting against her neck. "I seem to be gravitating toward dresses with giant flowers today. Sam said she could snip it right off. What do you think?"

Sam was right behind her, also a little disheveled, her hair now completely loose and free-falling over her shoulders. My mom looked terrific, but Sam... well, she looked... well.

"You're stunning," I said. Then I realized I might've been staring stupidly at Sam, so I quickly added, "Mom. Er—you should get that dress." I cringed because did I just call my mother stunning? Even worse, did I *mean* that Sam was stunning? This was disturbing on so many levels. I couldn't even look at—well, anybody.

Something else superseded my embarrassment—seeing my mom being spontaneous and laughing and dancing and living very much in the moment. "You *need* that dress," I said.

"That's what I said!" Sam said, laughing. She held my mom by the shoulders from behind and poked her head around. "See, Mrs. D., Caleb agrees. What do you think, Lilly?"

"Totally agree." She nodded. "It's a winner."

A shop employee walked up, dressed in jeans with felt flowers sewn all over, a fringy leather jacket, and sunglasses. "It really is a great dress," she said.

"Well then, I'll take it!" my mom said, beaming. She gave Sam a hug. "This was so much fun, honey. Thank you." They both walked into adjoining fitting rooms to change. Lilly and I browsed a little until they both came out at the same time.

My mom took the dress that Sam had draped over her arm.

"Don't pay for that!" Sam said in a panicked voice.

"Too late," my mom said, sweeping up the dress and carrying both over to the counter. She handed over her credit card. "Here you go."

Sam rummaged through her own purse.

"Save it," I said quietly, walking over to stand beside her at the counter.

"I don't need your mom to pay for my dress too." She looked genuinely distressed.

"How much is it?" I asked.

"Twenty bucks."

Was she really upset about twenty bucks? I put my hand on her arm to stop her rummaging. She looked up.

"She wants to do it. As a thank-you." I lowered my voice. "It would make her happy. I'd just let her."

She surveyed me with those big eyes. I saw the struggle. It spoke volumes.

My mom, still looking like a kid who'd just opened six birthday presents and was now ready to dig into the cake, gave Sam a squeeze. "Will you help me later with the flower amputation?"

"Of course," she said. Then added, "Thank you for buying my dress. It wasn't necessary but—I love it. Two great finds!"

"Oh, honey, you're welcome. I had the best time."

How had Sam found the perfect compromise for my Walmart-loving mom? I didn't know. But I was in awe.

I barely heard my mom ask me a question. "Where are you headed now, Caleb?"

"I'm going to walk Lilly back to her shop." I turned to Lilly. "If that's good with you."

"Of course. Sure. We can catch up a little more."

"Nice seeing you, Lilly," my mom said with a wave.

"Great to finally meet you," Sam added.

I gave a nod to both of them, making sure to barely look at Sam. I did not want Lilly thinking... well, anything. As we walked out of the dress shop and I held the door, Lilly said, "I thought Ani said you and Sam didn't get along very well."

"We've definitely had our moments," I said. "But Sam's all right." She really wasn't all right. She was stubborn and outspoken and a pain in the ass.

"That's pretty funny that your mom found a dress there of all places."

"My mom *is* the thrift queen."

Lilly fell silent. I knew that she was most definitely not a thrifter. I didn't know if her silence meant she was impressed or was thinking that thrift stores were not for the likes of her. Finally she spoke. "That orange color is really wild. Not many people could pull that off."

She was talking, of course, about the dress Sam had on. "That must be a girl thing," I said. "Guys don't really notice that stuff." The last thing I wanted to do was make her worried that I was noticing Sam.

Because I absolutely was not.

Chapter Seven

Samantha

As Mrs. D. collected our bags and her stuff, I perused a rack of extreme markdowns, my favorite thing. But I was distracted—I couldn't help but notice Caleb and Lilly walk out together, laughing and talking in quiet tones. He opened the door and momentarily rested a hand on her back as they walked out of the shop and onto the street.

They were perfect together. A stunning couple, actually.

It threw me. Maybe because I'm so competitive. I guess I felt uncomfortable because my vexatious colleague was finding love and I wasn't?

I realized that Mrs. D. was quietly standing there, assessing me. I took a random item off the rack and checked it out. Unfortunately, it was a neon green bodysuit with side cut-outs and rhinestones surrounding a deep V neck. Perfect for my next space adventure.

"Lilly's very pretty," I said to fill the silence. The last thing I wanted was for her to think I was—God forbid—jealous or something. Just because she was petite, blond and fair to my totally black hair and more ruddy complexion, polite and sweet to my sometimes brash outspokenness.

But I was *not* jealous. One did not get jealous of the would-be girlfriend of someone they disliked intensely.

"Yes, she is," Mrs. D. agreed. Which told me zero about how she felt about Caleb wanting to get back with Lilly. Not that it was my business, but well, I couldn't help but be curious.

"And she seems very nice," I said politely. I went to hang up the jumpsuit, but the slinky fabric made it slide straight to the floor, so I had to stoop to pick it up. "Just the fact that she came over here with Caleb is a good thing, right? Maybe she's really considering giving him another chance." I used a bright tone to make my intentions crystal clear.

"Samantha, may I ask you a question?" Mrs. D. put a hand gently on my arm, which made me stop trying to adjust the dress as it once again slid down the hanger. "Why do you care if Caleb gets back together with Lilly when you two don't even get along that well?"

Blood rushed in a hot flood to my cheeks. My stomach gave a nervous flop. "Um, I'm an altruist?" She stared at me as I shuffled nervously from one foot to the other. "A matchmaker at heart?" It was clear that she wasn't buying that either. One look into her kind, concerned eyes and I was done for. It was as if she saw clear through everything deep inside me, the good, the bad, and the desperate.

At that moment, all kinds of buried feelings swelled up. Longing for someone to confide in, to confess, to accept me just as I was, faults and all. I'd never had a mother like that, so why should the yearning be so very primal? "Because I did something awful to Caleb regarding Lilly," I blurted.

Frowning, Mrs. D. grabbed my arm and led me to a canary-yellow velvet-covered circa-1960s couch. I don't know what I was expecting. A lecture? A scolding? But all she did was smile.

How can a smile alone make you want to tear up?

She grabbed my hand before I could mentally put up my guard. "Whatever it is, it can't be that bad." She squeezed my hand tight. "I mean, he and Lilly are walking around town together, right?"

I realized that I was being ridiculous. I wasn't so much choked up over the bad situation I found myself in but rather because Mrs. D. was so... motherly. I was a caregiver, but I hadn't been on the receiving end of care in so, so long.

I shook my head to clear it and sat up. Then I forced myself to look her in the eye. I tried to think of something jokey to stop the flood of words that seemed hell-bent on rushing out of my mouth.

"It's no secret that Caleb and I are like oil and water—and sometimes we even clash at work. A few weeks ago, he switched my name out from one of his cases, which was embarrassing and upsetting, and I vented to a friend. I was mad—and ended up repeating some things about Caleb and someone he dated that I'd heard that turned out to not be true. Through a strange twist of fate, what I said got back to Lilly, and now she doesn't trust him."

I had to look away, certain Mrs. D. would be done with me after this. "I want you to know that I don't spread rumors, but in my anger, I caused damage. But I'm determined to fix it." I heaved a sigh. "Your son seems to bring out the worst in me."

She was smiling again. What was with all the smiling? "Watch out for those men that get your dander up," she said. "They're the ones who are dangerous."

"Dangerous?" I hardly thought Caleb was dangerous. Oh. She was talking about my heart. I immediately threw my hands up in a gesture of defense. "Oh no. No, no, no. You're misunderstanding. This is not an enemies-to-lovers situation. This is me trying to undo the damage I caused. That's all."

The shop doorbell tinkled again, and a mild breeze blew, bringing with it the scent of grass and blossoms and... life, sending my hair aflutter.

If it weren't for all this stress, this town would be a lovely place to explore. Full of nature and family and friendly people—a community.

Mrs. D. waved her hand dismissively. "Experience has taught me that if a relationship could be felled by a simple rumor, it probably wasn't going to make it in the first place." She gave me a poignant look. "Let's go to lunch."

I jerked up my head. Was she saying something about Caleb and Lilly without actually saying anything about them? "Caleb told me that Lilly was the love of his life," I said, catching up to her as she headed for the door. "Before all the stress of med school, he said that they got along really well."

"If that was true, they'd still be together right now." Mrs. D. gathered up her jacket, her purse, and our bag. "I'm like you. I don't ever want to be the one to ruin someone's dreams. Whether I like them or not."

"What do you mean?"

"I'll always be nice to Lilly, for Caleb's sake. But I don't agree that they're meant to be together."

That made me feel a little better. But I had so many questions. "Did Caleb tell you why they broke up?" I was asking solely for professional reasons, of course.

"The move to Milwaukee was really hard on Lilly. She had trouble finding a job, and Caleb was in class during the day and studying at night. She felt alone and miserable. One minute." She rummaged through her purse and pulled out her car keys. "Caleb tends to shoulder all the blame for everything. Of course, Lilly blamed it all on her loneliness and how she dropped her entire life for him and had difficulties starting another one."

My head was whirling. Mrs. D. was not painting a picture of the easygoing, uncommitted guy I knew. But maybe instead, he was romantic and impulsive. That could be just as bad, right? "Why do you think he wants to get back together with her so badly?"

She shrugged. "Once we had a dog named Larry. He was amazing, lovable, playful, smart. And he and Caleb were inseparable. When Caleb was eight, he visited Larry's grave in the apple orchard every single day."

"Aw, that's sweet."

"...for two whole years." She made a face that was *not* complimentary.

I tried to picture a little version of Caleb, kneeling amid the fallen apples, torn up about his dog. "That's a lot of loyalty for an eight-year-old."

"I'm being facetious. But the truth is, Caleb loves deeply. But, unfortunately, sometimes stupidly."

"You said that, not me."

"He thinks she's his soulmate. None of us do."

At some point, I realized that my mouth was hanging open. I managed to shut it. It was bad enough that I was determined to help my mortal frenemy get his true love back. How was I to know that apparently his entire family thought that was a very bad idea?

"I've probably said too much." Then she gave a little laugh. "Make that, I *know* I've said too much. Look, Caleb and Lilly were young. Maybe Lilly's matured. Caleb will have to figure that out. I just want you to see that there are layers here."

Layers I had no desire to peel back.

All I wanted to do was undo the damage I'd done.

My only job was to stay neutral and disinterested. And most importantly of all, to keep disliking him.

Because God help me if that ever changed.

Chapter Eight

Samantha

The next morning, I was up before Caleb. Mrs. D. and I chatted over coffee and I showed her my dress for Ani's wedding, a pretty salmony-pink satin gown with a lacy bodice. When Mr. D. refused any help in making breakfast, I decided to go for a run. As I was lacing up my sneakers, he handed me something. It was a UW sweatshirt, faded red and soft in the way that only a well-loved old sweatshirt can be. "Wear this," he said. "Mornings are still a little chilly."

I thanked him, put it on without thinking much about it, and went for a good run.

When I returned, Caleb was sitting at the island, talking animatedly to his dad about baseball as his dad loaded burrito shells with a mouthwatering mixture of scrambled eggs, cheese, and onions and peppers. I poured myself a coffee and sat down as far away from Caleb as I could get.

It wasn't long before his gaze wandered over to me. "That's my lucky sweatshirt," he said.

"Oh, for goodness' sake," I said, setting down my mug of coffee with a soft thud. "Your lucky *what*?"

"My lucky sweatshirt," he confirmed. "I was wearing it when I found out I got into med school."

I rolled my eyes. The man was a total sentimentalist. "At least it's not your *get* lucky sweatshirt."

Mr. D. gave a snort. "Good one." He handed me a steaming breakfast burrito that he'd tossed onto a plate, the cheese sticking in long gooey delicious strings to the spatula.

I took the plate and held my breath, knowing that Caleb's competitive streak would not allow him to be outdone.

"Hmm," he said, rubbing his chin and looking thoughtful. "Come to think of it, it might've been that too."

I set down the plate and smiled sweetly. "If I would've known that, I would've burned it instead of worn it." I took a bite of the burrito—which tasted as amazing as it looked—and immediately moved to take it off. Halfway through, I felt his hand on my arm. I poked my head out of the shirt to find him laughing hysterically.

His laugh was rumbly and hearty, reverberating in pleasant waves around me. "I'm teasing," he said, grinning. "Gotcha."

I pursed my lips and shook my head, pretending to be offended.

"Oh, come on, it was a little funny."

"No, it really wasn't. It was gross."

"Sorry," he said. I put on the most hardened, skeptical expression I could. "Really sorry," he persisted. "See?" He pushed out his lower lip and made a sad face.

He looked so ridiculous that I burst out laughing. Even though I didn't want to.

As my completely inappropriate guffaw faded, my breath caught, half from trying to stop and half from the realization that something strange was happening to me. I felt... caffeinated. A little tingly, a little out of breath.

I took another sip of coffee to buy myself some time to get it together. I remember thinking that his eyes were so intense, that odd shade of green, so, so... No. I was not interested. *Definitely not interested.*

I definitely did not see a spark of heat in those eyes aimed right at me, straight as Cupid's arrow.

That was when I choked on my coffee. I stood up, coughing and trying to catch my breath.

He stood too, poured me a glass of water, and handed it to me, slapping me on the back.

"What med school did you go to?" I asked between gasps, "Because that's not what you're supposed to do when someone's choking."

"If I tried the Heimlich on you, you'd probably elbow me to death."

I wanted to tell him he was absolutely right, but I was still choking. When I could finally breathe again, he was still standing next to me, his lips turned up in the slightest smile. Nice, full lips, I couldn't help noticing, probably because everything had gotten so weird, and once that happens, it's like I couldn't stop that inner voice from tormenting me. *He's hot.*

Out of the corner of my eye, I saw Caleb's parents exchange looks. I couldn't tear that shirt off fast enough. I handed it to him.

"Keep it," he said. "It looks good on you."

∿

Caleb

Sam caught me in the hallway, on her way upstairs to pack up for our trip.

I was a little off-kilter from what had just happened in the kitchen. Parleying with her had been fun. Exhilarating actually, if I was being completely honest. When I managed to forget the trouble she'd gotten me into with Lilly, that is.

"How did things go with Lilly yesterday?" Sam asked. She'd halted on the second stair, her hand on the railing. Her hair was messy from the run, and she was wearing a gray T-shirt that said *I got an A in Anatomy*. Which seemed just like her—I had no doubt that she'd graduated at the top of her class. Yet there was no denying that her personal anatomy *was* indeed A plus. But I digress.

I knew she was trying to help and that she felt bad about things. But unfortunately, the damage had already been done. Frankly, things hadn't gone that great with Lilly. Yesterday I'd tried to connect with her on the way to her shop. Oh, she'd been friendly enough, but when I'd tried to remind her of all our good times by bringing up a memory or pointing out a place we used to hang out, she'd gone radio silent.

I knew that I needed to show her, not just tell her, that I wasn't the guy she'd heard those rumors about. My sense was that she didn't quite believe me. Also, she kept fielding a beehive of texts on her phone as she walked, which also wasn't an ego boost.

"That good, huh?" Sam was regarding me from the step, from a vantage point of height. I felt like she could somehow peek right into my brain at all the jumbled thoughts swirling around there.

"It's early yet. I'm looking forward to spending time with her this weekend and showing her who I really am."

"I could totally help, you know."

"Thanks, but I don't need it." I didn't want or need Sam's help with Lilly, but I'm not going to lie, the matchmaking hocus-pocus stuff she'd mentioned sounded a little intriguing. Especially coming from a scientific, no-nonsense person like her who seemed to reject any kind of romantic notions about love. Wouldn't it be amazing if someone could really tell if a couple was meant to be? It would save a whole lot of money on divorce attorneys, right?

I wasn't that desperate. I felt certain that if Lilly could just spend some time with me, she'd see me for who I really was and realize how great we could be together.

I was going to be positive. I had an entire weekend to convince her. And I was going to make certain to clear this up once and for all.

"You should let me help," the pain in my tuchus said. "At least let me put in a good word or two."

Jeez, and my family thought that *I* had a tough time throwing in the towel on anything.

I studied her carefully. "I can handle this myself." *Please* let me handle this myself, I almost added. But I was afraid that would sound desperate.

"Okay, if you insist." She continued walking up the stairs. And I continued to not be interested in seeing her cute behind as she did that.

I had another way to get her off my case and keep her otherwise occupied. "Actually, there is something you can do." She froze halfway up the stairs. "Quinn will be riding with us after all. I know you won't mind sitting in the back seat with him."

"No, of course not," she said with a fake smile. "See you in the morning."

I was determined to make Lilly see how sincere I was, and for that, the only thing I needed was together time at the farm. Beginning with the ride there tomorrow.

～

Samantha

"Have fun this weekend," Mrs. D. said. "Here are some cookies for everyone for the road. Give Mia a kiss for me." She gave me the cookies and a squeeze. "And Samantha, thank you—for going shopping with me. It was so much fun."

"Thank you for making me feel so welcome," I said as I hugged her back. I meant it more than she could ever know. I moved to head down the steps when she grabbed my arm.

"You are welcome here anytime," she said, her gaze locking with mine so I couldn't look away. "With or without my kids."

A big ball formed in my throat. Those simple gestures—a hug, a kiss, someone handing me treats and sending me off into the world—brought a giant lump to my throat. She treated me like one of her own kids, and she had no idea how much that meant to me.

"Thanks for... everything," I mumbled. Not the most articulate thank-you. I could have done better if my throat didn't feel as if it were clogged with a Kleenex.

Just then, Caleb pulled up in his truck. He'd picked up Lilly and apparently had met up with Quinn and helped him park his car near the barn, and now we were ready to go. A quick glance showed the fuzzy outline of an unfamiliar face in the back seat surveying me. A sensation of dread diffused through me. I know that might sound harsh, but I'd been through this before: Guy desperate for love gives the hard push to go out. The last thing in the world I wanted was to cause conflict within this wedding party. I couldn't see him very clearly, but he looked fresh-faced and eager, just as Mrs. D. had warned me. But maybe I was just being an alarmist.

I didn't realize I was hesitating until Mrs. D. spoke. "Would you mind if I give you a piece of motherly advice?"

I felt my cheeks burning. Maybe she'd seen my apprehensive look. Or did this have something to do with Caleb and how we'd gotten caught up about that stupid sweatshirt in a way that might have seemed a tiny bit flirtatious? "Sure. Of course." I braced myself for what was surely going to be a critique.

"You don't have to be an adult all the time. It's okay to let down your guard and follow your heart once in a while."

That poor heart of mine plunged. I didn't expect that. But

Beth didn't understand that I couldn't have survived, let alone come as far as I had, by letting down my guard.

"I-I'm not sure what you mean." Let loose this weekend down on the farm? Definitely not with Quinn. What other choices did I have? Mia would be with Brax, Caleb would be hanging out with Lilly, and I would have my friend Gabe, the officiant, who was gay and engaged. I didn't understand what she was getting at.

"You need the chance to act young," Beth said. "There's plenty of time to act old and mature." Before I could ask how to go about doing that, she kissed me on the cheek and said, "Now that I've given you advice, you must call me Beth." Then she waved to her son, who had gotten out of the truck and took the front steps in two bounds. He looked hopeful and energized, probably from being with his lady love.

His glance bounced between both me and his mom before he gave her a puzzled look. "Am I interrupting something?" he asked.

"Just discussing last night's score," I said dryly.

He patted me on the arm. "Don't cry. The Brewers will pull it off next time."

I rolled my eyes.

"Actually, I was just telling Sam how wonderful she is," Beth said cheerily.

That wasn't awkward. With a shrug, he pecked his mother on the cheek. "Oh. Well, okay then," he said. "Bye, Ma. Thanks for everything and see you in a couple of weeks."

"Okay, honey. Bye." As she hugged him, she gave me a wink.

"Bye, Beth," I said with a wave. "Thanks for everything."

Was she telling me that I'd become old before my time? And what did that even mean, follow my heart? I'd always had to act mature. I'd had to put my responsibilities first. If not, what would happen to Wynn?

Chapter Nine

Samantha

I slid into the back seat of the Tacoma to find an earnest-looking guy sitting across from me in the not-large-enough space. Was I paranoid? Yes, but I couldn't help it. My instincts, aided by what Beth had told me about Quinn, had made me nervous.

He was good-looking, with short, close-cropped light brown hair and a Hollywood-worthy jawline. Yet he looked very apple-pie compared to Caleb's darker, more dangerous looks. "Hey there," he said, extending his hand. "Name's Quinn. Quinn Carlson. I went to med school with Tyler." He broke out into a huge smile.

He was obviously friendly, unlike some people I knew. Caleb turned his head, and I caught his eye in the mirror. I made sure to smile widely right back as I shook Quinn's hand. "Nice to meet you," I said. "I'm Sam."

"I've heard a lot about you," he said. "I'm from Milwaukee too. And I have a younger brother the same age as your sister. Actually, I have three of them. Oh, and I'm a huge Brewers fan."

"Oh, that's so funny," Lilly said, turning around. She looked fresh and put together this morning, from what I could see, in a crisply ironed denim shirt and gold hoops. Her lipstick was red and perfect, her hair styled in long pipe-curl waves, the kind that women pay big bucks for.

Did I even remember to put on ChapStick? And also, my thick, straight hair held curl for about thirty seconds, no matter what I did or how many products I used.

I don't know why I was comparing myself to Lilly. She certainly wasn't a threat to me in any way. Although I was firmly anti-love for myself, I still wanted to be the person the D'Angelos thought I was—a kind person. No matter what I thought of their son, I didn't wish bad things on anyone. It made me even more determined to make things right.

That meant that if I had to reach deep to find something positive to say about Caleb, by gosh, I was going to. "So, Lilly, Caleb tells me you own a floral shop?" I leaned forward while I asked, mainly so I could get out of the path of Quinn's stare, which seemed a little intense.

"My family's," she said, tucking her hair behind her ear, "but the plan is that when they retire, I'll own it."

She seemed nice. I know that Beth's view was colored by what had happened between her and Caleb, but I decided to keep an open mind.

"I also have a side business painting flowers," she added. "I sell my framed artwork in my shop."

"You're too humble," Caleb said, admiration radiating in his voice. "Lilly's paintings are going to be exhibited in a show at the state capitol building in Madison next month."

Wow. She was talented—running a business and with an artistic streak that spread beyond floral design to painting. She was also adorable—bubbly, petite, with tiny feet like Cinderella, whereas mine were more Prince Charming-sized. I was reminded of the time I'd worn fire-engine-red Converses with my prom dress because I refused to wear heels. Oma had said, "You're certainly not afraid to be yourself."

Either that or I was just a weird teenager. But the point was, I was always somewhere away from the norms of beauty and probably a lot of other things, but Oma celebrated me just as I was. I had serious doubts that anyone else ever would.

I was startled by a pair of piercing green eyes drilling into me from the rearview. I realized I hadn't responded. "That's really impressive," I said, and I meant it.

"Thanks," Lilly said in a humble tone. "I wasn't going to say anything." She waved her hand dismissively. "I mean, I love my job. But being able to paint flowers for actual money is part of my ten-year business plan."

My business plan was to get my sister off my payroll. Maybe then I'd have time to explore other interests.

"I think you should tell the whole world," Caleb said, beaming.

Ick. *Hey, buddy, eyes on the road* was what *I* was thinking. All we needed was to end up in a ditch because of his googly eyes.

"Thanks," Lilly said. "I've always been interested in all kinds of art, so it was a natural progression."

I had no other interests besides struggling to find time to work out, reading, and trying to stay solvent.

"Caleb is all math and science," Quinn said, which didn't help my plan to make Caleb sound avant-garde—or at least interested in art.

"We've always been as opposite as they come," Lilly said with a nod.

"Maybe not entirely," Caleb replied. He turned to her again, and I couldn't quite see his eyes, but I heard something in his voice. Something that sounded like longing. Or at least a sense of nostalgia. *We were good together, remember?* he seemed to be saying.

I felt something then, quite against my will. His pain. Oh drat.

I *had* to think of something to make this all work out, or I'd never be able to face my best friend again. I'd be steeped in guilt forever.

That's when I heard Oma's voice. *You know what to do. Get to work.*

I didn't come from a long line of matchmakers for nothing. "Well, you know what they say about opposites," I said cheerily. "Friction creates fire." I'd totally made that up. I decided to keep going. "Caleb *does* appreciate art." My mouth acted before my brain, as usual. The trouble was, I'd never even been inside Caleb's apartment. Nothing, absolutely nothing that I knew about him, led me to believe that he thought about, appreciated, or enjoyed art. *Yikes.*

"He does?" Lilly exclaimed.

"I do hang Emma's drawings on my fridge," Caleb said. "She's a very prolific artist. Her main media is crayons."

Aw, cute.

Lilly smiled a little, so she probably thought it was too.

"Does paint 'n' sip count?" Quinn said. "We did that once, right, Cay? It helped us get lai—dates." He cleared his throat. "It helped us get *dates*," he amended.

Caleb in the rearview looked murderous, reinforcing my gut feeling that Quinn was annoying on many levels—to men as well as women.

"So exactly how does Caleb appreciate art?" Lilly directed her question at me.

I didn't even dare to look in the mirror, but I felt Caleb's gaze burning into me. Quinn was half turned toward me expectantly. I had no clue what to say. All I knew was that it had to be good.

"Yes. Um. One time we visited the art museum in Milwaukee. Caleb fell in love with a particular section, didn't you?" I was flying into uncharted air space here. I only hoped he'd catch on and fly along with me.

"When we went...?" He processed the fact that we'd never gone to the museum together. "Oh yeah, of course. Ancient Egypt."

Oh come on, Caleb. I signaled via an eye glare in the mirror. *Give me something to work with here.* I tried steering him in another direction. "I was thinking more along the lines of famous portrait painters. Like, um... Van Gogh, Picasso, Sargent."

"I love the art museum," Caleb cluelessly said. "Best view of the lake from anywhere in the city."

Lilly opened her mouth, probably to say he sucked. I mean, that's certainly what I wanted to say. Ancient Egypt? Lake views? Come *on*.

"I love the Georgia O'Keefe's. She's from Sun Prairie, you know," said Quinn. "When I was in Spain last summer, we toured the Prado. I spent two days there. Goya, El Greco, Murillo, Velazquez... *Las Meninas* absolutely floored me."

"You know about *Las Meninas*?" Lilly said with surprise.

"That's like, the most appreciated painting in the world," Quinn said. "Not to mention the first selfie ever."

Lilly laughed. Caleb looked pained. Absolutely pained. And he wasn't saying anything either, probably because he didn't know *Las Meninas* from *las bananas*.

I took another tack. "Caleb is kind of an artist."

"I am?"

I squinted my eyes at his reflection as if to telepathically convey *Please let me help you to impress this woman.* This was *so* much harder than I thought. I cleared my throat and tried for sincerity, using my hands to demonstrate. "Well, you sculpt bone and piece —things—together—and stuff."

I had a very limited understanding of orthopedics. I really didn't know beyond a basic textbook-knowledge level what went on among the crowd of doctors, nurses, and surgical techs on the other side of my station in the OR. I was too focused on my own job to notice.

Caleb shrugged. "Ortho's really just working with power tools," he said.

Lilly stared. Quinn chuckled.

And this was the best Mr. Romantic could do? Power tools? Not romantic or related to art. So I dug even deeper. "Tell them about Joseph's surgery. Now *that* was artistry."

He sent me a confused look. I wasn't going to risk him screwing this up, so I plunged right in. "This little boy, Joseph, broke his leg so badly that after two surgeries, it was still shorter than the other one, so Caleb and his team did a graft. It took three specialists and many hours, but they let you do a lot of the work, didn't they?"

"How did you know that?" Forget confused. He was genuinely surprised.

"I was there, remember?" He'd done an amazing job. He had his faults, but he was a gifted surgeon, I'd give him that.

Before another word could escape from his mouth and ruin the moment, I added, "That little boy's dream is to play baseball."

Caleb nodded, and I saw the tiniest smile in the mirror. "I think he will one day," he said quietly.

I put a hand to my chest because I'd felt something viscerally. His pride. In his work and in Joseph's outcome. Hopefully Lilly did too. Finally!

"Aw, Cay, that's so sweet," she said.

Whew, all right. Success! At least, the start of success anyway. I sat back and quietly blew out a breath.

This was going to be a very loooong weekend.

"You still coach that disability basketball league?" Quinn asked.

Oh. New info here.

"Yep, every Tuesday evening. Those kids are great."

Oh jeez. He coached *kids*? I felt something else squeeze in my chest. My heart. Like a big block of frozen ice cream sitting on the counter, I felt one tiny edge get a little soft.

But just a tiny edge. *So you* do *have human qualities,* I thought to myself.

84

The eyes were back in the mirror. Except now they held amusement. "Sometimes, yes."

Oh no. I'd just said that out loud, didn't I?

Quinn pushed playfully on my arm. "She's funny, Cay. So, you two are good friends, huh?"

"Yes," Lilly said. "Tell us about that."

"Mia is my best friend," I said carefully, not wanting to lie. "So of course Caleb and I know each other through her."

"But we actually didn't meet through Mia."

My heart, which was getting quite the aerobic workout, flat out stopped. *Please, please do not tell this story,* I prayed. Actually, I'd forgotten all about a time when we didn't want to tear each other's eyeballs out.

"We met at a residents' party," he continued. "On New Year's Eve."

I'd managed to somehow erase that entire incident from my memory. Only the bitter aftertaste remained. I had no idea why he'd brought it up, but I really didn't want to relive it again, so I did damage control. "And we realized we'd be working together in the OR. And we figured out that Caleb was Mia's brother." I shrugged. "So voilà." I flourished my arm and smiled widely. "Instant friendship."

Caleb rolled his eyes. I glared—the most I could do outside of saying stop.

"It's got to be more interesting than that," Lilly said with a laugh. "Tell us more."

I struggled to think of something positive. *He'd* been the one to bring it up, but *I* was going to control the narrative. "Caleb saved me from the worst date of my life." Caleb's eyes narrowed. "On New Year's Eve."

And that worst date of my life? Yeah. It had happened to be *him.*

Well, technically, we weren't on a date, but we'd spent the entire evening together. We'd met in the bar line at a trendy East

Side bar a few years ago and started talking. Then we sat down together at a table. Two hours later, we were still talking. And then we danced. But every story has an unexpected twist, right?

My new share-a-ride friends asked for details. So I plunged in. Like I said, Caleb had brought this up, but I was going to tell it my way.

"My date disappeared right before midnight. Imagine that." I paused for drama. And also so that Caleb could sweat this out more—if he had a soul that was capable of feeling bad about things, that is. I embellished by waving my hands. "Poof, gone. Right into the snowy thin air."

It had been so embarrassing, I hadn't even told Mia. Neither had he, supposedly, because she never once mentioned it. And it was just as well.

Lilly spun around. "Get *out*. Your date ditched you right before the *countdown*?"

I confirmed that with a nod. "Ditched in the final minute. No, wait—make that *seconds*."

"Oh my God." Lilly covered her mouth in shock.

"Maybe it wasn't personal, as you seem to make it out to be," Caleb said in a measured tone.

My anger flared up. I told myself not to react, not to respond. But I couldn't help myself. "How does one *not* take that as personal?"

"Yes, really," Lilly agreed. "The jerk."

"I'm a little lost," Quinn said, which reminded me to calm down. After all, it happened a long time ago, shortly after I'd become friends with Mia. I hadn't even known that Caleb was her brother.

Lilly turned to Caleb. "So did you help her after that guy ghosted her?"

"I did." He looked directly into the mirror. "And apologized profusely for the bad treatment."

He did show up, ten minutes later, when I was gathering my

coat and heading for the door. "Hey, I'm really sorry about that," he'd said. "I had to take that call."

I just sort of stared at him. "Hope everything is okay?"

He cleared his throat. "Yeah. I-I enjoyed talking to you. But I've got to be honest—I'm not looking for a relationship right now."

Things had gone from smoking hot to icy cold. A complete one-eighty. And I was floored but trying not to show it. I mean, we'd been having such a fun time. It had been magical—for me anyway. Just goes to show you, I can't matchmake myself or call any shots on relationships. I'm just not meant to be a relationship person. I have no personal date radar.

"And we've been friends ever since," I said through gritted teeth. "And a pox on that horrible date, right?"

I really had forgotten all about that painful night. Except that it marked the beginning of a very antagonistic relationship that had continued to this day. I had no idea if that call he'd taken was legit or just an excuse to get away, but whatever had happened had changed everything.

Quinn sent me an admiring glance. "I can't imagine anyone abandoning you right before midnight any night of the year," Quinn said. "You're really funny. Pretty too."

Oooh no. Ouch. My hunch had been right. His tone, his sideways smile, his bright-eyed look. It all added up to interest I did not want.

"Pretty snarky, you mean," Caleb muttered under his breath.

I ignored that and smiled at Quinn. "Well, thank you. But don't you worry, I never gave that guy a second thought."

"Oh look," Lilly said, pointing forward. "We're here."

And it couldn't be soon enough. After miles of trees and highway and little else, we'd come upon a long white picket fence surrounding a stretch of woods and a wooden sign into which letters were carved that announced we'd arrived at Whispering Meadows Farm.

Caleb wound the truck up a winding drive past orchards and rolling hills with grazing cows, to a large white farmhouse complete with a giant covered porch with a swing and bright red flowers spilling out of planters. Two barns, one red and one white, stood behind the house. We saw a sign pointing toward the outdoor space where the wedding would take place in a few weeks, which was in a field by a creek. It looked gorgeous in Ani's photos, but I couldn't see it clearly from the truck. "We're definitely here," Caleb seconded.

Farm experience, here we come. I tried to think positively, but honestly, I couldn't wait to see Gabe. He was my only hope to survive this weekend, between whatever was going on between Caleb and Lilly and whatever Quinn thought was going to go on with me (but wasn't).

Lilly opened her door as soon as the truck rolled to a stop. "I made everyone's reservations, so I'm going to hop out and make sure everything's in order, okay?"

"I've got to use the restroom," Quinn said as Caleb and I exited the truck. "I'll come with you." He lifted his and Lilly's bags from the truck bed and followed her to the porch.

That left me standing there with Dr. Devil. A cow mooed. Such a foreign sound. Why couldn't we have done a girls' spa weekend instead?

I was so unsettled that I could barely think. I had to get something off my chest. "Why did you mention that party?" I asked Caleb, who had let down the tailgate and was zipping something into his duffel bag.

He stood up straight and faced me. Up close, his eyes were the color of sea glass. So startling. "Lilly asked how we met, and I wasn't thinking." He rubbed his neck, the first time I'd ever seen him look even slightly uncomfortable. "I guess I'm a little nervous. I'm sorry for mentioning that."

He'd sliced open a wound. It was a very old one, but I found myself with an opportunity to say what I'd never gotten off my chest.

"That was really humiliating, being left like that. Not that I've thought about it in years, but it was Harry and Sally gone awry. It was every New Year's Eve fantasy shattered to shreds." Especially since we'd had such a great two hours. Our relationship had gone downhill from there. I'd gone home with Mia not long afterward, and there he was, still without a real explanation. He'd left me assuming the worst, that he'd wanted to disappear rather than kiss me at midnight. Jeesh.

He gave a here-goes sigh. "The truth is, I'd seen Lilly over that Christmas break, and she called me right before midnight. I was still in love with her, and I took the call. It was rude, and I'm sorry."

I was momentarily stunned. It had been Lilly on the phone? Lilly had ruined my New Year's Eve fantasy of meeting the love of your life at random, hitting it off, and having a hot kiss at midnight to seal the deal forever? "For the record, why didn't you ever tell me that?"

"It was embarrassing." To his credit, he sounded sincere. "I was trying to move on, but I wasn't ready. I was really confused."

Apparently, he hadn't gotten his happy ending either. "So she wasn't calling to get back together?"

"It was more of a drunk happy New Year call. I honestly don't think she knew why she was calling me. Anyway, you didn't deserve that. I had a great time with you. But the call made me realize I wasn't ready for anything. So, I'm sorry."

He'd had a great time too? Why did that strangely matter, even now? Funny how old anger could deflate suddenly and leave you thinking about things in a completely different way. But in some ways, I suddenly thought, the anger had been a lot safer.

"Well," I said, relenting, "I got you into this trouble with Lilly, so call it even. And also, please try not to be clueless when I'm trying to help you."

"What are you talking about?"

"Egypt exhibits? Lake views?" I threw up my hands. But my tone was more joking than exasperated. "At least help a person out."

"I didn't study art, okay? I played sports and studied my brains out to get into med school and that's it. Give me a break. Also, as I keep saying, I don't need your help with Lilly, thanks anyway."

I pretended I didn't hear that. "You so obviously need help." I tried to explain. "Like, you need to build layers with her." I made imaginary layers with my hands in the air. "Layer after tiny layer, and she'll realize how great you are." Then I put my hands to my throat and gagged. "I mean, I forgive you for being a douchebag at midnight, but it really hurt to say *great* just now referring to you."

He snort-chuckled in a surprisingly loud way as he stood next to me, holding the trunk lid with one hand above his head. It made me suddenly aware of his height, his broad shoulders, his strong body. Plus he smelled pleasant and simple, like soap, no airs. I stepped back, out of range of the distraction.

"I get what you were trying to do," he said, "but that involved talking about things I don't know much about. Like art. I'm not going to lie to make myself look better. She's got to like me for who I am."

He had a point, but he had a one-weekend shot here. "I'm doing my best here with little to go on. I don't know you very well."

"The ortho part was good. I can talk about that." He folded his big arms over his chest, which I confess was quite a sight. "I don't need a sassy matchmaker to help me win Lilly back, okay? I can handle this myself."

An unwanted thrill of pleasure ran through me. Oma used to call me that—sassy. A lot. A quiet longing came over me. And the feeling of my heart ripping open all over again. Grief was something that caught you at the most unexpected times.

And it was always accompanied by the feeling of being scarily alone in the world. Which, for the most part, I was used to. But sometimes...

I decided the best way to honor Oma's memory was to use my matchmaking skills. Which I somehow had to believe I possessed. I wasn't Oma's granddaughter for nothing. I was determined to fix this.

Something made him soften. Maybe I hadn't been able to hide my moment of vulnerability. "But thank you for trying. I—appreciate it."

"Wait." I revved up my jokiness. That usually hid anything else. "Did you just say the *A* word?"

The corner of his full mouth tilted upward in the tiniest smile.

"I guess I did." He cracked open that smile. Lord, that smile. Slightly imperfect but really nice, set in a rock-hard jaw. I totally saw how women would light up over that. "*Appreciate* and *apologize*, both in the same day. And both directed at you."

"Miracles *can* happen."

Our eyes met. Something fluttered in my stomach. I sucked in a breath and sort of lost my balance, having to clutch the side of the trunk. What was happening here?

I shook myself out of whatever dazed state this was. It was just... the joking. The friendliness. It had thrown me for a loop. That was all.

The idea that I could be physically attracted to him was utterly horrifying.

It was just all this stress. And the crazy ping-ponging of emotions all over that truck just now. All that work trying to make him look good for Lilly while I was trying to not look good to Quinn.

I got it that attraction sometimes just happened for whatever confusing reason. Hormones, pheromones, whatever. You just had to deal with it. It didn't mean a thing. It was just chemistry.

He shut the tailgate with a definitive click. "That might be the first thing we've managed to agree on."

"Probably be the last too," I added. Still smiling, he reached into the bed of the truck and grabbed both his duffel bag and mine.

"I can take my own bag," I said, running after him and reaching out to take it back.

He stopped suddenly and turned to me. I'd managed to grab onto the handle. "Do you let anyone help you like, ever?"

The answer to that was obviously *no*, but even though I tugged on the bag, he wasn't letting go. Lilly walked out of the farmhouse, saw us, and stopped in her tracks. She glanced from Caleb to me and back again. My stomach did a nauseated flip as it occurred to me that it looked like we were holding hands. A little flustered, I gave a final tug until Caleb finally let the bag go. Then I quickly ran ahead, heading alone into the farmhouse.

Chapter Ten

Caleb

"Samantha is so annoying," I said to my friends Gabe and Brax as we checked out our cabin. I should have kept that to myself, but worry about this weekend was making my irritation spill out. I had two days to fix things with Lilly. To get to know her again. To resolve my *what-ifs* and see if we had a chance. I did not need interference from Sam, no matter how intriguing—and aggravating—she was.

"Sam annoys you?" Brax, who dated and adored my sister Mia, asked, exchanged knowing glances with Gabe. They knew all about our difficult relationship. And they knew about Lilly too. The guys started out as Mia's friends, meeting during pediatric residency, but when I came over to Children's to do pediatric ortho rotations, I started hanging out with them too. Now Brax and Gabe were done with residency and out working in the real world.

"She's so stubborn," I said as I paced the small sitting room, which had a couch, two chairs, a corner electric fireplace, and a killer view of the lake right in front of us. "She won't ever accept any help. And she refuses to listen to me when I say I don't need any help with Lilly."

"That's our Sam," Gabe said. "Determined and independent. And maybe you *do* need help. Once-in-a-lifetime chance and all that." Gabe had a charismatic personality that nearly everyone took to and an opinion about just about everything, which made him a great negotiator. His new job as part of the hospital administration was perfect for him. And his job as officiant of Ani and Tyler's wedding had landed him here.

"She wouldn't let me carry her duffel bag, and I was playing tug of war with her, and Lilly thought we were holding hands just now. I mean, Sam says she wants to help me, but she's already making everything worse, and we just got here!"

"Sounds passionate," Gabe said. "But typical. There are always fireworks where you and Sam are involved."

"The bad kind. Sam's the whole reason Lilly doesn't trust me." My friends knew about that too. I thought about the fireworks comment. When Sam was around, I felt that my whole body was on edge. I had nerves about Lilly, but this was different. With Sam, I felt this weird kind of anticipation. Like, I never knew what she was going to say next, but I was eager to hear what it was—probably so that I could hit her with a comeback. To be fair, she'd tried hard to make me look good in front of Lilly. Then, in the next breath, she let me have it about me flaking out on her that New Year's Eve. Which I admit, I totally deserved.

"Relax." Brax slapped me on the back. "This weekend will be a great opportunity for you to figure it all out."

"Sorry," I said, raking a hand through my hair. "Guess I'm a little tense." I made an effort to calm down by sitting down and checking out the great view. "How're you guys doing?"

"I'm fantastic," Gabe said, plopping down on the couch. "Now that Jason's coming."

"Here? This weekend?" Brax asked. "Isn't he about to defend

his dissertation?" Gabe's fiancé was about to finish his PhD in literature, his dissertation being about female voices in Shakespeare's plays. He was a great guy, and he always gave us science nerds a mind-widening humanities perspective on life.

"Ani thought that some change of scenery might do him good."

"Better not tell Sam," I said in a warning tone. "She was hoping you'd be her square dance partner tonight."

"*I'll* be her partner," Quinn said, suddenly appearing at the door with Tyler, our esteemed groom. "She's really cute. And funny."

His words churned my stomach, mostly because he was so... all out there. He seemed to be one of those people where you could read all his emotions on his face. Still crushed by his breakup but trying to prove that he was over it. And putting Sam in his sights. Scary.

Not that she couldn't handle him herself. So why did I want to take care of him myself?

Tyler walked through the door, looking a little agitated himself. He was tall to Ani's petite frame, with curly hair and fashionable glasses. He sneezed violently. "Bollocks. I forgot my allergy pills *and* my bug spray."

We laughed, but honestly, Tyler was the anti-Ani. Those two were absolute proof that opposites attracted. While Ani was bubbly, fun, and easygoing, Tyler was straitlaced, high-maintenance and very intellectual—he'd scored higher than any of us on all the standardized tests we were required to take in med school and beyond. He was from Connecticut, but he talked like an aged actor from an aristocratic family. Privately I thought that all he needed was a cigar and a smoking jacket to complete this persona.

He was a character, but he was also a careful, compulsively dedicated doctor, who would stay late, lose sleep, anything to get patients the good care they needed—but he could also be a rigid pain in the butt. His saving grace was his self-awareness of his pain-in-the-butt-ness. And the fact that he attended therapy regularly.

Tyler walked over to the window and looked out at the lake, blowing his nose. "I absolutely despise the country. I have never square-danced, nor do I ever want to. And I hate hiking. But I love Ani. So thank you all for coming." He pulled out his phone, checked it, and then tossed it to the couch, sneezing again. "Bloody hell. Why is the Wi-Fi not working?"

Brax held out his hand. "Let me enter the password for you."

"I have. Three times." He wiped his forehead on his sleeve. "It's too hot in here."

I exchanged glances with Gabe, who walked over to Tyler and sat down next to him. "Have this." He handed him a beer. "And take a nap. Then we're going to have a great time square-dancing and harvesting our own food and getting eaten alive by mosquitoes. And Ani will love you for every minute of it."

He grunted. Brax passed out more beers, popped his open, and lifted it into the air. "To a weekend of friendship and fellowship."

After we toasted, Quinn said, "I think I'll take a little stroll and see if I can find Sam."

The hair on my neck prickled, but I blocked out my agitation. Sam was not my concern, no matter how many emotions, positive and negative, she incited in me.

I suddenly had a plan—I would find Lilly and have a talk with her before Sam could wreak any more havoc. Why waste time? I'd see if there was still something between us once and for all.

Samantha

My head still spinning about the luggage fight and everything that had happened on the drive, I walked into the big white farmhouse, where I was greeted by a middle-aged woman with glasses, sitting behind a beadboard-paneled counter. The counter was part of a sitting room where a boy and a young dog played on a braided rug in front of a brick-lined fireplace. It looked tidy and bright and homey, and for the first time, my reservations about farm weekend lowered. A little.

The dog, a yellow Labrador retriever that looked not far beyond the puppy stage, came bounding toward me with a rag knot toy in its mouth.

I bristled but pretended not to. I was pretty good at hiding my fear of dogs—unless they jumped on me. I turned toward the desk, white-knuckling the counter, and tried ignoring the dog but he—she?—kept nudging the rag toy against my leg.

The boy stood up. "She wants you to play with her." He was tanned and skinny-legged, his face full of freckles. He bent down and rubbed the dog's head. "Don'tcha, girl? You want to play."

The dog bounded from the boy to me, shaking its head with the toy in its mouth, giving me an expectant look.

"She won't hurt ya," the boy said.

I smiled, but there was no way I could bring myself to touch the saliva-covered toy in the dog's teeth. "Cute dog," I managed with a nervous laugh. I drew the line there—because there was no way I could force myself to actually pet it—her.

But the dog persisted, looking up at me with dark brown, expectant eyes.

Jeesh.

The woman smiled. "Tater, take the pup outside." To me, she said in an apologetic tone, "She could play that game all day."

"Come on, doggie," the boy said as he ran toward the door. "Let's go."

The pup did not take the bait. Instead, she dropped the rag toy at my feet and thumped her tail.

Oh help.

The woman leaned over. "Tater, take this dog out right now. Not all our guests are dog people."

"She just wants to play, Mom," the boy said.

I decided it would be easier to scoop up the saliva-coated toy and toss it than to cause conflict between mother and son. So I did. Clear to the fireplace. The dog immediately scrambled after it.

I tried to give a dog-lover smile, but I was a dog-fearer, and if I didn't get out of there soon, that was going to come across loud and clear.

The woman smiled as she watched her son playfully wrestle with the dog. "She's a foster. Four months old and not potty-trained. Tater and I are training her."

Poor puppy. No family. I immediately identified. "What's her name?"

"Unbelievably, the people she was with called her Pup—I think that's an indication right there that they never intended to keep her. We foster for the Humane Society. Some people sadly don't understand that puppies require consistency and work. So she's here to learn some manners." She smiled and held out her hand. "I'm Marin Brown, by the way. That's Tatum—he's ten. We call him Tater."

"Mom!" the boy protested.

"Hi," I said to them both, carefully omitting the "Tater." I offered my hand to Marin. "Samantha. I'm with the wedding party."

"I have your key right here. The bride's already in your cabin."

As Marin explained how to put the farm app on my phone, which had a map and info, I felt another nudge. Another solemn, expectant gaze met mine as the pup dropped the soggy toy onto my sandal.

I couldn't suppress a chuckle. "You really are persistent, aren't you?" This time I did a sneak attack, quickly snatching the knot and tossing it as far as I could. The dog flew after it, grabbed it, lay down, and play-growled with it.

"She's really a nice dog," Marin said, peering over the counter. "Labs are high energy. I don't think those people had a clue what they were in for."

I couldn't imagine, but I just smiled.

After giving me directions to the cabin, she added, "Hope you brought some tennies." She gave a chuckle. "It's an active weekend. The square dance tonight, hunt your own breakfast first thing in the morning, then a long hike. You're gonna love it."

Ani, Ani, Ani. The things we endured for friends' weddings. Square-dancing? And did she just say *hunt*? That would be a hard pass. I hoped there was a vegetarian breakfast option, because I absolutely was not hunting anything more animal than milk for my coffee.

"Don't worry if you don't know how to square-dance," Marin said. "Ted, our caller, is great with beginners. My husband Brent and I usually come too."

Okay, great. I thanked her, waved goodbye to boy and dog, and began my trek on a winding path that led down a rolling hill toward a necklace string of log cabins surrounding a little oval lake. I counted two down as Marin had instructed and walked up a few concrete stairs onto a porch with blue ceramic pots overflowing with red flowers.

The main room had a little sitting area and a kitchenette. There were potted plants near a big window and the same clean white decor as the main farmhouse. Cute. I found Ani in one of the two bedrooms, lying on a twin bed, scrolling on her phone. She was wearing a white sweatshirt that said BRIDE. Mia sat across from her on the other twin bed. She gave me a weak smile as I dropped my duffel and jumped into bed next to Ani, giving her a giant hug. "Hi, bride. Nice place."

Her smile seemed a little weak too. The fact that she was lying down seemed strange too—I wouldn't have been surprised if I'd walked in to see her practicing her do-si-dos. "It's a great farm, isn't it?" she asked in a lukewarm tone.

"Yeeees," I said, literally knowing nothing about farms. Ani usually didn't ask basic questions, and she looked a little off.

"How was the drive with my brother?" Mia asked.

"Great." You know the first thing I thought of? Not the luggage fight. Not the dumb answers to art questions. But rather the apology.

I never thought of Caleb as someone who would apologize, and it had thrown me. It did more than that. It had dissolved the grudge I'd carried for years.

Uh-oh. That was not a good thing, I realized.

"That good, huh?" Mia said. "I hope you two can keep it together this weekend."

I was a little offended. "Of course we will. We worked it out."

"You and Caleb actually talked about getting along?"

"We actually did." Sort of. Somehow, I knew that we both understood that this wedding wasn't about us. Besides, I was committed to getting Lilly on his side.

Wasn't I?

Yes, of course I was.

Maybe I needed to lie down too.

I was pulled out of this inner turmoil by Ani holding out her hands and wiggling her fingers (including the one with the honking huge emerald-cut diamond that was glinting in our eyes) for both of us to hold her hands in support. "I'm so glad you both are here."

Mia and I grasped her hands. "Me too." I glanced at Mia. *Was something wrong?* I telegraphed. She gave a tiny shrug in return.

"Where's Lilly?" Ani asked.

"She went out on a hunt to find some flowers to sketch," Mia said.

I found it a little odd that she wasn't with Ani having some bonding time, but art was calling, I guess. Historically, Lilly was Ani's best friend through grade school and high school. I knew they often saw each other when Ani went home, but my sense was that they weren't quite as close as Ani, Mia, and I were.

"You two should go check the place out too," Ani said. "We have some time before the square dance." She sat up and seemed to force a smile. "What did you think of Quinn?" she asked me. "He stopped by and said he'd love to be your partner tonight."

My stomach did that queasy thing again. I decided to tell it like it was and prepare for the consequences. "He's good-looking and he seems nice, but I'm not interested." I pressed my lips together, prepared for what I knew was coming.

"Sam, you always scoff at nice guys," Ani said. "You always pick the bad boys."

"I pick bad boys because they're fun. And fun is all I want right now." And maybe ever. "Besides, there's no shimmer." Oma was a *huge* believer in shimmer.

She heaved a sigh. "Dating a nice guy might change your life."

Mia nodded vehemently and grinned. "No pain, no gain."

Pain being the key here. My friends were as persistent as that little dog up at the main house. I was used to this, but I was going to shut them down quick. "Thanks for thinking of me, but no, thanks." I had a solid backup plan—I was going to pair up with Gabe, who would save me from Quinn for sure. "This weekend isn't about me. How are you doing?"

Ani looked anything but relaxed and unstressed.

"Out with it," Mia said.

She went quiet.

I put a hand on her arm. "Ani, what's wrong?"

"Things just aren't... going well."

"Wedding planning is really stressful," Mia said hurriedly. "That's why Brax and I aren't even attempting it this year, what with me starting my heme-onc fellowship and him starting practice."

Ani's clear blue eyes brimmed with tears. It was clear she took no comfort from Mia's answer.

"You can tell us," I said. The three of us had been through a lot together these past few years. Our friendship had been one of the best things to come out of residency.

Ani sat up and crossed her arms. "We're just not on the same page about a lot of things. Tyler seems so frustrated with—well, everything. I'm worried he's having second thoughts."

Mia and I exchanged looks of hidden worry over Ani's head. We both half believed what she'd just said. Of the two of them, it was no secret that Ani got along with everyone and found humor in nearly everything. Tyler was introverted, serious, and in general, uptight.

Ani attributed that to his tough childhood. But frankly, I had as tough a childhood as anyone, and I'd retained the ability to get a joke once in a while. But I guess I had different issues. I vowed to try harder not to judge.

We loved Ani, and she obviously loved Tyler, so we wrote it off as an opposites-attract thing and hoped for the best.

But there was a little wrench thrown into all this that also gave us cause for worry: Ani had been a nurse. She'd married young, at twenty-two, and was divorced by twenty-five. Anyone could forgive a youthful mistake—except for Ani herself. She seemed to think *she* was the difficult one in the relationship and seemed to us to go above and beyond to placate Tyler. In our opinion, she was the gem in the relationship.

It didn't help that her parents helped to perpetuate her sense of failure, treating her divorce as an embarrassment. For a long time, they wouldn't even tell their friends that it happened.

"This is a beautiful place," I said, "and we're all here to celebrate you guys. You have a whole weekend to unwind, relax, and have fun together." That was the most positive spin I could think of.

Mia approved, telegraphing me a stealthy thumbs-up and mouthing *Good job*.

"That's why I chose it," Ani said. "But Tyler is already saying that the pollen is activating his allergies. He wants to stay in the air-conditioning."

Of course he did.

"You guys should go explore the place," Ani said, shooing us out. "Don't let me stop you."

"You want to come for a walk and explore with us?" Mia asked.

"It's been a week," Ani said. "I think I'm going to lie down for a while. Everything will look brighter after a nap, right?"

"Totally." To Mia I said, "I think I'll pass on the walk. I've got some work stuff I've got to take care of."

"Okay then. I'm going to find Brax and see if he wants to find a place to fool around," Mia said.

We both laughed, but Ani looked a little wistful. This might have been my imagination, but I wondered if she was thinking that Tyler was never spontaneous—or fun—like that.

I didn't want to take a nap or explore the farm. I had other things on my mind. After the luggage fight, I didn't want there to be any question—in anyone's mind—that I was interested in Caleb. So I was going to repay my debt to him, the sooner the better. It was time to take matters into my own hands.

Chapter Eleven

Samantha

A little way along the wooded path, Lilly was sitting on a bench overlooking the lake, lost in an artist's zone, her chalk pastel box spread open beside her. A batch of bright orange and yellow tiger wildflowers bloomed in a profusion of color right at the lake's edge, which were clearly her subject.

I felt a little bad interrupting, but I was on a mission. "Could I talk to you?" I asked.

She glanced up and smiled. "Oh hi, Sam. Sure." She moved her art supplies so I could sit. In front of us, the sun was shining on the calm water, illuminating the trees and grasses in dappled light as only a bright May sun can. One glance at her sketchbook told me she was a seriously talented artist.

After watching her work for a few minutes, I said, "I want to say something that's been on my mind. I feel like I need to get it off my chest."

She put a hand to her own chest. "You're scaring me a little."

I sounded a little scary to my own ears, but this was serious. I glanced around, making sure Caleb wasn't about to pop out of the woods and burst in on us. I knew he wouldn't like what I was doing. But I plunged ahead, having only two days to accomplish the impossible. "I want to clear up something you might've heard about Caleb."

"Okay," she said carefully. "What is it?"

"At the hospital, he and I had a professional disagreement that made me upset—I mean, we often disagree—but I didn't handle it in the best way. In my anger, I repeated what I'd heard about him from one of my friends. It was pure gossip, and it did damage—to you."

"You're talking about what Stacey told me?"

I nodded. "Caleb is—well, he's a good guy. He didn't two-time anyone, and he didn't cheat. I wanted you to know that." I found myself actually believing the good-guy part, which threw me a little.

I really, really hoped I was doing the right thing. Caleb had to get going or he was going to lose this woman forever.

Lilly set down her sketch pad. "You know we used to date, right? Caleb called me to say hi a few weeks ago. He said he wanted to make sure we were okay before the wedding, but I think he might've been working up to ask me out." She turned to me. "I have a lot of conflicting feelings about that. I mean, we were young, but it was a bad breakup."

"I get that." Okay, here goes. My chance to make Caleb shine. "I know him mostly professionally, of course, but I can tell you he's a very good doctor and also a very compassionate one." I'd seen him interact with patients before their surgeries. He had a great way with kids and their parents. Once, he stayed long after his twenty-four-hour call shift was up to make sure that one of his patients was out of the woods. I'd found him at the patient's bedside post-op, falling asleep in a chair. Most residents would've gone home long before and learned their patient's fate the next day.

"Being Mia's best friend, I see that Caleb really loves his family," I continued. I thought of the cute, casual way he called his mom *Ma*. How he'd playfully rubbed his beard against her cheek. How tight he was with his parents and siblings.

"He's *really* into his family," Lilly said. "When we'd have time off during his first year in med school, he'd always want to head home to see them."

She'd said that like it was a bad thing. That was hard for someone like me to imagine, who struggled on a daily basis to keep that sense of family alive for Wynn. "That must've been a very hard year for both of you," I said.

"It really was. I still have hostility." She laughed. "But it's nice to connect with him again. I think this weekend will help us to resolve some things."

"He doesn't seem to hold grudges." Even though he detested me, he'd still somehow offered me a ride. Which was kind of incredible. "I mean, I think he'd welcome connecting with you and making amends."

"Caleb never gives up on anything. Once, the D'Angelos' dog got sick, and for weeks all he did was research senior-dog ailments and try to find alternative therapies."

"Larry?"

"Yes, Larry!" She laughed again. "How did you know his name?"

"I think he's a family legend. Did anything work?"

"The dog was fifteen." She lifted her hands in a shrug. "I mean, it was just time to go."

We both pondered that. I wondered what that must feel like, to be loved like that. It didn't seem like something to take for granted—unless it was stalkerish. Was Caleb a stalker?

"He's not bad-looking," she said.

"That he is not." I suddenly thought maybe I shouldn't have agreed so quickly, so I added, "He's also not beyond apologizing." That damn apology was still rerunning in my head like an Instagram reel on loop. I kept trying to understand how it had still really mattered, even all this time later.

As I strained to come up with more compliments, I thought about adding that fact that he liked kids—I mean, he chose peds ortho for a fellowship—but thought that might be a straw too much. We fell silent in the afternoon heat. An occasional frog made a strange trill.

Something was churning inside my brain, niggling at me like a toddler yanking on their mother's coat, creeping up on me like a sneak attack.

Good-looking, kind, funny, smart. A golden quadrangle of traits, one of Oma's favorite expressions.

Caleb had it. The golden quadrangle.

I could never find all four in one man. I usually settled for good-looking and smart. And if funny was thrown in, I was okay for a while.

"Thanks for all that," Lilly said, patting me on the arm. "You must care about Caleb a lot to want to explain all that to me."

"I feel terrible for what happened," I said honestly. "I just wanted to correct the damage I caused."

There. I'd said it. I'd done what I came here to do. I'd given Caleb his best shot. If he was angry, it would only be for me telling the truth. I felt like I'd done what I needed to do, like shaking sand from my feet.

Caleb. His stupidly handsome, smiling face was stuck in my brain like an earworm song you can't stop singing all day. *Baby Shark do do do do do do…*

"Hey, you two." Suddenly there he was, emerging from the forest path, striding toward us in his confident way with his lean, muscled legs, his tanned skin, and his bright white smile.

He hadn't heard me, had he?

That seemed the least of my worries. At that moment, my head was spinning, my hands were clammy, and the rest of me was sweaty. Had I forgotten to drink water? Sometimes I did that at work.

But this felt different. I felt like a Mack truck had just hit me, knocked me off-kilter and sent me flying.

I was falling for the guy I was trying so hard to convince Lilly to love.

And that was very messed up.

∿

Caleb

I took in the two women on the bench. They couldn't have been more different. Lilly's hair was sun-kissed, backlit by the warm afternoon sun, her eyes blue as the water in front of us. She'd somehow managed to find time to change outfits and was wearing a sundress with daisies on it and sandals. She looked like a perfect work of art.

My heart ached with nostalgia, because how many times had I seen her like that? Knees up, supporting a big sketchbook, head cocked a little to the side, hand poised above the paper, lips pressed together, every part of her in total concentration.

Sam, on the other hand, looked stricken on seeing me. Guilty maybe. After all, I'd just overheard her telling Lilly I was a great guy.

Sam with her dark silky hair bound into a ponytail and the fresh, honest smile. Who wore a plain gray T-shirt and jeans shorts and white tennies that were a little worn.

I wasn't angry that she'd gone to bat for me. How could I be? I'd heard her list all my sterling qualities—and it didn't seem like she was lying.

Before I could wonder why I was more interested in what Sam thought of me than Lilly, Lilly scooted over, so I sat down on one end of the bench. I'd brought a book with me, just in case I couldn't find her, so I set it in my lap. For a moment, I took in the lake, shaded by willows, some lily pads floating on its mirrored surface. A peaceful place, but I was feeling the opposite of peaceful.

It wasn't because the stakes were high with Lilly. Sam had set me up for success, and now I had only to take the ball and run with it and see what would happen.

The confusion was that Sam wasn't at all who I'd initially thought she was. She was nice and funny and kind—and stunning in a very different way than Lilly. I was struggling to untwist my thoughts and actually say something when Sam stood up and walked around us, placing her hands on the bench behind us.

I glanced up to see her closing her eyes, concentrating deeply. My heart started pounding. She was about to do her Oma thing. *On us.*

My mouth went dry as I tried to pretend nothing was happening. "This place reminds me of that camp we went to once when we were kids," I said, just to say *something*. "Remember?"

"Oh, I forgot about that place," Lilly said. "What was it called again?"

As Sam rested her hand purposely on my shoulder. I felt my skin prickle beneath her touch. A frisson of electricity.

I reminded myself that I was a doctor. Science was everything. Experimental studies, statistics, results—those were the foundation of medicine. In ortho we had tests, signs, and maneuvers for diagnosis—the Abbot method, the Achilles bulge sign, the squeeze test, the Addis test, the shoulder abduction sign, the active glide test on the knee—not Oma's ill-defined match-making hocus-pocus that Sam seemed to think could be inherited.

As if such a thing was even possible.

Too late to worry about it. Belief had to be suspended as she touched Lilly's shoulder too and masked this by nodding toward the pond and saying, "Will you look at that? A mama duck trailed by a million babies. How many are there?"

She managed to sound genuinely amazed. I thought about how she said that growing up, she hadn't had wild, untamed spaces to run free in as I had. She seemed truly awed by nature.

"Camp Rockbottom," Lilly said, clapping her hands together, "that's what we called it. But what was its real name?" I couldn't remember, because my mind had gone blank. Sam's hand rested gently on my shoulder and upper arm. I felt her warmth. The soft but steady pressure as I sat frozen, holding my breath.

"I know!" Lilly said. "Camp Rockymount!"

"Right, right," I said absently.

Whatever Sam was doing was nonsense, I knew that.

But her touch held me spellbound. Made me want more.

She lifted her hands off but then replaced them, as if she was repeating the process. "Is that an eagle high in that tree? And is that a nest?"

I bit down on my cheek so as not to smile. I suddenly wanted to take her all around this farm and show her all the wonders being in the country had in store—hawks and herons, monarchs and geese, and even the chickens.

The hand came down again. A third time? How many times did it take? I didn't believe in it, but I had to admit that I hoped it would yield a magic solution to all my confusion.

What if it said that Lilly was my one and true soulmate? That was what I wanted, right?

Sam withdrew her hands and gave an exaggerated yawn. "Okay you two," she said, giving both out shoulders a squeeze, "I'm going to take a rest before dinner. See you all later!"

Once she left, I decided to figure out once and for all if Lilly and I had a shot. "You haven't changed. You still love to sketch flowers."

"Caleb, I *have* changed a lot." She assessed me carefully, her expression unreadable. "But yes, I still love to draw flowers." She smiled. "That wasn't a slap-down. You just remember things in a certain romantic way. But neither of us is the same."

I rubbed my neck and found that I was sweating. "I just meant that your artistic spirit is the same. Your love of flowers." I sounded ridiculous. But I was trying.

She set down her tablet. "Okay. I accept that. Sam just went through that whole hospital gossip thing and said the same thing you did. So no worries there, okay?"

Okay, great. "So... we're friends, right?"

"Yeah. We're friends."

And then I paused. Blew out a breath. Now was my chance to say more. But I didn't—couldn't—say "I want another chance," or "Let's try again." Or even, "Do you want to go out sometime?"

We fell into silence. Still, I hesitated.

Inside, I was a little panicked. Sam was in my head—dancing with my mom, wearing my lucky sweatshirt, doing her hocus-pocus and telling Lilly the truth to help me.

And then suddenly I looked across the pond, and there she was. I could barely see her through some trees, sitting on a lounge chair, reading a book in the side yard of the women's cabin.

"What's your book?" Lilly finally asked me.

I picked it up and looked at the dark cover with bold gold lettering and a scrolled border. "It's this cool story about four friends who get stuck in this dystopian universe and can't get back to their own, and these evil beings who are taking over the world and the friends have to stop them. But it's much more than just sci-fi. It brings up all kind of important issues like taking care of our world, getting rid of waste, conserving resources..."

She laughed.

"Sorry. I guess I get a little excited." Lilly had never gotten my thrill of reading a great book and then wanting to tell everyone I met about it.

She smiled. Maybe a little wisely. "You always wanted to save the world. I just wanted to draw flowers."

I shrugged, but inside, I felt like a bomb had dropped. I think she'd pretty much summed up our entire relationship right there —and not in a good way. I was always pushing, never accepting defeat. I was practical, she was whimsical.

Also, she wasn't into aliens or heavy book discussions. I'd have to save that for my bros in book club.

I thought about Sam's matchmaking advice. That couples trying to get back together have to fix what happened in the past. I knew I had to attempt that by saying something difficult that I'd said in my head hundreds of times. "Lilly, I just wanted to say I'm sorry about the way things ended between us. I had no idea how difficult that year was going to be for either of us."

She gave a tight smile. "It was definitely... challenging."

The first year of med school had hit me harder than a solid brick wall. To say that I'd been overwhelmed was an understatement. "I couldn't find balance at all that year," I said, "and I know you suffered for it."

"Caleb, you always give one hundred percent plus. The problem was that when we were together, there wasn't any percent left for me."

Across the way, Sam was quietly reading. I wished I was reading too instead of fielding these hard issues. Except who would suddenly show up there but Quinn, who flopped himself right down on the grass beside her. She promptly sat up. I felt annoyed at him for no reason. How about leaving her alone so she could enjoy that book? How about getting the hint *period*?

Why was I thinking this in the middle of a discussion I'd longed to have for years?

"I love my job," Lilly said. "I'm very passionate about it. I have so many ideas. Maybe getting to where I am wasn't as hard as med school, but I want to find an equal partner who respects my career too."

"I've always respected you," I said. "I admire what you've done to your family's business."

"When we were together, it was all about you."

I flinched. I knew I had to do better, be more honest. Admit the truth, which was hard for me. I often saw the glass as half full, even in retrospect. I knew that I tended to minimize my vulnerabilities, and maybe if I hadn't, we might've made it. "That first year, it was all I could do to keep my head above the water. The workload was beyond anything I could imagine. I was terrified I wasn't going to make it."

"You did make it," she said in an even tone. "With flying colors. But *we* didn't."

Through the trees, Quinn had picked up Sam's book. Sam had moved to the far end of her chair, away from him. Judging by her body language, she wanted him to leave. Who does that, parks himself next to a woman when he's not even invited? A strange, protective urge came over me.

"Caleb?"

I faced her. "Look, in retrospect, I didn't know who I was or what I was capable of. I'm so proud of you, Lilly. I'm sorry for the pain."

She stared at me. I knew her well, and I could see a struggle going on inside her. "I'm glad we had this chance to talk."

"Me too."

Lilly got up from the bench. "See you at dinner, okay?" After she tossed her art stuff into a canvas bag, slung it over her shoulder, and left, I sat there for a minute, thinking. Carefully rehashing our past as I'd done so many times. I had great memories of our close moments, our romantic moments, and not so many of the arguments we'd had—like, the blowups over whose family to have dinner with on a rare day off, or the fact that I always seemed to be studying, or the times when she felt isolated and lonely and my exhaustion and stress had made me less sensitive of her.

Across the way, Sam got up and went inside the cabin, leaving Quinn to do whatever it was Quinn did. In this case, he found the trail. I could see through the trees that he was traveling all the way around the lake, headed back to our cabin. I was strangely relieved that he'd left Sam alone.

I should've come away from this discussion with clarity, but I felt more confused than ever. I mean, I was glad we'd talked honestly. It helped the wounds to heal.

But I didn't feel... invested.

Or attracted.

I wasn't pining for her. I wasn't wanting... more.

I was thinking more about the complicated woman who'd just done everything she could to get me what I wanted.

I just wasn't sure it—rather, Lilly—was what I wanted anymore.

I felt like my chapter with Lilly was finally ending, not beginning.

~

Samantha

I tried to sit out in the sun for a while to calm down after that stupid, horrible matchmaking test, but Quinn came out of nowhere like a puppy dog and literally wouldn't leave until I confessed to having a whopping migraine.

That wasn't far off. He was giving me a pain in my head, my brain, my stomach, but most of all, in my butt.

I hated having to tell guys I wasn't interested, something I'd done a lot. Except this was extra tricky because I'd have to see Quinn for more events before the wedding. So what were my choices? Oh, I didn't have many.

I hadn't lied about my head—it was throbbing from stress. And it was all Caleb's fault. I put myself on the line for him. Going around touching people's shoulders and mumbling things about eagles and ducks.

But my real problem wasn't Quinn. It was that the test hadn't worked.

Either that, or Caleb and Lilly were a dud match.

My head started throbbing so badly that I barely made it into the cabin to rummage through my bag for some ibuprofen.

Had I done everything right? I'd touched Caleb and Lilly at the same time. And I'd focused hard and said inside my head what my Oma always said. *Are these two people meant to be together?*

And I felt... nothing. A big zero. Nil. Naught. Zip.

I lay down on my bunk and threw my hand over my forehead. The worst thing was, I was an unprofessional matchmaker. Caleb had his arm on the back of the bench, and I aimed for his shoulder, but I sort of got his biceps.

It had been downhill from there. Because he had a big, hard biceps. A mound of muscle—and it had distracted me. Not only that, it... thrilled me. After that, it was all I could do not to think of him. But he was there, right there, and I was touching him and smelling his soap and feeling myself grow hot and tingly all over like a teenager.

He kept furtively glancing at me, probably to wonder what the hell I was doing, and that didn't help.

I felt a lot of energy coming from him and nothing from her.

And worst of all, it felt directed at *me*.

Oh *no*.

And all that energy... might have thrown off the test. It was like static interference.

The one other time I'd done this maneuver, with Mia and Brax, it felt—well, it felt like peace and harmony and great energy. Which was exactly the vibe they still had with each other.

This time I couldn't even say what the end result meant. Everything was so muddled. But even when I concentrated as deeply as I could, I couldn't get any positive energy from either one of them going out to the other one.

I rubbed my right arm, which still felt funny from when I'd

touched Caleb's arm. Like pins and needles. Truthfully, my entire body felt like pins and needles.

There must be something I was doing wrong. Why had I thought I could do this? Why had I thought I'd inherited my grandma's gift? And why was I so upset I hadn't?

I knew why. Because it was a little piece of her I thought I still had within my reach.

A little piece that... wasn't.

I should've paid more attention when she was still here with us. I should have learned what she'd always been trying to teach me.

Even though Oma was all drama and one heck of a storyteller, I didn't actually believe the matchmaking. But I felt that her art was being lost, and now it was my fault because I hadn't learned enough.

But I believed in my grandma. And oh, how I missed her. Somehow, by keeping this ritual of hers alive, I was keeping her alive.

On top of all this, I couldn't shake off the creeping feeling that Caleb and Lilly were a mismatch, regardless of how fervent Caleb felt about her. This had nothing to do with Oma's test. It was just an observation I made all by myself.

"Sam, are you okay?" Mia's voice pierced my bad thoughts.

I was never so relieved to hear her. At the same time, how could I ever tell her? This was about her brother. And me *feeling* things. Life was so much better when I hated him.

She walked into the dimly lit bunk room and perched herself on the end of mine. "Headache?"

I nodded. "I just took something for it."

Another voice. "Want me to run up to the farmhouse and get you a diet soda?"

I opened one eye and saw Gabe. My two best friends. A wave of instant relief welled up inside me.

"Do they have those here?" I was suddenly parched and craving a delicious, bubbly, caffeinated beverage.

"Good question," Gabe took a seat on the bottom bunk across from mine. "I did see a sign about all-natural green juice. But I think you might have to go pick some spinach to get one. You want that?"

I shook my head. "If it doesn't have caffeine and aspartame in it, I don't want it."

"Why are you here?" I asked Mia. "I thought you were with Brax."

"I was, but my brother is convinced that Quinn is stalking you. He said something about having a talk with him. He asked me to see if you were okay. Is that valid?"

Wait... Caleb was worried about me? I forced myself up, propping myself on my elbows. I was surprised and grateful that Caleb had noticed. Not that I couldn't handle Quinn by myself, but still. "Quinn's just not getting the hint, and I'm not sure what I can do other than spell it out for him." All this reminded me of tonight, so I turned to Gabe. "Could we be partners at the square dance? If not, then I'm going to get stuck with him."

Gabe's face fell. "Oh honey, I'd love to, but I can't tonight."

"You're not going?" My throbbing head just got throbbier.

"Jason's on the way," he said a little sheepishly.

"Jason's coming... here?"

Gabe nodded. He couldn't contain the elation in his voice. "He's been working really hard on his dissertation, and we've barely seen each other. Ani had the idea that he should bring his work up here for the weekend."

"That's really nice." I tried to mean it. "But I hate you."

"I can help you with Quinn, don't worry," Mia said. "But is something else wrong? I mean, I've never known rejecting a guy to get you upset."

Mia knew me so well. A mere mortal man—especially one who

was a pain—wasn't something I ever lost sleep over. And here's the thing with Mia. The reason we're best friends. I can't lie to her. There's something about this woman that makes me instantly unburden my heart. I wondered if it was genetic, because I'd felt the same way with her mom. But this—how could I tell her any of it?

She pointed to my lap. "You've been shredding again."

I looked down to find that the tissues I'd been clutching had indeed been shredded to pieces. I swooped down and picked up the mess and balled it all up.

I took a deep breath, finding my courage. Mia was my best friend. No matter what happened, she deserved to know the truth. "I spread a rumor by accident about your brother, and it somehow got back to Lilly, just as he was trying to get back with her."

Mia frowned. "That's not like you. What kind of rumor?"

"That he cheated on someone that he dumped. It wasn't true. But I thought it was, and I was mad about something else that happened between us at the hospital."

She put a hand to her chest. "Caleb's a pain, but he's absolutely not a cheater."

"I offered to straighten things out with Lilly, but he said no. But I had an opportunity to talk with Lilly just now and I took it. And then I did Oma's matchmaking move, just to reassure Caleb that all was well."

"That thing where she puts her hands on the couple?" Mia asked. "She did that with Brax and me." She smiled proudly. "We were a great match."

"Your grandma did it with Jason and me too," Gabe said. "We passed with flying colors. But judging by your face, something wasn't magical about this time."

"With Caleb and Lilly, I got nothing. No energy. *No simpàtico.*" I rubbed my pounding temples. "I didn't pay enough attention to my grandma to understand what I'm doing wrong. And now it's lost." I was now bawling into my shredded tissues.

Mia ran to the bathroom and gave me a long tail of toilet paper. I promptly blew my nose.

"There's something else," I managed. "It's awful."

Mia clutched my hand. She and Gabe exchanged grave glances. "What? What is it?"

"You know how I hated Caleb? Well, the energy I picked up wasn't between Caleb and Lilly." I hesitated. Was I really going to spill this? "It was between Caleb and me. I really screwed something up. And I think I might have a crush on him! How is that possible? I mean, the last crush I had was Justin Bieber in high school!" I dissolved back into tears.

"Wait a minute," Gabe said. "You and Caleb?" He started to laugh. "Girlfriend, you're not telling us anything we don't already know."

Mia nodded. "We've been seeing the fireworks between you two for ages."

"Yes, angry ones," I said. "It's not anything," I rushed to tell Mia, because... her brother! "It's just one of those thoughts that you get in your head, and once it's in there, it won't dislodge. I'm sure it will pass. I swear, I would never ruin his chances with Lilly. Hopefully I said enough to Lilly just now that she'll give him a chance."

Mia put a hand on my shoulder. "You're just... human." She paused. "It's been a long time since you've allowed yourself to be." That hit me hard. What did she mean by that? "Besides, somebody's got to love Caleb. It might as well be you."

"You don't understand. I don't love him. And I definitely don't want to like him. It's just... attraction. I'm sure it will fade."

"I've never seen you like this," Mia said.

I looked up at her and wiped my snotty nose again. "Like what, a mess?"

"No. Vulnerable. I mean, you never ask for help or support. It's refreshing to see you do that."

I rolled my eyes. "I'm really sorry—for all of this."

"Sam, like who you like," she said in a solemn tone. "Love who you love."

"Here's a question," Gabe said. "Just for funsies. What if Caleb actually doesn't want Lilly? What if he wants you?"

"I would *never* interfere with what he wants with Lilly." That was rule number one of matchmaker code. And I already knew *my* rule number one—never get involved.

Mia sighed. "Deep down, I know you know this, but I'm going to say it out loud. Someday you're going to have to stop running from love."

I rolled my eyes. "Or else?"

"Or else you'll stay closed off your whole life." She reached over and hugged me. "And you're too much of a gem to do that. And don't tell me you don't want love. Once you find it, you'll want it. It's hard, but it's worth it. Trust me."

"That's all wonderful," Gabe said, giving me a hug too. "But what are you going to tell Caleb?"

Chapter Twelve

Caleb

I entered the white barn (as opposed to the red one, which held animals) at seven that evening to find that it wasn't really a barn at all but rather a large event space complete with big wooden beams, glossy wood floors, and tables lining the sides for tonight's square dance. No animals in sight. Unless you counted the guys, who were hanging around at the bar, drinking beers—no doubt quelling their nerves about square-dancing.

The place was crowded with people that I heard later were neighbors and avid square dancers from near and far. On a stage in the corner, musicians were warming up and adjusting mics. Just then, Sam walked in and spotted me. She was wearing jeans, a white T-shirt, and a red-and-white bandanna.

Gabe was suddenly at my side, following my gaze to the doorway. "She's looking good tonight," he said, nudging me with his elbow.

"What are you, switching teams?" I asked, ribbing him back.

"Not on your life." He gave me an assessing look. "I just want to make sure you don't miss the right gal."

I didn't have to respond to that, because Jason walked in just then, shook my hand and exchanged greetings. As he went to stand next to Gabe, his gaze trailed to the door too. "Sam's looking hot tonight," he said.

I shook my head. "There are *way* too many matchmakers here this weekend."

Gabe grinned. "I don't know about you, but I wouldn't be standing here talking to us." He gave me a gentle push. "Get to work now. Your lady love awaits. Shoo, shoo!"

"See you in a few," I said, happy to leave them. But I was sure they'd be pleased with what I did—I met Sam at the door.

"Cute scarf," I said, but that wasn't really what I was thinking. The guys weren't wrong. The woman was stunning in an unfussy way that she didn't even realize. A *natural beauty* is what my mom would've called her. I finally understood what that meant.

"Your sister made me wear it," she said, flapping the bandanna end. "She said she wanted me to look more 'square-dancy,' whatever that is."

"Well, I'd say you look very square-dancy." And *kissable*, is what popped into my head. "Thanks for talking with Lilly on my behalf."

"You're not angry?"

"No. I appreciate what you did."

She paused. "I hope things go well with you two. And if you want, we can talk about the hike tomorrow before breakfast. I'm happy to talk you up more and give you a feel for what she's thinking."

I wanted to tell her that I was pretty sure that I didn't want that anymore, but what could I say? She would only think that I was a fool, flipping my attention from Lilly to someone else—i.e., her—so easily. I wouldn't trust someone like that either. So I simply left it at "Sure. Thanks. Great idea." Then I said, "So, what's my strategy for tonight, matchmaker?"

"Easy," she said with a shrug and a smile. "Dance with her."

"I've never square-danced before."

"Neither have I." She looked around at the band—two fiddlers, a guitarist, a banjoist, and a guy on a mandolin, all poised to play. "But I'm getting excited."

She looked excited, not reluctant, ready for a new challenge. The caller, a man with a gray beard and a gray-and-white checked shirt, tapped his foot and spoke into a microphone, telling everyone to break into groups of eight.

Someone grabbed my elbow. Brax. He'd rounded everyone up, and they were all standing nearby. "We've got our group, right?" Gabe and Jason joined an adjoining group, so ours would consist of Ani and Tyler, Mia and Brax, Lilly and me, Sam and... Quinn. *Dammit.* There he was, in blue jeans and a blue denim shirt, already sidling up next to Sam. Mia stood next to Sam in what I'd call a protective stance, but even she had to eventually join Brax as all of us couples started to line up opposite each other in a square. I had to hold myself back from intervening. I'd even start with "Hey, buddy, didn't anyone ever tell you not to wear denim-on-denim?" But in the end, what could I do? Nothing but watch it play out.

"Where's Lilly?" Brax asked, looking around the crowd.

Just then Lilly ran into the barn, a little breathless. Or maybe I should say sashayed, because she skipped in a lively way and waved and nodded to people on the way in like she was going down a red carpet instead of entering a barn. She wore a black skirt that swirled around her knees, red boots, a cute plaid shirt, and bright red lipstick to match. My instincts told me from experience that she was late because it had taken her a looong time to get ready.

The caller taught us all the basic moves—do-si-do, swing, promenade, allemande. Through the lessons, Tyler's eyes were puffy and his nose was running, a consequence of the forgotten allergy medicine, no doubt. But he kept sneezing and blowing his nose, and absolutely no one wanted to stand by him and therefore have to hold his hand. Finally, Ani disappeared and came back with a giant bottle of hand sanitizer and made him use it.

And that's how the night began. I should've known it would be downhill from the Purell.

Lilly agreed to be my partner, except the first thing she said was, "Chambray button-down and jeans? Not very original." Maybe not, but I thought I'd cleaned up pretty nicely.

I don't usually get nervous, but I wasn't a great dancer. I figured I'd be okay as long as I could learn the moves, but during the first promenade, where I had to hold her hand behind her back and another one in the front, I tripped up a little.

"Cay, you're so clumsy," she said loud enough that Sam turned her head. "It's your *right* foot first."

By the time we ran through the Texas Star a few times, I started to feel a lot better. When we all finally got it, we cheered.

A little while later, we got a break, so we all sat down at a round table and ordered some drinks.

"I'm so happy we're all together," Ani said, raising her beer. "I can't tell you what you all being here means to me. Even if a farm weekend is out of your comfort zones."

"Nothing's out of our comfort zone with you, babe," Gabe said. "We're thrilled to be here."

Tyler looked like he had to pass gas.

"Thanks for letting me crash," Jason said to Ani.

"Love you, Jase," she said.

"Love you too." Jason lifted his glass. "To the happy couple."

"To being together." Mia raised her glass, and we all followed suit.

Marin and her son walked in, Tater holding the little yellow lab in his arms. On seeing all the people, the pup wiggled out of his grasp and bounded straight over to our table. To be fair, we were right by the door, so that explained that. Unfortunately, the dog chose Tyler as the first recipient of its love and youthful dog energy, leaping up on him in the middle of our toast.

He immediately used his arm to keep the dog away, splashing some of his vodka tonic down his shirt. "Down, animal," he said nonchalantly—and frankly, a little coldly. "Anyway, as Ani said, we appreciate you all being here."

Sitting a few chairs away from Tyler, Sam stiffened. I got it. Tyler could come across like that, unlike Ani, who had warmth and love enough to fill this barn forty times over. "Tyler, it's a puppy, dude," I said as the dog bounded over to me. I reached down and playfully scratched behind its ears. "You just need some time to learn your manners, don't you, girl?" Maybe Tyler did too, but I didn't say that.

Ani immediately called the puppy over and petted it, cooing to it as it placed its paws on her legs. "How do you know it's a girl?" she asked me.

"If he has to explain that to you, then you might have to repeat med school," Tyler said. Then he sneezed.

"Give her a break, Tyler," Sam said, calling him out. "She didn't do a physical. Marin said it's a girl. But she doesn't have a name yet besides Pup." At the sound of Sam's voice, the puppy turned and bolted over to her.

Sam stiffened, immediately putting her hands up on the table, as if to protect herself. But the dog jumped up on her, placing its paws on her leg and wagging its tail at high speed.

I half got out of my seat, unsure of exactly how frightened she was of dogs, half ready to swoop the dog up and away from her if she showed any signs of distress.

"Well, hello," she said, cautiously looking down. The dog looked up and wagged its tail in that puppy way.

Sam gave a nervous laugh. She was so still that I could have tipped her straight over with one flick.

I got up and stood behind her chair, then reached over to pet the dog—and gently steered her away from Sam. "That's the puppy butt-wiggle."

She glanced up at me and laughed. "The what?"

I stooped down and let the puppy jump up and put her paws on me. "She likes you. The butt-wiggle is a barometer."

"She's got big feet," Sam said, a little more relaxed since I was keeping the puppy at bay.

My turn to laugh. "Those are called paws. And if they're big, that can mean the dog is going to be big too."

The dog was staring at Sam. Going nose to nose with her, practically. Like, in love.

"You have the prettiest brown eyes," she said to the dog. "No one on the planet will be able to refuse you." The dog licked her leg.

She burst out laughing.

I did a little roughhousing with the dog. I mean, I didn't want Sam to get freaked out or anything. But as soon as I stopped, she jumped up on Sam again.

She didn't seem frightened. But she did seem unsure of what to do.

"It's okay to pet her," I said, "if you want." I kept my hands right there, rubbing the puppy's head, scratching behind the ears. My way of letting her know I'd be right there if something went wrong.

Sam lowered her hand. But she didn't actually get to the dog's head. The puppy began to lick her fingers.

Sam giggled. A sound I'd never heard before. But it made me feel warm all over.

She bent down to examine the pup up close. "You're pretty cute."

So the puppy responded by licking her nose. And that unleashed a giant snort of laughter. She sat up, rubbing the dog saliva off her nose, still chuckling.

Then Marin ran over and scooped up the dog. "Sorry about that."

"Did you think of a name yet?" Sam asked.

"No, but if you've got an idea, we might take it. I agree with you, being called Pup is just plain sad."

"Bye," Sam said as Marin carted her away. The dog gave a little whine, unhappy to be taken away from all the fun.

"Hey, watch it, Sam," Ani warned, "or you'll be taking her home."

"Not me." Sam put up her hands. "My landlady can't bear it when I tiptoe on the floor after nine p.m. A dog would throw her completely over the edge."

Mia stifled a yawn and stretched her arms. "This was really fun, but I'm post-call and I'm going to hit the sack early. We have hunt-your-own breakfast tomorrow at seven. Does anyone care if I turn in?"

"I'll go with you," Brax was quick to say. "Full moon tonight. We can take a stroll around the lake."

Tyler sneezed and blew his nose with a napkin. "I'm sorry, baby," he said to Ani, "but I'm going to head back and google when the pharmacy in town opens tomorrow morning. If you all will excuse me."

"I'll go with you." Ani rose to go with him. But she looked like she wanted to stay.

Lilly said, "I think I'll head back to the cabin too."

"I hope it's not because I crushed your foot," I said. I was a little thrown she'd want to leave this early.

"No, not at all," she said with a smile. Then she dropped her voice. "I'm just a little bored. Square-dancing just isn't my thing."

What *was* her thing? I suppose my ego felt a little offended—for about ten seconds—her leaving certainly saying everything about her desire to spend time with me. But my thoughts immediately strayed over to Sam. Maybe she'd stay. Maybe we'd get to talk some more.

A young teenage boy wearing blue jeans and a white shirt placed a giant order of french fries that we'd ordered onto our table. Lilly immediately looked distressed. "I hate to cause a problem," she said to the server, "but these are burnt."

I can't call myself a french fry connoisseur, but I didn't see the issue. Maybe there were a few slightly more brownish ones on the top. I reached over and grabbed them and put them into my mouth. "Problem solved," I said with a smile, trying my best to repair the cringe factor.

Lilly gave me the eye. And her color was up, both indicators that she was angry. But I didn't regret trying to defuse things. I was coming to suspect that Lilly routinely expected James Beard-rated food.

"Caleb, I was making a point," she huffed.

More cringe. Before I could answer, Quinn pulled the plate over, examined the fries, and snagged one. "Did you say you're a florist?" he asked Lilly as he calmly chewed his fry. I was so relieved he'd said something that I got over the fact that he was talking and eating at the same time.

"Yes," Lilly said.

"So, customer service." He sat back and examined her.

A frown creased her pretty brow. "What's your point?"

"That server is just a teenager trying to earn a buck. Have some compassion, lady."

She immediately stood up, looking like she wanted to leave, like, yesterday. "I didn't mean anything by it. It's just that you should get what you pay for."

"I'm going to grab us another pitcher," Sam said cheerily, getting up from the table and effectively cutting off the discussion. "Unless anyone wants something else?" I didn't have the heart to tell her that she, Quinn, and I were going to be splitting that whole pitcher among ourselves, because at this point our troops were dropping like flies.

After everyone left, Quinn sat back and smiled. "She's got it all," he said to me because, well, there was no one else.

I felt my brows shoot up with surprise. "Sam or Lilly?"

Quinn smiled. "I was a waiter all through college and med school. Being chewed out for food issues that aren't really issues is abominable."

I could hear my mom's take on this now. "Anyone who is nasty to anyone in the service industry is not a good life partner."

Ha. But I had to say, it was kind of true, in an obnoxious way.

"So how long have you and Sam been friends?" Quinn asked.

And... I was back to disliking him, just like that.

My gaze wandered over to where Sam was in line at the bar. She was chatting with an older woman dressed in a red-and-white checked skirt. Suddenly she burst into laughter.

Part of me wanted to get up and join her conversation instead of listening to Quinn pry me with unashamed questions. Although for a few minutes, I'd found a new respect for him for calling Lilly out.

"Sam's pretty and smart and funny. She's not seeing anyone, is she?"

"She's not interested in dating," I said before I could think. "Bad breakup." I let that settle and hoped that Sam would forgive me. "And she's dancing the next round with me. Sorry, buddy." Maybe that sounded a little harsh. But somehow it just flew right out of my mouth.

Sam was going to either kill me or thank me, I wasn't sure which.

Quinn leaned forward. "Really? How bad?"

I leaned forward. "Oh my God. Really bad."

"Me too. I just got dumped after six years. Six *years*. I bought the ring too. She kept it and won't give it back."

He looked torn up. "Sorry. That's harsh."

Quinn rubbed his forehead. "It's been six months. I decided I have to get back in the dating pool. It's the only way forward."

"That's a positive attitude."

"Sam's tall and she's got that shiny black hair and those big brown eyes... totally different from my ex."

That statement was so loaded that I didn't want to touch it with a ten-foot pole. I pretended to check my watch. "Hey, I'm going to help Sam. Can I get you anything?"

"No, thanks." I got up and beelined pretty fast, pretending not to hear his "So you don't think she'd date me?"

I passed Sam in line. "Everything okay?" I pulled some money out of my pocket. "I forgot to give you this."

"I got this round," she said, pushing my hand back.

She looked worried. Distracted even. "What's up?" I asked.

She sighed heavily. "Do you think you might stay just a little longer? Mia asked me for a little bit of time before I head back to the cabin."

"Sure, I'll stay." That sounded a little too enthusiastic, so I added, "I mean—Brax told me to take my time heading back there too."

"Wait, so—which one are they using?" She laughed and shook her head. "Why didn't they just get their own cabin? I feel like I'm back in college again where a blue ribbon on the doorknob means hanky-panky going on inside."

I would've laughed, except something was bothering me. "Has Quinn done anything to make you uncomfortable?"

"Nothing like that. I hate to be blunt when we've got to interact more before the wedding, but I might have to."

"I might've told him you were devastated by a breakup and weren't interested. I hope you don't mind."

She laughed. "I hope that works, but I'm not sure it will. Has Lilly left?"

"She wasn't into the square dance. Also, I might've stepped on her foot. Even worse, I put a giant scuff on her shoe."

"Yikes." Her eyes danced with humor. "Sorry about that."

I smiled. Mostly because she made me want to smile. I felt

relaxed and comfortable around her. "I want to stay and dance anyway."

She grinned widely. "Me too."

"But first, food. What are you getting?"

"Grilled cheese. French fries. A shake. Do they have that? I'm starving!"

"I got you," I said, and moved on to the food counter.

We chowed down pretty fast. Good thing, because the caller announced another round. Before I could think about what I was doing, I asked, "Sam, be my partner?"

And so we walked onto the dance floor. She stood across from me, grinning widely. "I have to warn you," I said, "I'm not very good at this. I might step on *your* foot."

"I might step on yours," she said right back. "Come on." And then she whisked me away.

∾

Samantha

Caleb and I danced the entire set together. All too soon, the caller announced the final song, the music came to a sudden stop, and everyone cheered, whooped, and clapped. We were breathless and laughing as we left the floor.

"You're... having fun," Caleb said in a quiet voice, his eyes twinkling. He appeared to be very satisfied that he'd called me out.

I *was* having fun. I really, really was. We'd learned all the calls and the steps, poking fun at each other's missteps and making funny faces. I didn't want it to end even as I knew it had to. "No. I'm not," I answered, but I'm sure I was grinning from ear to ear.

He reached out a hand and pushed a strand of my hair back. "Look at you. You're all untidy and glowing. I'd say definite fun was had."

I stared at him, frozen. He'd just touched my hair, and that was... unexpected. And confusing.

He didn't seem to notice, just kept staring at me. Finally, he gave a low chuckle. "Samantha unleashed," he said in a low voice, shaking his head incredulously.

He looked as thrown and surprised as I was.

I tried to think of a snappy comeback, something about all my bones being intact and not stepped on or something, but my mind was blank, dead as my uncharged phone. I felt flushed and hot, and my knees felt wobbly, like I might collapse in a heap if I didn't reach our table ASAP. Yet we both stayed rooted to the spot.

I steeled myself away from all that feeling. It was *nothing*. Just a fun, unexpected moment. Nothing more.

Tell that to my heart, which was beating more rapidly than during a decent round of cardio.

Every time we promenaded, held hands, swung our partner, or had a reason to touch, it was electric. Call it a square dance high. Make that a *Caleb* high. As we'd learned the age-old dances, his eyes sparkled, he smiled, and we'd both let loose. We'd laughed and squawked like chickens and do-si-doed and had a great time.

He didn't even step on my feet, I thought with pride, even though they were a lot bigger than Lilly's.

Dancing, the music, the moves, the fun. And something more that I did not want to admit even to myself. I thought about what Mia had said. That I tended to run from relationships. What would it be like if I didn't run? If I took a chance?

The caller thanked everyone for coming, and the fiddlers began packing away their fiddles. Somehow we were still standing there, connected in some unspoken way. I knew that once one of us moved, it would be broken forever.

Across the barn, Quinn spotted us and started walking toward us.

Go *now*, I told myself.

"Thanks for dancing," I said, tearing my gaze away. I couldn't keep looking into Caleb's eyes. I was losing my sense, my direction.

With this crazy energy, if it were another time, another guy, I'd expect an invite. Or give one. To get a drink. To go out. To go to bed.

But this was not the time, and this was definitely not the guy.

How could we have barely touched, not even have kissed, and yet I felt this way?

This was a man who, until three days ago, was on my most unlikeable persons list. Who believed in romantic fairy tales. Who was here to discover if he was truly still in love with his first love.

Remembering that woke me from my stupor. I was not going to—could not—interfere with his plan. It would only lead to heartache. And I would never, ever do anything to endanger my friendship with Mia.

"I'm going to cut out now," I said at the same time that he said, "I'm going to head back to the cabin."

"Let me walk you back," he said.

"No, I'm fine. Thanks. See you in the morning. You still want to meet before breakfast and discuss some strategy about Lilly for the hike?" I couldn't believe I'd just said that. As if I could offer a useful strategy to use with Lilly. As if I wanted to! That was laughable, really.

Considering the fact that Lilly had shown up at the last minute, complained about being bored, and then left, it didn't seem like things were going that well. And that didn't even count the french fry fiasco. I wasn't sure what else I could do to turn that tide, especially with all the emotions churning inside me. But I'd put it out there, and I was nothing but good on my word.

"Yeah, sure," he said. "Thanks."

Great. I was thinking what an idiot I was as I turned and started walking toward the path. What was I doing? Not what I was supposed to be doing. I was muddying the waters. Interfering in decisions Caleb had to make all by himself. Suddenly I turned around and called his name.

I was surprised to find him still standing there, watching me.

That threw me a little, but I focused on what I wanted to say. "The matchmaker test—you and Lilly passed with flying colors." That seemed to catch him by surprise. "Just wanted you to know."

Then I left before Quinn could figure out where I'd gone. But I didn't really care about Quinn. I had to get away before I could think any more about what the hell had just happened.

Mia was right. I *was* running away. But I had no choice.

Chapter Thirteen

Caleb

At around six forty-five the next morning, Brax and Gabe spied me outside the barn. They caught me carrying a cup of coffee with a lid on it that I'd gotten from a coffee station near the front desk. I was on my way to meet Sam to supposedly talk about a good plan for Lilly, as we'd all be spending the entire day together.

After a restless night, I'd already come to a few conclusions. One was that the Lilly of now was definitely not the Lilly in my imagination. The real Lilly was not who I'd thought and dreamed she was. And the Samantha of now was not my enemy. Far from it. But that was as far as I got, and I decided that the safest plan for the weekend was just to survive it and to go home and try to process everything then.

I had to admit something that I never dreamed I'd think, that Samantha was fun. She was friendly and kind and open to new experiences. And she'd gone over and above for me and Lilly. Even worse, something between us was building—make that threatening to bowl me over—and it was nowhere near friendly in nature. It made me question myself—how was it possible to fall for someone so quickly? I never really fell for anybody. I didn't have infatuations. I'd clung onto my vision of Lilly, my regrets, my what-ifs, for all these years.

What I was feeling couldn't be real. Could it?

"Who's that for?" Gabe asked poignantly. "I might grab some for Jason. He's up working already and he's not really into the hunting-your-breakfast stuff."

Who was?

"It's for Samantha," I said calmly, "but don't get your knickers in a knot. We're going to discuss some strategies I can use today with Lilly."

"Sorry she left early last night," Gabe said. "But the french fry thing—"

"I don't want to talk about the french fry thing." I cut that discussion off fast.

"You okay with the low-energy test results?" Brax asked.

I studied his expression. He didn't seem to be joking. "Low energy?"

"Sorry," he said, looking a little embarrassed. "I thought Sam told you. I mean, Mia knew, so I thought you knew too."

It occurred to me that these doctors were talking about the hocus-pocus matchmaking test with the same scientific objectivity as a patient's blood chemistry panel. "Sam told me the test was fine." I left out "flying colors." My head was spinning a little. Low-energy test? Failed? Why had Sam told me exactly the opposite?

"Maybe it doesn't matter so much anymore," Gabe said carefully. "You were with Sam most of the night anyway."

"Let's be clear," I said quickly. "We did a round of dancing together after Lilly left. That was it." And I'd gotten sort of swept up in the moment—enough that I'd touched her hair. A mistake.

"Leave him alone," Brax said. "He's discerning, right, man? You've wondered *what if*, and you're seeing if Lilly lives up to the hype in your mind. Besides, that matchmaking stuff is just family tradition for Sam. Even she doesn't actually believe in it."

I wasn't so sure, but I let that go.

"I believe in feelings," Gabe said. "I mean, think about relationships. When something feels extraordinary between two people, it usually is. Or else no one would get married or make a commitment. Sam's empathic. I think she can naturally sense if there's chemistry between two people."

"I thought I had that something special with Lilly," I confided to my friends. "But now I'm not so sure." It wasn't just that I wasn't feeling any chemistry. The way we viewed life seemed different—like, family was always number one with me, hands down. The way we viewed food (I ate and she didn't), the way we viewed new experiences (me with anticipation, not skepticism), not to mention the way we treated anyone in the service industry were completely opposing. Her entire lack of interest in discussing books was also a blow. How had I not seen any of this before?

"Lust clouds the brain," Brax said matter-of-factly.

"What?" I cracked open the coffee lid and watched the steam pour out into the cool morning air.

Gabe gave an enthusiastic nod. "Basically, he's saying that the sex was great once upon a time, and that colors everything. Makes you look back on that time with rose-colored glasses."

"Exactly!" Brax high-fived Gabe. "Plus she dumped you, right? If you aren't the one doing the leaving, you always wonder *what if* because you didn't have a choice."

I frowned and shook my head like that wasn't the case. But I had to admit that the feeling of being in love for the first time had been pretty amazing. It had been a powerful, heady time. But it hadn't lasted. And I didn't feel those feelings toward Lilly now at all—in fact, I was struggling to summon them again. As for being the one who was dumped—that had hurt like hell. I hated giving up on anything.

"Sam doesn't believe in love," I said. "I'm surprised that she's even involved in this matchmaking stuff."

"Everyone believes in love deep inside," Gabe said softly. "It just takes the right person to make them feel safe wanting it."

Interesting. Did Sam talk the big talk about not caring about love because she was afraid? Why had she told me the test with Lilly was ragingly positive? I left the guys thinking about the things that had already kept me up way too long at night.

As I walked through the wide-open doors of the barn and passed horse stalls and hay bales and farm equipment, I spotted Sam outside the far end, standing with her elbows on a wooden split rail fence, chatting with a brown-and-white horse. More horses grazed in the distance under the canopy of a lone tree. Beyond that, the morning mist blurred watercolor hills and the light of the rising sun that promised a warm, clear day.

"You're a pretty thing, you know that, don't you?" she murmured as she quietly stroked its mane. "Here you go." She reached into a back pocket of her hiking shorts to pull out a giant carrot, which the horse delicately took between his teeth.

"Looks like you finally found a male you could trust," I said. Probably not the greatest line to lead with. I set the coffee on a pile of logs behind us—didn't want to seem too eager.

"Yep." She tossed me a smile. "He's a sweet boy. His name is Jetson."

I liked this soft version of Sam—the one who forgot to be a cynic. Her smile lit me up, clear and bright as the dawning light behind her. The sun was shining on her hair, dark and silky as her horse friend's, and it was up in a high ponytail again. No nonsense. Like her, dressed in hiking shorts and shoes, ready for the day's adventures.

Glancing at her watch, she said, "Is it time for breakfast yet? I'm starving."

"You might have to starve a little longer. I heard we have to fetch the eggs and milk the cows." I paused to let that sink in. "But then Marin told me that a chef named Pierre is going to whip everything up into a fantastic meal."

"Milk the cows?" The color drained from her face. "Are we processing the sugar cane and picking the coffee beans too? What does it take to get a cup of coffee around here?"

"Already did that." I produced the cup of coffee. She shot me a startled look followed quickly by a grateful smile. She immediately took the lid off, rich fragrance and wisps of steam and rich fragrance escaping.

Somehow, I knew she'd be pleased. Her reaction made me happy.

"What's for breakfast anyway?" she asked as she blew on it and took a sip. "Thank you for the coffee. It's good."

"You're welcome." For a moment, our eyes met and held in an inescapable hold. In the distance, some pigs squealed, excited to be served breakfast by one of the farm hands, who dumped a giant bucket of something into their area.

"Bacon," I finally said. "Bacon's for breakfast."

"*Stop*," she said. But she was wearing a little smile. As the smile faded, she glanced down at the cup and then up at me as if she wanted to say something, but she didn't.

"Hasn't anyone ever brought you coffee before?"

"No," she said honestly. "But you're two for two days. You're setting a bad precedent."

"Hey, it's my love language. Er—I mean, my *friendship* language." Great. A vivid scene flashed uninvited in my mind, triggered no doubt by the *love* word. Sam in bed, her long hair down and tousled. Me handing her coffee. Her taking it with a smile—a welcoming one. A get-over-here-right-now-and-kiss-me one.

I blinked. Cleared my throat. Made a big show of visually scanning the entire area from the barn, the fenced field, and the wild field beyond to the tree line. A soft, low moo or two came from the barn. Jetson nickered. In the yard, a rooster crowed.

She downed another sip. "Oh wow. It's ridiculously delicious."

And I was ridiculously pleased. She had deep brown eyes, warm and rich like the coffee. When she wasn't frowning at me, she was noticeably pretty. I mean, not that I noticed—except in a purely clinical sense. We docs were trained to observe, of course. The sun was rising far across the field in front of us. It was a beautiful almost-summer morning. I stepped back a step and pointed to a railroad-tie fence overlooking a rolling meadow. "Want to sit and talk about today?" Business. Purely business.

"On the fence?" she asked.

I looked around. Barn, dirt, fence, field. "No patio furniture for miles." I made a gesture like a stirrup with my hands. "I can help you up."

"I don't need your help."

I held back a smile. "Of course you don't."

She made several unsuccessful tries to get up on the fence, holding the coffee.

"Are you always determined not to ask for help?" I asked. Although admittedly, I had quite a nice view from down here.

"Did you just mumble something about a nice view?" She gave me a cold stare from the top plank of the fence.

Oh no. Had I said that out loud? "I—what I meant was," I said, going full damage control, "that meadow." I pointed out to the lush green meadow, covered with slanted rays of morning sun. "I mean, come on. It's as nice as the one where Lizzy met Mr. Darcy at the end of *Pride and Prejudice*. With the sun just peeking through the trees. I mean, yeah." I whistled. "*Quite* a view."

Her frown was accompanied by a big effort not to smile. "How do you know about *Pride and Prejudice*?"

"It's Mia and my mom's favorite movie." Then I looked into her eyes, which were brown, with pretty gold rims. "'You have bewitched me, body and soul.'" Not a bad impression, if I could say so myself. I'd had a lot of practice tormenting Mia with that Matthew MacFayden line.

She laughed, but then a weird thing happened. I couldn't stop staring into her eyes. I got tangled up in that big, brown gaze.

Finally, she turned to look out at the fields. "Thanks for helping me with Quinn last night."

"He's like, head over heels. He couldn't stop talking about you."

She put her hands up defensively. "I'm not looking for anything, especially not with anyone in this wedding party."

"Aw, come on. One of the bridesmaids always sleeps with one of the groomsmen."

She tossed me a glance. "We'll save that for you and Lilly."

Oh. Lilly. Hadn't thought of her for a while. And right now, I was wondering about Sam. "What turned you off of love?" I asked before I could censor myself.

Another withering look. I definitely should've censored myself. "The day I discuss my love life with you will be the day the earth freezes over. I will literally *never* discuss my love life with you."

"As it should be." What was I doing? Flirting, asking her out-of-the-blue personal questions. I couldn't tell her that I no longer thought Lilly was everything I'd thought she was—she'd think I was as unreliable and superficial as she'd initially believed. I cleared my throat. "Now then. Back to business."

I took her cup, and she hiked herself up to sit on the top rung of the rail fence.

Then I stole a sip while she was getting situated. "You're right. It's good."

She took a sip. "Really good." Then she held it back out to me.

"Aha, so you *did* learn to share in preschool after all."

She rolled her eyes.

A weird idea popped into my head. On impulse, I pulled out my phone. "Let's take a selfie."

She laughed. "A what?"

"Oh, come on. It's the perfect moment." I held the phone at

arm's length, got the rising sun behind us, and said "Smile," while I clicked.

She humored me, standing close and putting our heads together. And it turned out to be a really nice shot. I took a bunch of photos, somehow desperate to capture this exact moment. "There. Farm weekend captured for posterity." That wasn't why I did it. I wanted to remember forever exactly how she looked right at this moment, sort of glowing, fresh and beautiful, with the rolling hills and the dewy new morning as a backdrop. And I wanted me in it too. The two of us together. Like I said, it was an impulse, and I went with it.

"So, did you see Lilly last night?" Sam asked. "Did you go for a walk in the moonlight? Did you take her down by the lake and pour out your heart? Did you get all those pent-up feelings out on the table?"

"You're making fun of me."

She blinked.

"You said you would help me. So that should mean not judging me."

Silence. I could feel her considering that. "You're right. I'm sorry. Sometimes I can be a little sarcastic."

My turn to lift a brow. "A little?"

A flash of vulnerability sparked in her eyes, but it passed quickly. She heaved a sigh that sounded sad and resigned. "Sorry. You called it. I don't really believe in love," she said. "I mean, I just don't."

I respected the admission, but I wanted desperately to understand. "How can anyone not believe in love? I mean, love is... everything."

She took another sip of coffee and glanced out across the misty meadow. "It rarely works out."

"I wonder, with a magical grandma, why you're such a cynic." I scanned her face intensely. This was the most honest thing she'd ever said. But she stared into the distance, her eyes focused straight ahead, and they weren't revealing any secrets. At least not to me. "Haven't you ever been in love before?"

"I never wanted to be," she said. Then she faced me. "Look, my mom—she got pregnant young. And she married my dad, but she shouldn't have. She didn't go to college—she just worked and struggled endlessly to make ends meet. And tried to find a better guy. Only none of them were better, you know what I mean? She'd come and go, in and out of my life, and then she got pregnant with Wynn. By the time Wynn was eight, she left for good. Which was probably the best thing, because our grandma was amazing."

I was so bowled over that I almost had to sit down. How had she accomplished all that with all she'd been through? How had she survived? I had to stop myself from asking more questions, because I sensed she'd shut me down, but I wanted to know everything about her. Hell, I had to stop myself from gathering her up in my arms. I wanted to hug all that pain right out of her.

"So you see," she continued, "your assessment of me is spot-on. I *am* jaded and cynical. Nothing can convince me that love is a big old fairy tale. How are you so certain that Lilly's the love of your life?"

"I'm not. But I needed to see her again to find out." That was the truth. And I forced myself to stop there. I'd already found out that my romantic fantasies hadn't panned out, but I kept that to myself. "My mom and dad—they're still in love, even after all these years. I wouldn't say what they have is a fairy tale. They'd be the first to call it hard work, but they still stick together through everything. From them I learned that your true love is someone who gets you. Who has your back no matter what. Who you miss when you're not with them because you find yourself wanting to tell them all the little things that have happened through your day. Who's kind and smart and fun." I grinned because she looked so perplexed, like I was speaking a foreign language or something. "Someone who doesn't frown at you and give you a headache every time you interact."

"Ha, okay, I get that last part. Has Lilly had your back?" She must've seen my surprise, because she said, "I'm asking because I'm worried that this romantic notion of love you carry has clouded your vision."

I stiffened. "You're starting to sound like my parents." And my friends, to be honest. Had everyone figured this out before I did?

And what was the answer to that question? I'd always thought of myself as needing to have Lilly's back—but failing. Had Lilly ever had *my* back?

"Maybe they don't want you to get your heart broken again." She assessed me carefully, then said, "I mean, I hope that's not the case. But a lot of times if someone's friends or family doesn't agree with their choice, they might be right."

"That year Lilly and I moved to Milwaukee—we were very ill-equipped for real life. I couldn't stop wondering if we would've made it if our situation was different." The look on her face appeared to be pity. "But I'm not naive. I know that if I don't take a chance and let people in, then I'll never know. Love requires risk."

She hit my sore spot, but I could put my finger on hers too.

She seemed to grow distant. Like if she were a teenager, this would be the part where she'd stopped listening. "Risk leads to pain, is all I'm saying. Just be careful, okay?"

"I'm more worried about you. You're too young to give up on finding your person."

We stared at each other a moment. I had this burning desire to know what made her sound like my own grandma instead of a person in the prime of their life, with all the hopes and dreams of love and life ahead.

She shrugged and looked out into the fields. "Not everyone needs a person."

I wanted to say more, but then Marin suddenly emerged from the barn, gesturing for us to join her. "Come on, you people. Time to gather eggs."

"Time to kill your breakfast," I said with enthusiasm.

This time Sam burst out in a laugh. It was big and messy and spontaneous. Her whole face lit up. Her eyes too. It seemed to me that not many people knew how to coax a laugh out of her. I must say, I was pretty proud that I had. It was like unlocking a secret. And that was a sight to see.

As we headed in, I realized then that I'd completely forgotten to ask her about the matchmaking test.

Chapter Fourteen

Samantha

Marin's husband Brent, aka Farmer Brown, stood before all of us in the barn and said, "This morning we're going to collect some fresh eggs, churn some butter, milk a cow, and pick some fresh herbs. Then we'll go into the kitchen and stir up a delicious breakfast. Are you all ready?"

My stomach growled again—loudly, as I considered that breakfast appeared to be hours away. How long did it take to churn butter anyway? Thank God I'd at least had coffee, or I wouldn't be able to function.

I stood in the background, near Mia and Brax, with the intention to stay as far from Caleb and Lilly as I could. Just as I was planning to walk off by myself to check out the chickens, Caleb fell into step beside me.

"Those little piggies back there sure were cute," Caleb said, just to torment me.

"If Wilbur's on the breakfast menu, I'm outta here," I shot back. That made him snort with laughter.

"Oh, come on," he said. "What's a farm breakfast without ham and sausage?"

"Healthier," I retorted. Why wasn't he with Lilly?

"But not as much fun." He let that sit. "Oh, that's right. You're not into fun."

"That's not what you said last night," I reminded him.

He chuckled and rubbed his neck. "Okay, you're right," he said a little shyly. "Last night *was* fun."

The tiny smile he sent my way sent my stomach aflutter. Only for a moment though, because Brent began to explain how to gather eggs. He walked us over to a row of chicken condos—that's what I called them—wooden boxes on a platform, each with a grated window. According to him, you reached in and collected the eggs, right there for the taking. I couldn't tell if most of the chickens had already flown the coop. Or if they remained, were they unfazed by egg gathering?

I raised my hand. "How do you know there aren't—um—baby chickens in the eggs?"

"This part of our farm doesn't have roosters," he said. "But to make sure, we always candle every egg with a flashlight. If an egg is fertilized, you can see veins and a little chick embryo growing in there. Otherwise, it's pretty clear."

At the barn door, Lilly appeared, late, as I was coming to see was normal, but fresh-faced and perfectly dressed, her hair a golden halo of curls. "Sorry I'm late," she said with a smile. She walked into the barn and joined us, looking photo-shoot ready in a cute sundress and full makeup. Beside me, Caleb's gaze followed her as she joined the group.

On the other side of me, Mia whispered, "She's done all that before coffee?"

I gave a little shrug. I'd never spent a lot of time getting ready, even before I entered medicine. With our training, all those nights on call where you had to show up and be on your toes at a moment's notice, you learned to get no-frills presentable quick.

Lilly looked gorgeous, but then the woman would look gorgeous in a potato sack.

"Okay, kids," Brent said. "Take one." He handed everyone a basket. "We throw the feed on the ground so the chickens leave their nests. Just give them a gentle shoo if they don't. Once they're gone, take the eggs and put them in the basket. Then we'll show you how to clean them, okay?"

He scattered the feed around the yard, and sure enough, the hens popped out of their condos and began pecking at it.

I took a basket and followed cautiously after Mia.

"Got my eggs!" Lilly said shortly, holding out her basket, which somehow held six. "Aren't they pretty?"

"Nice," Caleb said, lifting one out of her basket.

"So," Tyler said, "did you know that you can tell what color eggs a hen lays?" He looked considerably less miserable than last night, thanks to the modern wonder of allergy meds.

Ani flicked her gaze up, all interested and wide-eyed.

"You look at their ears," Caleb said.

"Chickens don't have ears, silly," Lilly said.

"Caleb's right." Tyler pointed out the small oval of skin next to a chicken's ear hole. "If it's brown, they lay brown eggs, and if it's white, the eggs are white."

"Cool. You're so smart, Ty," Ani said with a wink. Tyler smiled, proud to be complimented for his smarts. I was glad the two of them seemed to be getting along better today.

The couples were together, except for Gabe and Jason, who'd taken a hard pass on breakfast, so all looked well on the Western front. As for me, I walked with purpose around the coops, getting up the courage to stick my hand in one to grab my breakfast.

After most of us had found eggs, Lilly said, "I'd love to get out of this hen yard before I get my tennies messed up." She called to Caleb, "You coming?"

"Yeah. Sure, as soon as I grab a couple of eggs, I'll be right there."

"'Kay," she said. "I'll save you a seat at breakfast."

Okay. I didn't know what had changed after the square dance, but she actually seemed eager to be with Caleb this morning, and that was a good thing, right?

Caleb was checking for some eggs nearby when I reached into a nearby coop to grab an egg, just as Farmer Brown had directed. A sudden stabbing pain pierced my index finger. I withdrew my hand from the coop as if I'd been burned or stung and gave a cry, stumbling backward. Caleb caught me, preventing me from falling on my ass, just as a chicken flew out of the coop, squawking angrily.

I felt two things at the same time. The first, I admit, was pain. A trickle of blood dripped from the tip of my finger. I didn't want to put it in my mouth—I mean, chicken saliva and all that—and I certainly didn't want to wipe it on my shorts, so I stood there, holding my injured finger with my other hand.

Caleb was at my back, hard as a tank and so big I felt completely enveloped by him.

For one millisec, I felt... safe. Breathless. Embarrassed. And very aware of his hands on my arms, holding me, steadying me. Preventing me from falling into the hay under the coops which I felt certain would be full of surprises I didn't want to encounter.

But I didn't need safe. I regained my balance and examined my finger. "I think I just got pecked."

Brent walked over, took a quick look, and said matter-of-factly, "Some of the hens think they're hatching actual chicks," he said. "I should've told you not to reach in if the hens haven't left. Sorry about that."

"Not your fault," I said.

"Did you just reach under an actual chicken to get the eggs?" Lilly asked, somehow right next to Caleb, wide-eyed.

I laughed it off. "I guess I stuck my hand into places where it doesn't belong." And into other people's business where it *definitely* didn't belong, I added to myself. I decided I didn't want to know what happened between Caleb and Lilly anymore.

That was my job. To help them connect. But now that they seemed to be connecting, it was painful.

The chicken who'd pecked me was hopping around near the coops, still protesting loudly. I didn't blame her. Still cupping my bleeding finger, I bent over the chicken crates and said "I'm so sorry, girlfriend. I get it." She was unimpressed with my apology, because she flew right back into her coop.

"Are you sympathizing with that chicken?" Caleb asked, brow lifted.

I straightened out. "I invaded her privacy. I tried to take something she's been working on for a long time."

Lilly walked up and stood beside Caleb. "It's just a confused chicken who, like, thinks she laid an actual egg."

"She did lay an actual egg," I said. "It's just not the kind that will turn into a chick, but she doesn't know that."

"Crazy chicken," Lilly said. "I think you're thinking a little too deeply."

"And I think you should go in and wash that off," Caleb said.

"Great idea," Lilly said as Caleb, not waiting for me, grabbed my elbow and started to haul me toward the door. "What's that smell?" Lilly asked, sniffing daintily.

The smell of chicken poop was already in the air. But it suddenly seemed especially fresh.

I stopped and sniffed. Held on to a couple of stacked hay bales and hiked up my foot so that I could see my sole. *Ugh, gross.* I raised my uninjured hand to my forehead and groaned.

"There's a hose over there," Caleb pointed out. I walked over and grabbed it. There was a wire brush hanging near the hose and I grabbed that too.

Caleb took the hose from me and pulled it out into the grassy yard. "Here's a good place."

A quick glance over my shoulder showed me that Lilly was taking in the whole scene, thinking God knows what. I wished he'd just go with her and stop trying to help me, the do-gooder. "Caleb, please go in to breakfast," I urged in a whisper. "I'll be there in a minute."

Instead, he held out the hose. "Just give me your hand," he insisted. "You don't want to get some kind of nasty infection."

"Death by chicken peck," I said as he blasted my wound with cold water. "How would I explain that to an ER doc?"

He took my hand, which was now freezing, and examined it from all sides. A bolt of warmth spread through me despite the discomfort.

"Cay, you coming?" Lilly was waiting at the end of the courtyard, past the chickens, her arms folded.

Oh no. Last night I'd thought Lilly was apathetic toward Caleb, but now she was... jealous?

I took the hose from Caleb. "I got it. Thanks."

Still, he hesitated. He was eyeing the brush, as if he might help me with that too, but I drew the line.

I dropped my voice. "Don't miss your chance," I whispered, tilting my head toward Lilly. "I'm fine."

Lilly had walked back over and looped her elbow through Caleb's. "We'll save you a seat," she said.

It was a relief to carry on alone without an audience. Of course, on dousing my shoes, I got my socks wet. But I managed to blast and scrub every speck of chicken poop out of those grooves in my soles, which was all I cared about. That smell... it was... well, a little too farm-fresh for the likes of me.

Besides, by this point, I was so hangry I could hardly think.

Still, I was determined to show up with eggs. I wouldn't suffer the humiliation of being the only one who didn't. Also, I felt that I could eat a dozen by now.

Just then, the chicken—my chicken, that is, literally flew the coop. She was brown with white specks, and she completely ignored me. But she left behind two brown eggs.

"Thank you!" I cried, snatching them up and placing them in my basket.

Just as I turned around, I spotted Caleb standing in the doorway, a puzzled expression on his face.

"Hunger is a fantastic motivator," I said, tilting the basket toward him so he could see.

He laughed. A nice laugh, deep and a little rumbly so that I felt it in my chest.

"You *are* determined."

"Totally," I said as I walked toward him. "My middle name." What was he doing back here? It was crystal clear to me that Lilly was unhappy that I'd diverted his attention. Heck, I was unhappy too. And nervous. I did *not* want Lilly getting the wrong idea.

He held up a small, rectangular piece of paper.

Except it wasn't a piece of paper. It was a Band-Aid. "I'm a doctor," he said as if that wasn't obvious. "It's against the Hippocratic Oath to leave people bleeding."

I snagged the Band-Aid. "Thanks. But you didn't have to do that."

"Hey, I keep telling you that I'm a nice person. Besides, you were nice to me." He moved his hand back and forth between us. "See, it works both ways."

At that exact moment, the sun broke through the clouds, dappling down through the trees, bathing the plain barnyard in golden light.

His smile broke through to me. Made me feel all fuzzy and hot, like I'd just quickly downed an entire mug of hot chocolate in the middle of a summer day. Made me realize that Caleb was not only a good human being but also a really handsome one.

Just as suddenly, a more ominous feeling moved through me. A warning kind of feeling, telling me to watch myself. Because I could get myself in big trouble with a man like that.

And maybe I already had.

Caleb cleared his throat. A horse nickered.

He held out his hand, palm up. "Here, give me your hand."

Why was I not able to think coherently? I found myself surrendering it. And I was sadly on the verge of surrendering the rest of me.

He opened the Band-Aid and placed it expertly on my finger, which was still oozing. He was so gentle, so careful, that I felt a sudden panic. I wasn't used to anyone doing such a thing. As he bent over me, focused, long fingers steady, I noticed his hair, wavy and thick, dark brown but with golden strands lit up by the sun. He had the thickest hair. I wanted to sweep it back. Touch it to feel its silky-coarse texture.

What was happening to me?

"Boo-boo fixed," he said with a magnanimous smile.

My knees felt weak. I realized I'd been holding perfectly still, not even daring to breathe.

And then he turned to go.

I shook myself out of the strange fugue. "Caleb," I called after him.

He turned. He was tall, but he had a way of moving fluidly, with ease. I would bet a paycheck that he'd been one of the cool kids in high school, based solely on his grace. I understood how that confidence would translate into being a great surgeon. "What is it?"

"Thanks. For the Band-Aid." *Thanks for caring. For not leaving me alone.* Those were the things I didn't say out loud.

I'm not going to lie, but my hands and feet felt a little tingly. Probably from the ice-cold hose water. And the awful, stabbing hunger. And the nagging mental stress that I was way in over my head.

I headed into the farm kitchen with my eggs, proud to have earned my breakfast.

I decided that if there was bacon, I swear I was going to eat every last bite.

Chapter Fifteen

Caleb

We set out on the big hike right after breakfast, with Marin and Tater leading us straight toward the woods. The summer morning was glorious, sunny and warm, birds chirping up a storm high in the trees above us on the dirt path. It seemed like a low-key, tame adventure that I wanted to be all-in for Ani. But I couldn't help thinking that the karma of the universe seemed a little off—Lilly seemed different, more attentive, but I had no idea why.

"We've got a waterfall, some caves and hieroglyphs, and some stunning cliffs to see," Marin said, cataloging what we were about to experience. "So everyone stick together, okay? Tater, watch where you're going!" Tatum, who was walking along playing a handheld video game, shot her an obstinate look and kept playing as he walked.

How many doctors did it take to keep an eye on a bored ten-year-old? Maybe just one, because no one else besides me seemed to be noticing.

I had a lot of questions about how athletic this hike was going to be if it was led in part by a ten-year-old, but I deferred to sweet Ani and decided to do my best to liven up the group. Besides, it was Saturday, our last day, thank goodness. I vowed as a solid member of the wedding party to make it a good one.

Sam seemed to be walking as far away from me as possible. Maybe I shouldn't have done the Band-Aid thing. But I hated that she was alone—I mean, she was surrounded by friends, but existentially, she went it alone. I wanted to help her. And talk with her. And I had so many questions, from how she got to med school with the struggles she'd had, to what did she really like to eat for breakfast?

Meanwhile, Lilly seemed to do a complete one-eighty, showering me with attention, sitting near me at breakfast, chatting with me. She seemed strangely possessive, considering she'd barely given me the time of day before. She'd even said, "Jeez, Caleb, you're running out with a Band-Aid for someone who was careless enough to get pecked by a chicken sitting on her nest," which I thought was a little over the top.

Sam was up at the front of the group with Brax, listening to Quinn give an impromptu lecture on poison ivy, oak, and other plants to avoid. Lilly eventually ran up front with the others to listen. Gabe walked with Jason, clearly happy that he'd decided to take a break and join us.

I caught up with Tyler, whose skinny, pale legs looked like they hadn't seen any vitamin D in quite a while. "Hey, Ty, your face looks a lot less puffy today," I quipped. "I can actually see your cheekbones."

"The miracles of allergy meds," he said. "And I've sprayed myself from head to toe with bug spray."

"Such a trouper." Ani, who was wearing a green brimmed safari hat and green utility shorts with her hiking boots, said, patting him on the back as she passed us up.

"Anything for you, my love," he said back.

Okay, so they were getting along better. That was good to see.

A quiet moo and a faint nicker sounded from the barn, which was now fading into the distance as we entered the woods. I reminded myself again that this was a very low-risk hike. If a ten-year-old could play a video game while hiking a well-worn path, why could I not dispel a strange feeling of doom?

Tyler joined Ani up front. That left Mia and me to bring up the rear. "Hey, wait up," Mia said in an insistent voice as she ran to catch up, hands on hips.

I gave my sister a big smile and an elbow nudge as she appeared beside me. "How are you this fine morning?"

"Great, but don't try to deflect. What's going on between you and Sam?"

Once Mia grabbed onto something, she didn't let go until she'd wrung out every bit of info possible. She wasn't beyond threatening to use it to get what she wanted either. Case in point: I'd done a cross-country road trip during spring break freshman year with four other guys in my buddy's barely functional ten-year-old Kia, knowing that our parents would never approve. I'd told them I would be visiting one of my friends, which was technically true—in San Francisco, that is. Mia had kept her mouth shut, even when our car broke down outside of Vegas and I'd run out of money after pitching in for the repairs. The price I paid for her Venmo financial bailout was having to set her up with a friend of mine she had a crush on. Besides paying the cash back with interest, that is.

This time I decided to protect myself. "Oh that," I said in a mock-serious tone, lowering my eyes to the ground.

"What do you mean?" She shook me by the arm.

I gave her my most saintly smile. "We've decided to get along—for the sake of the wedding."

She frowned deeply. I have to give my sister credit—she was smart. It was difficult to pull one over on her. But not impossible.

"You two have decided to suddenly 'get along'?" She did air quotes.

I nodded. "Yup. We've buried the hatchet. And it wasn't easy." That was all true, wasn't it?

"Cut the baloney, bro. I know everything. And just in case *you* might not know, Sam's gotten through school on scholarships and worked to pay for everything they didn't cover, and she doesn't care what anyone thinks because she's been single-handedly raising her younger sister since their grandma died. And you do know that Sam is financially responsible for her sister in college, right?"

She took a deep breath after that mouthful. "Wait. *Paying* for her college?"

"She moonlights. And took out loans. It hasn't been easy. But then, nothing about her life has been."

I guess I looked stunned. I certainly felt that way. But that didn't stop Mia from laying into me.

"So I would be very careful about giving Sam flirty personal first aid or trying to come to her rescue by offering to clean chicken shit off her shoes. She doesn't need the help. I especially wouldn't do it with cutesy banter and a big dopey grin on your face."

Wait. Big dopey grin? No. That wasn't me. I was *not* flirting. Was I?

"Also, I don't really understand how or why Sam happened to be helping you with Lilly but put a stop to that immediately."

So bossy. Some things never changed. "That's over. And you don't have to worry about me and Lilly," I said in a firm tone.

"What do you mean?"

"There's nothing between us." I winced. Mia had a way of forcing info out of me, and it worked. Every. Single. Time.

"Wait." She halted on the path. "Repeat that?"

"You heard me. She's not who I thought she was."

"Okay. All right. Good." She seemed to be trying to calm herself down. "Now say I don't have to worry about Sam. Right?"

I was silent.

She punched me in the arm. Again. "Ow! Hey, stop that right now." God, I hated sisters.

In front of us, Tyler was standing in the middle of the path, rubbing his arm and fuming.

"That *child*," he said, "Tater Tot or whatever—just winged a rock at that tree, and it ricocheted right into my arm."

"My name's not Tater Tot!" Tater said in an angry tone.

"Tyler!" Ani exclaimed. Then she turned to Tater. "He didn't mean to make fun of your name." Then back to Tyler. "Did you?"

Tyler rubbed his arm. "He could've really hurt me."

"But he didn't," Ani said. "It was an accident!"

"Tatum Albert, no more rocks!" Marin said, walking back to see what was going on. "I'm sorry, folks. Tater's a little out of sorts because his friend is sick and couldn't come today."

Oh well, that explained it. So far literally no one was bonding this bonding weekend—at least of the people that should be. We trudged onward, Ani walking far away from Tyler. On one side, a drop-off appeared, rocky and steep and of course unfenced, something else to worry about. Tater had stopped throwing rocks and pocketed the video game, thank God. But then he started tossing stones off the cliff, standing precariously close to the drop-off.

And Mia had not lost her train of thought. "I want to know your intentions. Sam doesn't ever put herself out there. I don't want to see her hurt. So tell me the truth, Caleb."

She said my name, with emphasis on the *Cay* like the zillion other times she'd lectured me in our childhood. Even though *I* was the older sib. "I'm *trying* to tell you the truth, if you'd just listen. Sam is different. Sam is... special. I've never met anyone like her. And I'm not going to do anything to hurt her."

She gripped me hard enough that I stopped walking. "I cannot reinforce enough what I am capable of doing to you if you hurt my best friend, do you hear me?"

"Could you please reinforce that without hurting my arm?"

She released me, fortunately. But now Tater was standing on a rock, taking selfies of the drop-off behind him.

"Just a sec," I said to my sister. "Hey, buddy," I said to the kid, "that's a big drop-off. Want me to take a photo for you?"

I glanced over at Marin. She was oblivious, settling an argument between Quinn and Tyler about a plant that might've been poison sumac, but no one knew for sure. The kid was fooling around, pulling faces, leaning over to get better and better shots. Below was a scenic fork in a river—*way* down below, that is. If I could get him away from the edge, I'd have less of a heart attack. I didn't want to yell at someone's kid, as Tyler seemed to have no problem doing, but I couldn't stop picturing imminent disaster.

That was the thing with being an ortho resident—with being a doctor in general. You heard about everybody's accidents, because that's what usually brings on the broken bones. Falls on an outstretched hand, tripping over the dog, toppling over on the bicycle, crashing the scooter, bouncing off the trampoline. The list was endless. I wasn't a catastrophizer, but I was one step away. If I was ever a parent, I would probably consider locking my kids in the house and never letting them leave.

Tater gave me the okay about taking some photos, so I did, but I made him stay far from the drop-off. Then I stepped away so that he had to get down from the rocks to get his phone back. But a minute later, he'd wandered right back to the edge of the drop-off again.

I jogged to catch up to his mother and tapped her on the shoulder, "I'm a little worried about Tater. He's a little bit of a daredevil, getting close to the cliffs like that."

She guffawed. "Aw, Doc, don't you worry. We lead this hike three times a week. He knows all the ins and outs."

"Yes, but—" Tater had run ahead, where he'd climbed even farther down the incline to take more selfies. I could hear pebbles and rocks scraping and bouncing their way into oblivion as his feet scrabbled for purchase. "A lot of folks get injured taking selfies." I didn't say *die*, but that was a fact. Tourists on hikes for one.

Marin patted me on the shoulder. "Don't you get your britches in a twist, Doc." She yelled at her son, "Hey, Tater, you're making Doc here a little nervous. Keep to the path, okay, kid?"

Tater made a face at his mom. *Figures.*

Marin pulled us over to show us a view of some beehives in the valley below. I looked down to see bee boxes lined up in a clearing. She was discussing the ins and outs of honey production when Sam met my gaze. I could see worry in her eyes. She lifted her chin and pointed—there was the kid, standing on a jutting-out rock, shooting yet another selfie with the winding river gurgling in the valley far below.

I was just about to call out to him to get down when he lost his balance.

Why hadn't I just done it, yelled out? I never thought I'd say this, but I should've been more like Tyler. I should have shouted at that clueless kid, no holds barred, to get the hell away from the edge.

His phone dropped, clattering downward as it bounced off the rocks. "Wh-wh-*whoa*," he cried, his arms flailing.

Without thinking, I dove forward, grabbing his skinny-assed ten-year-old body by the torso like I was a defensive end sacking a quarterback and pulled him forward with all my strength. He landed on his butt, but I stumbled, tripping on something—a raised root maybe?—or something harder, because pain seared through my foot as I hit the ground hard, scraping my leg and right shoulder as I pitched down the steep hillside.

"Grab that branch!" a voice cried. *Sam.*

I tried to clutch onto scrub, tree branches, grass—anything—but objects were passing me fast, and the hill was too steep. Around me, dust kicked up and small rocks rolled along right beside me as I plunged downward.

Unbelievably, I felt a tug on my foot. It dawned on me that I wasn't alone. *Sam.* In horror, I realized she must have plunged right behind me, attempting to hold me back. But now she was sliding down the rocky incline with me.

Of all the foolish stunts. Was she out of her mind? Was I out of mine, having all these jumbled thoughts when death seemed imminent?

We landed with a thud in a pile of limbs about thirty feet down the cliff on a plateau that was about ten feet wide. I found myself clutching hard onto her waist and leg, trying to save us from pitching right over the edge like Niagara Falls daredevils. Below us, the cliff plunged precariously down to the water below.

"What were you thinking?" I exclaimed as she lifted up her head, her hand on my thigh. I would've thought that was erotic if I hadn't hit my head and I wasn't terrified out of my mind that she was hurt.

"I almost had you," she said in a defiant tone. She was covered with dust. Her leg was scraped and bleeding. As she blew her hair out of her eyes, she said, "I thought I could grab you before you lost your balance."

"You almost got yourself killed is what you did."

She grinned. "I'm not dead. And neither are you." She untangled herself and started looking me over. Checking my arms, looking in my eyes. I knew exactly what she was doing. She was assessing me for injury.

"I didn't hit my head."

"Yes, you did." She ran her hands over my scalp. It felt soothing, except I felt stabbing pains. It took me a minute to realize that they were coming from my leg.

"You have a bump on your head. But more urgently, your foot's messed up."

My anger and shock at her careless bravado had caused me not to notice that I was in pain. Quite a lot of it actually.

A cautious peek showed me that my foot was rotated inward at an odd angle. A giant bruise was forming over the front of my lower calf. I let out a curse. My leg felt like someone had driven a stake straight through it.

"It's not broken," I said, more to reassure myself.

Sam got up and dusted herself off. "Remind me to cross you off my preferred ortho providers list."

"It's not broken," I repeated foolishly as I stared up the steep incline above us. "We have to climb back up."

"I don't think you're going to be climbing anywhere."

I felt her poking around my lower leg. The bruise was blooming a deep purple, and the swelling was now the size of an orange. "Ow!" I said as she pressed on it.

"I'm not an orthopod like you, but I think it's your fibula."

An awful, sinking feeling went through me. If my leg *was* broken, then we were both effed. I'd have to have help getting up that rocky, steep incline. That meant EMS, harnesses. And a rescue team somehow being able to get near enough without plunging to their own deaths—as well as hauling us up safely. A million scary scenarios went through my mind, including plunging down the rest of the cliffside.

"Are you two okay?"

Gabe's voice. I looked up. At the top of the cliff, a good thirty feet above us, tiny heads came into view. I'm not exaggerating—in my panic, they looked absolutely microscopic.

"Oh my God, Cay," Lilly called out, panic in her voice, "are you okay?"

I tried to speak, but a sudden burst of pain made me grimace.

"We're fine," Sam called, sounding quite calm. "Everything's okay."

"Someone call 911," Lilly cried. "Hurry!"

Sam stared at me, all seriousness, her pretty brown eyes wide. "No bars out here."

I managed a half smile, half grimace. "Guess we're going to have to stick around and appreciate nature for a while."

Standing there on the narrow plateau, she looked like a person in a car commercial, standing by a fancy SUV on a mountaintop with impossible drop-offs everywhere.

"Sit back down," I managed to grunt. "You'll plunge to your death."

"I'm grabbing you some water." Pulling a bottle out of a sling she wore around her chest, she knelt beside me, twisted open the bottle, and lifted it to my lips.

"I can hold it," I said. But my voice sounded muffled. The pain was making everything hazy.

After I took a drink, she cupped her hands around her mouth and shouted up to our friends. "Looks like a fibula fracture. And he's a little stunned. We'll need a rope harness to get him out of here. And can someone please throw down some water?"

"Tell them I want a beer," I called out.

Sam ignored me. Brax poked his head over the side of the cliff. "Sit tight. We're going back to get a rope and some help. He's okay?"

"Tell him to make it a six-pack."

Sam stared at me, a small smile on her lips. "He's just as ornery as ever. Thanks, Brax."

He tossed her a water bottle, which she caught and then walked over to me.

"I was doing that for your benefit," I said.

"Doing what? Starting a bar tab?"

"No. Joking around. I don't want you to worry about me."

"That's sweet, but the fact that you have to explain to me that you're joking makes me worry." She tugged on my arm. "Scooch over into the shade and lean against the cliff."

I nodded, and didn't even try to stand, because frankly, even sitting, the pain was too great. I scooted back on my butt, each scoot sending a burst of pain through my leg, until I was in the shade cast by a tiny frail Charlie Brown Christmas tree. But I was grateful for it.

"I'm so pissed," I said through gritted teeth. "I can't believe this."

She was busy digging around in her pocket. She produced a little white plastic tube, which she opened into her palm. Then she handed me two pills.

I shook my head. "I don't want any Advil before they set my bone."

"I'm not lucky enough to have Advil for my cramps today. It's just travel Tylenol Mia handed me before I left. So take a couple."

I tossed down the pills and some water, then leaned my head back, closing my eyes against the pain. "Thank you."

"I'm sorry it hurts," she said. Her face was drawn, her eyes full of concern. I wanted to make her laugh, distract her from the worry, but I was out of jokes. The situation sucked, but I trusted my friends. Hopefully, they'd get us out of here alive.

I opened one eye and managed a sorry bit of a smile. "Like a *mother*."

She laughed and scooted up next to me to share the shade. I handed her the water, and she took a sip. Then she reached into her pocket and took a couple of Tylenol too.

"Is this where we tell each other all our secrets before we die?" I squinted up at the top of the cliff. How were they going to manage to lift me up there?

"We're not going to die. Just sit back and close your eyes, and I'll tell you a story."

I felt her prodding my leg. I knew what she was doing. Checking my circulation.

"Can you..." she began.

"...feel my toes. Yes," I confirmed. I leaned forward to examine the swollen purple bruise on my lower leg. "It's probably a simple fracture. But that will still get me two months in a boot."

"You saved that dumb kid's life," she said.

I shrugged. "I didn't think. I just acted."

"You acted fast."

A glance over at her showed she was twisting the bottom of her shirt with her hand, clearly a sign of nerves. "You did too. Some might question your sanity with a move like that."

She thought about that. "I didn't think I could stop you. But I figured I could slow you down a little."

"Well then. Thanks are in order." I tried to smile through the biting pain but failed.

"Don't mention it." There was a softness in her eyes that made me calmer. "How long have you been afraid of heights?"

"I'm not afraid of heights." She frowned deeply and gave me a knowing look. "Okay, fine. How did you know?"

She shrugged. "You keep clinging to the wall. And avoiding looking down."

"Ever since I was a kid and we went to Niagara Falls. I stood close to the falls on the Canadian side and watched a toddler try to sneak under the railing. His mom grabbed him, but that stuck with me." A short distance away, glinting in the sun, was a phone. Tater's phone. I pointed to it. "You'd better pocket that. I'm having an uncontrollable impulse to kick it right over the edge."

"Ha." Sam crawled over to near the edge of our plateau and grabbed it.

As she sat back against the rock again, I asked, "Why didn't you tell me the truth about the matchmaking test?"

She looked a little startled. "You're thinking about that stupid matchmaking test *now*?"

"Would you rather me think of death?"

"I'd tell you, but I'm still not a hundred percent sure you're totally all there." She tapped the side of her head and lifted a knowing brow.

"I'll prove to you I'm not delirious," I said. "Here's a fact: you sing while you're cooking."

Her eyes widened. "You can hear me singing across the hall?"

"Either 'Bad Blood' or Italian operas, I couldn't say which."

That made her snort. Good. But I still wanted to get some things straight with her while we were alone.

"Fine," she said. "I didn't tell you because you have to figure out your own truth with Lilly." She crossed her arms. "Besides, it's just a dumb test that doesn't mean anything."

"It meant something to me." I stopped and looked straight into her eyes. "Because the test was right. Lilly and I aren't compatible."

Sam shook her head vigorously. "The pain and the fear of death *are* making you delirious."

"Lilly was my twenty-two-year-old fantasy that I was forced to give up. In my mind, she grew into something that she just... wasn't."

"Besides the fact that she needs to calm down in restaurants, what's wrong with her? And today she certainly seems to be paying you plenty of attention."

I turned to her urgently. "Do you ever stop joking?"

"Not in life-and-death situations," she said. "Especially with men who are hopeless romantics. I don't want to hear any more."

"You are so... exasperating." I grabbed her elbow. "I'm trying to tell you something important."

"You're in shock and in pain and have a head injury." She shooed me away with her hand. "Save your breath."

I put a hand on her arm. "Lilly doesn't have wonder and awe."

She spun her head toward me. "What the hell is wonder and awe?"

"Just looking around and being amazed at every single thing. Like trees out the window or a thrift shop dress or a square dance. You're curious about everything and excited about new experiences. It's addicting."

"Maybe I'm just a new experience for you."

"Yes, you are, because I've never met anyone like you. Someone who can infuriate me yet who calls me out on the things no one else sees. Now I see that your absolute refusal to take risks with relationships is related to something I didn't see before —fear."

"I'm not afraid of anything," she said, pulling her arm away. "Stop analyzing me."

Just then, Brax called from above, "We have the harness. I'm lowering it down."

"Coming," Sam called back as she braced herself to get up.

I grabbed her hand, which made her look at me. She looked troubled. "Take a chance with me."

Ignoring that, Sam got up and caught a rope harness made of knots that looked as flimsy as a macramé plant hanger. "Your ride's here."

She knelt down next to me and demonstrated the tiny saddle made of knots.

"I don't want to move." For a moment, I closed my eyes and tilted my head back against the rock. Fear was seeping in, but I fought it back. And I wasn't done with this discussion. I needed her to know how I felt.

"I get it," she said. "We've got to immobilize your leg somehow."

She started looking around for something—sticks, I guess. I could see her reasoning it out.

"Would you do something for me first?" I asked.

She turned and looked down at me. "What?"

I lifted my hand.

She stared at it. "What?"

"Take it." She frowned. "Come on," I said, insistent. "It's important."

She did and I used my strength to tug her down next to me. Before she could protest, I said, "I want one favor. Since you said so yourself—this is life and death."

"Caleb, it's not life and death. You're going to be fine. We just have to—"

"Kiss me."

"No. No way." She tugged back, but I kept holding her hand. "Just one time."

"You're not just a hopeless romantic, you're also a drama queen. You need to get to the hospital. We've got to get you hauled out of here. Our friends are waiting."

"I want us to be honest and talk about what's really going on here. And it's not about Lilly."

"Two days ago it was," she shot back.

"Take a chance. One kiss." I met her panicked gaze. I truly believed that she thought I was delirious. "I would never hurt you, Samantha."

"Everyone says that."

"But *I* mean it."

She huffed. "If I do it, will you let me help you into this thing?"

I answered by giving one last tug that placed her body right up against mine. I felt the sudden shock of her softness, her heat. She let out a tiny gasp of surprise as our bodies collided and our lips met. For a suspended moment, we stood there, pressed up against each other, unmoving. I began to kiss her, slowly, carefully, gently exploring her lips. At last she began to kiss me back, at first small, light-as-a-feather kisses. Then she wrapped her arms tightly around my neck, pulling me closer, kissing me deeper, moving her lips against mine. I savored every second—her soft lips, the quiet exclamations, the feel of her in my arms. Everything felt so right.

I was lightheaded—from her nearness and the pain—and my leg was throbbing. But I'd never felt so certain that this was different. This meant something. I hoped she felt it too.

I finally broke away and pulled back. My head and my leg—and other parts of me—were throbbing, but those kisses... had been one small, perfect thing in an otherwise heinous day. "That's much better," I said, smiling. "I didn't want to die without doing that." I forced myself to scoot away, dragging myself into view of the top of the cliff and waving to our friends.

I turned to take one last look at Sam. She was a little out of breath, her hair tousled, her eyes dazed, her lips a little kiss-swollen. In that moment, she was so breathtakingly beautiful and clearly as impacted by those kisses as I was that I could easily have said the hell with being rescued and stayed. But it was time to go. I could only hope that she knew that was just a small sample of how I really felt about her. I gave her a big smile, then gave a thumbs-up to the people above. "Okay, folks," I called up, "here I come."

Chapter Sixteen

Samantha

I got up and walked over to the dangling harness, struggling to untangle it and all my emotions as Caleb dragged himself over, bracing himself against the side of the cliff for support.

The makeshift harness was made of rope and knots, and I fretted as I tried to figure out how to get him to climb into it. I was afraid that he would refuse and say something ridiculous, like he was climbing up himself or something I couldn't even predict. Anyway, I braced myself for an argument.

Figures that the first great kiss I'd gotten in I-don't-remember-how-long was from someone dehydrated, concussed, and in shock. Oh, and let's not forget to add "out of his mind." No one should go around kissing people in that state, because someone could actually believe it was real.

"Let me see that." By this time, he was standing on one leg, leaning against the cliff. He reached over me and took the harness from my hands. I could feel the shade from his big body, the heat, smell the scent of his soap and the smell of warm sun on skin. I made sure not to look him in the eye because honestly, I was feeling so many things.

How could this be happening? Maybe I was the one with a concussion. My heart was pounding, I felt flushed (but to be fair, it was sunny and very hot), and I felt an impossible rush of awareness. He'd said he wasn't into Lilly. But could I believe that?

I needed to get both of us out of here ASAP and get this entire weekend to end. Then, with a little luck, I'd go back to work and start hating him again and things would go back to normal. Easy peasy.

Caleb figured out the ins and outs of the harness and held it in a ready-to-go position. Then he nudged his head at it. "Get in."

"Excuse me?" Was there *nothing* he wouldn't fight me on?

"You heard me." He sounded a little out of breath from the pain. "Get in."

"Um, no." I grabbed hold of the harness. "You're going up first."

"I'm not." He cupped his hands over his mouth. "Sam's coming up. You guys ready?"

Maybe he wanted me to go first to be the guinea pig, but I didn't think so. This appeared to totally be a Caleb-being-protective move.

He said, "Thank you for trying to save me. But I want you to go up first. If something happens, I'll be here to break your fall. And that might not make sense, but you can't change my mind, so just do as I'm asking. Please. Okay?"

He wanted to make sure I was safe. Not only that, but this was also *important* to him. I could see it in his eyes. This astounded me, someone hurt who put himself second. And me first. Had that ever happened in my life? It nearly brought me to tears, but I didn't have time for tears now. I had to help us both out of here.

His expression was unyielding and formidable. I seemed to be learning when there was no point arguing. "If you insist," I said,

171

then shoved a leg through the leg opening, then a second. I ended up with a bunch of ropes supporting my legs and my ass.

"One more thing." He was holding on to the rope above my head and on my leg. His face was very close, a little flushed from the heat, a little sweaty. But his eyes were urgent, demanding me to listen. "One more kiss—a goodbye one."

"You *are* delirious." I was afraid, because getting him up was going to be challenging—not to mention painful. I was pumped full of adrenaline, shaky and lightheaded, and I wasn't sure how much of it was from this harrowing experience or from being so close to him and from everything he'd just said.

"Maybe. But you'll regret it if you don't. I mean, anything could happen." He gave me a crooked, winning smile that I know took effort.

"Don't make light of this." I felt elated and close to tears. Dizzy, hot and clammy, all at once.

"You ready, Samantha?" Brax again. "I can't see you. You're going to have to move over a few feet."

"One—one second," I said.

Caleb was standing there, holding on to the side of the cliff for support, vulnerable, expectant.

I started to cry.

"Women don't usually cry when I ask to kiss them."

"This isn't a joke to me."

He pushed himself off from the cliff and grabbed me for support. Yet he steadied me with his hands on my arms. "It's going to be okay."

Somehow I sensed he wasn't talking about his health or my health or getting us both back to safety. I was almost sure he was talking about *us*.

He leaned in and kissed me on the forehead.

I reached over and held his face in my hands. His precious face. I was teary, my emotions overcoming me. I kissed him on the lips quickly, intending to pull back, but he wrapped his arms around me and kissed me again, softly, pulling me closer, then kissing me deeply.

If I was dizzy before, I was positively vertiginous now.

The kiss was sweet and earnest and confident, expert and deep and promising. And it was over way too soon. Caleb drew back, and then he spoke. Which was more than I was capable of.

"There you are." He tugged on the main rope. "All trussed up like a Thanksgiving turkey."

I gave him a look.

"A cute turkey." He winked. Which made me incredulous because how could he crack jokes now?

"I really wish you'd—"

"Bye," he said with a satisfied lift of his brow. Then backed up into view of our friends and gave the thumbs-up sign to everyone above. Suddenly, with a jerk of the rope, I was on my way.

Being pulled up was awkward even though I could brace myself with my legs and arms to keep from crashing into the jagged rocks. Not to mention the harness dug into my skin. But Brax and Gabe and two EMS guys from the local fire department got me to the point where I could crawl up the rest of the way on all fours.

Everyone was yelling and cheering. The other guys were on the distal part of the rope—Jason, and Tyler—steadying it with their weight. Mia stood with three more paramedics, whose white SUV was parked nearby. Lilly was off to the side with Marin, wringing her hands and gingerly looking over the drop-off. Fortunately, Tater was nowhere to be found. Good thing, because I was feeling uncomfortably feral impulses toward him and his mom.

Gabe gave me a hand up.

"Caleb's so damn stubborn," I said. "I don't know how he's going to get himself into that harness without help. He insisted—"

Gabe reached over and gave me a big, calming hug. "He's going to be fine." He pulled back and looked me over. "Pretty ballsy of you to try jumping overboard to save him. You okay?"

"I'm good."

"You're worried about him."

"Yes." I couldn't make light. I couldn't lie.

I wandered over to the edge. Somehow Caleb had gotten the harness around his middle and was suspended, his good leg out to protect the rest of him from the jagged cliff face. "Hope you guys ate your protein for breakfast," he said as the guys hauled him up.

As soon as he rounded the crest, relief flooded me. I moved toward him, ready to—I don't know—do something, anything, to help him into the waiting ambulance.

But Lilly ran straight in front of me. "Oh, Caleb, Caleb, I'm so glad you're okay." She ran to his side, crying, instantly grabbing his hands. "I'm going in the ambulance with him, okay, guys?"

I backed up, stunned at today's sudden zeal, her studied indifference all but vanished.

All my emotions toppled around inside me like clothes in a dryer. I was torn between worry and the intense emotional hit from being kissed—and kissed well. I was afraid and agitated and *jealous*, all at once.

Caleb had decided to navigate away from Lilly when she was indifferent. But what would he do now?

Marin ran up to the back of the EMS vehicle, Tater in tow. "Dr. D'Angelo," she said, "I am so sorry for this. And I can't thank you enough for what you did for my son." She turned to me. "You too, Dr. Bashar. I'm so sorry."

She pushed Tater forward. His face was beet red from embarrassment. "Yeah. What my mom said. I'm sorry."

I couldn't see Caleb's face, but I saw him reach out a hand, which yet again made me understand what kind of man he was. "Hey, buddy," he said. "It's okay. Just be safe."

Caleb grasped Tater's hand and shook it and then slid his hand back in some complicated hand thing in that way guys do. To Tater's credit, he backed away and hugged his mom tight.

"We'll be happy to cover whatever your insurance won't,"

Marin added as the EMS team closed the doors. "And Tater will be cutting *a lot* of grass this summer."

As Caleb was whisked off to the hospital, Lilly glued his side, I turned to find my backpack. It appeared that I'd abandoned it somewhere, along with my common sense.

~

Caleb

"There, is that better?" Lilly asked as she pulled and pushed pillows behind my head, jerking my neck accidentally in the process. Which in turn maligned the rest of me and sent a shock wave of pain radiating from my throbbing leg.

We were in the ER, and I didn't even know how she'd managed to confiscate three pillows from somewhere. It was embarrassing. "Thanks," I said, "but I really only need one."

"But three is so much better for your spine." She rearranged them all again. "Trust me on this."

Had she always been this bossy? Or was that yet another thing I'd never noticed before? I think I had loved her once, a long time ago, when I was young. But I didn't anymore. Not in a lasting, give-and-take way.

Also, I needed my phone, which was taken from me before my head CT scan. I'd quietly asked Brax to text Sam and find out how she was doing. He assured me that she was fine and also that they'd sent her all the updates about my sorry ass, in his words.

I was waiting for the okay to be discharged, and I couldn't bust out of here quick enough. Meanwhile, Lilly patted my shoulder and stood so close our shoulders practically touched. "You saved that boy's life. You're a hero."

To say that Dr. Blumenthal, the ortho doc that I had literally just interviewed with a few weeks ago, was a bit surprised on seeing me, not as a doctor but as a patient, was an understatement. Apparently, he helped to cover the ER in several small communities as well as in Oak Bluff. First of all, he'd laughed. Then he'd said, "Well, hello, Caleb. Glad to see you're experiencing how our group operates firsthand, eh?"

Then he set my bone and put me in a short-leg cast and crutches, a routine I knew all too well. The pain was still dull and aching, but I felt grateful that things were taken care of. Despite the weeks of crutches and inconvenience, I would be good as new.

Except he probably thought I was an idiot.

I had a little concussion, was a little dehydrated, my leg a little bit broken, my pride a little bruised, but my head CT was okay, and they were booting me out.

At this point, I was also a lot starving.

I was also worried. My right leg was the broken one, and therefore I couldn't drive. Which led to another question—how was I going to get to work next week? And all the weeks until my cast came off?

I had other worries too. Lilly was being awfully attentive. At one point, she'd even hand-combed my hair. And frankly, all of it was terrifying.

After my cast was done, the cast room tech had wheeled me back into my curtained partition in the ER. Brax and Gabe were each on their phones with suffering expressions on their faces, while Lilly leafed through magazines, sipping something from her giant sparkly pink tumbler. I felt guilty that they were all stuck here on a beautiful spring day.

Brax looked up as I was wheeled into my spot. "Hey, there you are. Whoa, neon green?" he exclaimed, checking out my cast.

"It's very fashionable," Lilly said.

"I love it," Gabe said. "White is boring."

I shrugged. "Since this is an extended body part for six weeks, hopefully green will hide some dirt. I figured the kids at the hospital would like it."

Lilly checked her watch. "Glad you're done. We'll be back to the farm in time for the cookout and a bonfire."

I suppressed a moan and forced a smile. I wanted to do a cookout and bonfire about as much as I wanted to get my bone set again. I'd had pretty much enough of farm weekend. All I wanted to do was go home, turn on a game, and put my foot up, which felt like a throbbing hunk of cast iron.

Lilly walked over and rested a hand on my shoulder. "I brought you something full of protein to hold you over until then."

Oh hurray, food. She handed me a cardboard take-out container. I was appreciative for the thoughtfulness.

A peek inside revealed... lettuce. Lots of it. I mean, I like salad, but my appetite by this point was tomahawk-steak sized. Another glance revealed seeds, cranberries, couscous, and tofu—at least that's what I thought that was—and kale. I loved healthy food but right now, my appetite was army tank sized. "Thanks," I said in the most enthusiastic voice I could muster. Which, after all I'd been through, was probably not very much.

"I know you like meat, but it's really not healthy for you," she said. "Hope that's okay. Do you need a pillow for your foot?" She reached down to adjust the pillow propped between my cast and the wheelchair right-leg rest, which was elevated.

As she adjusted the pillow, searing pain ripped through me —again.

At least it temporarily took away my appetite. I bit back any show of agony. "No, it's fine," I managed as my pain finally subsided. I caught Brax's eye. It was full of doom-concern, the kind of look your bro gives you when they know things have gone south fast.

An ER nurse popped her head in our room. "Your paper-work's almost ready. Someone can go get the car, and we'll wheel you out to the parking circle in front of the ER. Sound good?"

Lilly left to go to the bathroom or something, and I was left with my friends, neither of whom were speaking. Brax bit down on his cheeks to keep from smiling.

"Eat your seeds," he said.

"I blame you both for the über-healthy food choice," I said.

"Lilly offered to grab you something," Gabe said. "We didn't have control of what."

"It's okay," I said. "It's the thought that counts. Thanks for being here. Thanks for everything. I mean it."

"We can order a pizza and grab it on the way back," Brax offered.

"I don't want to make Lilly feel bad. And we should get back —tonight's the last night. I feel like I ruined the weekend for Ani."

"I don't think Ani's had that great a day either," Brax said, "but it has nothing to do with you. She's still angry with Tyler—I guess he told Marin straight-out that her son almost got you and Sam killed."

"He's not wrong," I said. But knowing Tyler, that probably didn't come out in a civilized way. "Tater's not a bad kid. He just needs all that boy energy directed somewhere else besides trouble."

"That's very generous," Gabe said.

I shrugged. "How's Sam doing?" I asked. I looked around. "Does anyone have my phone?"

"Lilly took it," Brax said. "She said you were getting a lot of texts from Sam."

Was that why she wasn't giving it back? If that was the case, this situation was more complicated than I thought. "Sam's okay?"

"She's more worried about you," Brax said. "We've been updating her."

"Lilly's also aware of you two square-dancing the night away the other night, just FYI," Gabe said. "She's mentioned it several times."

Aha. I wondered if that had been what started Lilly down this path of suddenly being interested in me again. "I care about Sam," I said.

"Sam?" Brax cleared his throat. "Sam, as in *not Lilly*?"

"Yes. Sam," I said firmly.

Gabe heaved a sigh. "I speak for Brax when I say we're both thrilled." Across the room, Brax gave a thumbs-up as he scrolled his phone. "But be careful," Gabe warned. "Lilly seems to be really shaken up by your near-death experience. I can see this train crashing from miles away. I don't even need the red lights or the guard rails at a crossing." He made flashing-light motions with his hands.

"Okay, I'm back," Lilly said, bursting through the door. A plastic bag with more magazines hung from her wrist. In her hands, she held a drink carrier holding four coffee drinks. "I couldn't resist a skinny chai. And as a special treat, I got you all one too. With soy milk."

Forget the throbbing pain. I was literally going to starve to death. As I viewed Lilly, I seemed to see her for the first time. Cute, bubbly, agreeable. But not perfect. Not someone who understood who I was on the inside but who saw me as someone who needed dance lessons, nicer clothes, and a taste for vegan food.

Lilly handed me a coffee, dumped the plastic bag in my lap, and then added her massive purse and chunky sweater. "You don't mind carrying a few things, do you?"

I held out my hand. "Only if you give me my phone back."

"Oh, I must've forgotten," Lilly said, rummaging through her purse. "Here you go."

Funny, but the woman who gave me grief on every front, who openly said she wasn't looking for a relationship and wouldn't ask for help if her life depended on it was all I could think of.

"Cay, I was just so frightened," Lilly said as the nurse wheeled me to the entrance where the guys would pull up in Gabe's car. "I'm so relieved you're okay. I-I've been thinking about what you said. How this weekend was good for us. How we needed a chance to reconnect."

The ER nurse was getting an earful, which didn't seem to

concern Lilly. "I'm glad too," I said. "It's good to call you *a friend*." I put as much emphasis as possible on *friend*.

"A friend?" she asked, teary-eyed.

I wasn't sure what she was getting at. Was she glad of that or... was she wanting more?

I did not want more.

This I knew. The realization came as a relief, not a disappointment.

I found my answer. "We spent a lot of years together. I'm glad we can finally put everything behind us and be friends." I'd said the *f* word twice. I could only be clearer if I was cruel, and I didn't think that was necessary. At least, I hoped more elaboration wouldn't be.

"I mean, when I saw you fall down that hill, I-I just—"

She got even more teary. That was another thing I'd just recalled: her emotions. So many of them. Up and down all the time.

The nurse had backed up and was now examining items in the gift shop windows behind us, undoubtedly still hearing every word.

I didn't have an urge to comfort Lilly physically. Which also surprised me. "I'm glad you didn't want me to die," I said, joking. "That's a good sign. I mean, there was a time when you probably came pretty close to feeling that way."

She laughed. "You're too funny."

That broke the more solemn mood and stopped the discussion about our past. The past was done and over. And I couldn't wait to move on.

"Okay, kids," the ER nurse said. "Time to go. I'll wheel you right up to the car."

I thanked her and managed to fold myself into the passenger seat, managing a nod of thanks to Gabe. As soon as I buckled in, I sent Sam a photo of my cast, told her all was well, and begged her to let me know how she was doing. She responded with three thumbs up emojis and wrote that she'd see me later.

Fortunately, Lilly didn't say anything else beyond the norm in front of the guys. I was ecstatic when we finally pulled into the gravel lot near the farmhouse. "Home at last," I said. I grabbed my discharge instructions—and the bag with the salad—from the floor. "Thanks, everyone, for everything."

"I'll help you to your cabin," Lilly said when I managed to get myself out of the car.

"We got him," Gabe said, intercepting Lilly physically by standing between us and taking my stuff from her. "You can get ready for tonight if you want."

"Are you coming to the cookout?" she asked me.

"I'll do my best." What I really wanted was to go home, but that would mean Sam would have to leave early too, and I figured I'd already put enough of a wrench into Ani's weekend. I could rally one last night for her sake.

I awkwardly placed my crutches on the uneven ground and headed down the path to the cabin, Brax and Gabe at my sides. How many times had I instructed patients to avoid mashing them into your armpits? Now I got how hard that was.

Somehow I felt like I'd shut a door. One that had been closed for me long ago. But now this time I was the one doing the closing. And it felt like a relief. I just hoped that Lilly got the memo.

Chapter Seventeen

Samantha

As soon as I knocked on the guys' cabin door at around four that afternoon, a flutter of nerves made me second-guess my errand. *It's all right,* I told myself. I'd find out how Caleb was doing. Simply a friendly gesture from someone who'd shared his scary ordeal and cared about him. I left just as everyone was getting ready for the evening. I'd be back shortly and never miss a beat.

I didn't know how he'd feel about company. Maybe he was irritable and exhausted. Maybe Lilly had won him back with her sudden attentiveness and care.

That was the real issue here. How had he received her emotional outpouring, her insistence to be with him?

I scratched my leg. And then my arm. The bugs were terrible out here.

Who was I kidding? This was more than care. I was worried sick about him. What if his head injury was worse than they'd thought? What if the break was much worse than it had seemed?

What if he'd injured his internal organs when he rolled down that hill or—

"Come in," a groggy voice called, interrupting my catastrophizing.

It sounded like I'd probably just woken him up, and that made me second-guess myself even more. I pushed open the door to find the main room full of slanted rays of sunlight in the late-afternoon light. In the bedroom, Caleb was lying on a bottom bunk with his leg stretched out, toes sticking up from the bright green cast. With all his height, he seemed pretty squished into that bed. His head was a little sideways so that his cast could fit. Otherwise, his leg would be hanging off the bed.

"Hi," I said. I thought about trying for a joke with dumb lines like "That cast is so bright I need my sunglasses," or "It took a broken bone to finally keep you from springing to the door," but I was too nervous to say anything.

"Hi," he said back, looking a little surprised. He instantly started smoothing down his hair, which cracked me up a little inside. His voice kind came out kind of wobbly—the way it does when someone *feels* something. Could he have been nervous like I was?

I didn't know. I'd always been someone who made sure she didn't ever feel too much. This was novel territory.

Everything seemed different between us. There was nothing to argue about. The air, void of our usual back-and-forth, was quiet —too quiet. It was charged with something else entirely.

I was so relieved to see him. And then—how embarrassing—I got a little teary. I had to swipe at my eyes because—well, because tearing up was just plain weird.

"Are you okay?" he asked. Oh no. He was asking *me*.

"Yes! I mean, there's nothing to get emotional about. You broke a bone, and it wasn't even bleeding or sticking up out of your skin. It wasn't even your femur, which would have been a *much* bigger deal, and your head injury wasn't even enough to keep you in the hospital overnight." Could I have babbled on any worse?

He was going to be just fine. Yet I sank down on the bed, trying to control my shaking.

His gaze resting on mine in that intense way of his threw me. Wiped my mind of all thoughts, humorous or otherwise. And so I just sat there, brown paper bags in hand.

He inhaled deeply. "I smell meat. You *do* care about me."

"Of course I do, you lug head. I mean, jeesh. You could have plunged to your death!"

"But I didn't. Because of your quick thinking. You slowed me down enough that I didn't go straight over the edge."

A sob escaped me. I clamped my hand over my mouth, but it was no use. This time I couldn't hide the emotion. I was overcome with tears.

"Sam, come here." His voice was calm yet commanding in the nicest way. He scooched over in the creaky bed and tugged on my arm, which brought me down lying sideways with my back next to him on the narrow bed, his arm around me.

Oh, it was heaven.

"You're shaking," he said.

"I think I just realized what could've happened."

He cleared his throat. I felt the warmth of his body through to my skin. And his gentle strength. "But it didn't. Thanks to you, I live to torment you another day."

That wonderful, joking way of his. I never wanted to move.

I laughed, which meant I was laugh-crying, which was terrible. And now my back was itching. And my legs. Like, furiously itching.

Finally he pointed toward the items I'd abandoned on the other bunk. "Is that food?"

"Oh. Yes. Here." I shook out of whatever trance I'd been in, bolted upright, and grabbed the bags. "Mia said you didn't eat much lunch." Actually, she'd told me the salad story. That's how I got the double cheeseburger idea. Because if I'd been through all that he had, which in a way I had, minus the broken bone of course, that's what I would've wanted. Plus fries. And a shake, which I pulled out and placed it at his bedside, then fished out a straw. "You'd be proud. I didn't even have to kill anything to get Pierre the chef on board."

He laughed, shoving a handful of fries into his mouth. "How'd you do that?"

"I asked Pierre to fire up the burgers. And I might've said that it was a matter of life and death." I snuck a fry. I'd had no appetite all day from all the worry, but now suddenly I was starving. "And of course you're a big hero around here, so he did it ASAP."

He peeked into the other bag. "There are two giant burgers in here."

"One of those might be mine." I turned red. "You don't mind if we eat together, do you? I mean, if you're in too much pain..."

"Please stay. I need a distraction," he said with a full mouth. "Also, I'm starving."

"Near death will do that to you."

He held out the fries to me while he took a bite of the giant cheeseburger.

He grinned. Then I grinned. And then I opened the container of ketchup Pierre had tucked in the bag. We reached at the same time for the same exact fry.

Awkward. But also funny. I withdrew my hand.

"You let me have this fry?" He sounded incredulous as he held it up between us. "Just like that?"

I shrugged and snagged another one. "Well, you *are* the one who had to go to the hospital," I said.

"You must *really* like me."

"I don't hate you." But not hating him, I was learning fast, was very dangerous.

Hate is a powerful emotion. It keeps people away. So does disdain and disinterest. I was great at those. I was a literal star at driving men away. Now it felt as if some kind of barrier had come down between us. I felt raw and naked. This had been so much easier when we argued all the time.

"Kind of you." He reached for the shake. "Is this chocolate?"

"Yes."

"Then I *love* you."

I laughed, the tension finally broken. "From like to love in seconds. Your favorite?"

He held it out to me. I took some from his straw.

Suddenly my autonomic nervous system went off the rails again. My hands were shaking, and I felt warm—too warm—all over. I could feel my heartbeat thumping in my ears. Why did drinking from the same straw feel kind of... intimate?

"Oh, I almost forgot." I pulled a permanent black marker out of my back jeans shorts pocket. "You can have everybody sign your cast before we leave."

He pointed to it. "You be the first."

"Oh. Sure." Somehow I wasn't expecting that. As I turned and leaned over his leg, some impulse grabbed me to make my signature memorable. Before I could think about what I was doing. I wrote Sam in cursive, right at the base of his cast near his toes, my signature ending in a giant curlicue with a heart inside. Then I colored in the heart.

As I sat back, remorse promptly kicked in. The heart was a big, feminine touch in a place where he—and everyone else, for that matter—would be sure to see it. What had I been thinking?

As I sat back, he assessed my handiwork and wiggled his toes, clearly unbothered by those kinds of thoughts. "Nice," he said.

We ate for a few minutes in companionable silence. "I better stop eating your fries," I pushed the remainder toward him.

"I like it when you eat my fries," he said. "What I mean is, I like sharing my food with you."

I changed the subject. "Are you in a lot of pain?"

"At least now I don't have hunger pain on top of the other

pain." He'd devoured the burger in no time. Balling up a napkin and tossing it into the bag, he said, "Thanks for the food. Can I say something about today?"

"Depends on which part of today." Hopefully not the Lilly part.

"Thanks for what you did—it was good to have company on that ledge. You were calm and levelheaded. But then that's how you are in the OR too."

"Well, I guess I wouldn't be an anesthesiologist if I wasn't." I flicked my gaze up at him. "And you're welcome."

More awkward silence.

I didn't want to, but I guess I needed to ask about Lilly. I wanted to know what had happened, why she'd suddenly seemed so into him now.

I rubbed my forehead. Jealousy of Lilly, the shakes when I tried to eat or drink, not eating at all while he was gone because I was upset—all this was adding up to something that I didn't want to admit to myself.

I hated how I felt around him—giddy and excited and fluttery. I hated that I loved how his face had lit up when I'd walked in, and that *I* was the one—not Lilly—who'd figured out what he wanted.

Anesthesiologists had kahunas. Why did I keep forgetting mine?

He was right that I never took risks with my personal life.

I decided to grow some. And take a risk now. "I'm not sorry we kissed," I said firmly. "But—are you? I mean, were you delirious and didn't mean it? Because if you didn't, I need to know that right now, before this goes any furth—"

He grabbed my hand and held it. "I wasn't delirious." He smiled and rubbed his thumb inside my palm, something that made me even more giddy. "I told Lilly I was glad we were friends —twice. I hope she got the hint."

Oh joy. Relief flooded through me. I blew out a breath I didn't know I was holding.

He still chose me, even on solid, safe ground.

I felt safe and solid with him. I didn't doubt what he said. I *knew* he didn't love Lilly anymore. I knew he wanted a chance with me.

He kept hold of my hand, his solid and warm and a little rough. "I know all this with Lilly has been... a lot," he said. "But I want you to know that I was serious about everything that I said on that cliff. And while I loved the life-and-death kisses, I wondered if you might go out with me on a real everyday-life date when we get home?"

I thought that was really sweet. I respected that he wasn't just rushing to kiss me again. That he wanted to make it official.

"I'll have to check my calendar." I pulled out my phone and pretended to check. "I'm free Monday, Tuesday, Wednesday, Thursday, and Friday."

Caleb oddly didn't laugh at my antics. Suddenly he released my hand. I became aware that he was examining me—my entire face, specifically, with a puzzled expression.

"What is it?" I brought my hands up to my face, which felt flushed. At first I thought I was just revealing all my embarrassing feelings. But then I realized my face was not just warm but also a little bumpy.

"What's wrong with my face?" I asked in a panicked voice.

Caleb calmly placed his finger under my chin and tipped my face this way and that, the practiced move of a clinician. "Did the bugs get to you?"

I realized just then that I'd been scratching my sides without even realizing it. Come to think of it, my butt and legs were feeling kind of itchy too. I lifted my arms and examined them. There were bumps there too—tiny, all-over ones. "Darn mosquitoes." But a creeping dread was coming over me. I knew it was far worse than bug bites.

"I think it's more than mosquitoes, Sam," he said gently.

In a panic, I stood up and crossed the room to a spot on the wall where an old mirror hung.

My face was covered with the same tiny, angry red bumps. A scratch mark ran up my cheek, and that was filled with bumps too. On my sides, more of the same, some of which were filled with fluid and blistering.

Oh *no.*

Caleb frowned. "Lift up your shirt."

"Excuse me?"

He gestured from the bed with his hand. "Raise the end up a little. There you go."

I complied, only because by this time I knew something was really wrong.

He let out a long, low whistle. "Holy shit, Sam. You're covered in poison ivy."

Chapter Eighteen

Caleb

"What do the other people look like?" Mrs. Von Gulag asked from the doorstep around seven that evening as we made our way from the truck, Sam with a rashy face and one eye swollen half shut, me lumbering awkwardly along on the uneven gravel drive with my crutches. Step-crunch-step-crunch, a slow, painful process.

"The other people?" I asked, looking around. Mrs. VG was usually sober as a minister and firmly grounded in reality, but who knew?

"From the fight." She gave a laugh that was more of a raspy smokers rattle. "You two look worse than two rats that escaped a drowning." She examined us with an eagle eye, her gaze dropping to my cast, where Sam had written her name and colored in a big, obvious heart.

Why had I allowed that? A moment of weakness. Seemed that I had a giant weak spot for Sam.

"I had a little accident," I said quickly.

Mrs. VG's thick brows lifted. "And what happened to you, missy?" She looked Sam over. "Your face is all red and puffy."

"It's a blush," I said to distract her. "The girl is head over heels for me."

Mrs. VG guffawed at that. Sam, however, looked like she was ready to kill both of us. She was lumbering along, carrying both our duffel bags, something I ordinarily wouldn't have ted if I'd had the choice.

Mrs. VG crossed her arms and tapped her foot. I sensed what she was thinking before she said anything. "Don't you worry, Mrs. VG. You won't even know I have these things." I held up a crutch to demonstrate.

"I'll hold you to your word." She motioned to Sam. "Especially if you're over at *her* place. That one's right above my living room."

Sam halted so abruptly that I almost crashed into her, crutches and all. I shifted a crutch to my right hand and gently squeezed her shoulder, hoping she'd get the hint to just keep moving.

"Yes, ma'am," I said, "these crutches will be as silent as an electric vehicle. Don't you worry."

"Oh, I almost forgot. Here's your package." She held out a brown mailer bag to Sam.

"Package?" Sam shot me a puzzled look. "Must be yours. I didn't order anything."

Mrs. VG pointed to the name and address on the front. "Technically, I can only turn over the package to whom it's addressed, missy."

Sam glanced at the label. "Yep, that's me. Missy."

I managed to grab it and hold it along with my right crutch, and fortunately, Mrs. VG didn't protest.

Mrs. VG appeared to be pondering something. "If you move in together, I'll let you both out of your leases early."

"We're not dating," Sam said, quicker than her next breath. "But thanks."

I leaned a little closer to Sam and shot her a sweet smile. "That's not what the justice of the peace said, honey."

A one-eyed glare is a scary thing. Sam's response was to leave me there to figure out how to butt-crawl up the stairs. "Thanks for getting the package," I said to our landlady. "You have a good evening now."

Sam didn't say a thing until we were upstairs, across from each of our apartments in the middle of the hallway. "Why would she be so eager to let us out of our leases?" she asked, digging in her purse for her key.

"Because then she can raise the rent for a new tenant. Wanna move in together?" I moved my brows in a nefarious fashion that made her laugh.

"Watch that cast," a voice called up the stairs. "I don't want that heavy thing scratching up my floors. You hear that, Doctor?"

"Yes, Ma'am," I called.

Sam got her door open. "I don't know how you can be so pleasant," she said in a quiet voice.

I shrugged. "Oh come on, Missy. You managed it even though she's a lot nicer to me than to you."

I got the tiniest smile. Maybe. "With my teeth gritted and cursing under my breath. The fact that there's no cheaper rent anywhere keeps me here. What's your reason?"

"It's all about the charm for me. Charming old building, charming landlord." She rolled her eyes. "Okay, seriously, we're ten minutes from work. And I'm basically a cheapskate." The truth was that I was saving for a little house. Preferably in Oak Bluff.

"Charming place for a charming guy," she said with a shrug.

"I love it when you give me compliments," I said as I followed her through the door. I knew I was pushing her patience. But I needed to make sure that she was okay before I left.

She spun around quickly and pointed to my door. "Um, in case you forgot, you live over there. Across the hall."

"Don't you want company?"

She tossed up her hands. "I look like a giant red puffer fish. Every body part is itching. And I'm super cranky, in case you haven't noticed."

"Yeah, I know." I turned up my mouth in the slightest smile—any more and she might've tossed me out the door. "Let's open the package." I balanced on my good leg, moving my crutches to one hand.

She shot me an expression that told me she just wanted to be left by herself to maybe crawl into the bathroom trap door and die alone. But, of course, I wasn't going to allow that.

"Later, okay? I just want to—"

I shook the mailer bag so that the pills rattled.

Placing it on the kitchen counter, I unzipped the cardboard zipper. Three bottles of pills, a tube of steroid ointment, calamine lotion, and some packets of oatmeal bath tumbled out.

"You had my medicine delivered." Sam teared up. Well, in the eye that opened all the way anyway. She sorted through the contents. "Prednisone. Anti-itch pills—two kinds."

"One makes you sleepy, which might be great for tonight. But the other kind won't." I paused. "Oh, you already know that. I forgot you went to med school too."

She ignored that quip, still perusing the items. "Calamine. Oatmeal bath. You shouldn't have bought all that extra—"

I held out the bag. "There's one last thing."

Frowning, she dove back in. I watched her face, imagining her fingers closing in on the small rectangular object, rounded on top.

She pulled out a giant Snickers bar and then really started bawling. "How did you know I love Snickers?"

"Mia told me. She feels really bad for you, by the way." I pulled her in for a hug—one-armed, but hey, the best I could do. Not thinking, just acting on impulse. Sort of like what she did trying to save me from death. In doing so, one of my crutches crashed to the floor. Of course we got the broomstick for that. But that didn't stop me from holding her as tightly as I could with my one arm until I felt her slowly relax. I knew I should let go, but she was soft and warm, and her skin smelled nice, a subtle scent that I was coming to learn was uniquely hers, a mix of soap and something lemony. "This has been a really long day," I said in a low voice, barely daring to move.

"The longest," came her muffled reply.

She was way too used to handling everything alone, and I knew how she struggled to accept help. That made my heart hurt for her. And right then and there, I vowed to cure her of that.

She pulled back, starting to scratch her arms until she realized she shouldn't. "Thank you for my medicine. You're taking care of me, but who's going to take care of you?"

I held her at arm's length, staring into her good eye. "Sam. You threw yourself down a cliff for me. You brought me a lifesaving cheeseburger. And you just drove us home, which was a little scary seeing as you only have one usable eye. So I feel very taken care of. But it would make me feel great if you'd let me stay and help you get settled, okay?" Before she could protest, I steered her to the couch and sat her down. Then I brought her a glass of water so she could take her pills. Finally, I went and filled up her old claw-foot bathtub, tossing in a packet of the oatmeal stuff, and guided her into the bathroom.

Twenty minutes later, she walked out in a fluffy blue robe, carrying a bed pillow, a white towel wrapped around her head, and spied me on the couch with my foot propped up on her ottoman. "You're still here?"

"I was afraid you'd fall asleep in the bathtub or something." Not really. Truth was, I wanted to be here—I didn't want to leave her alone. And to be honest, I wanted to be with her.

She sat down beside me, tossing her pillow nearby. The intoxicating scent of soap and shampoo filled the air. Feelings churned deep within me, warm and exhilarating, desperate and overwhelming, feelings that I had no control over, dashing every which way like water in a drive-through car wash.

She grabbed the tube of steroid cream and touched my arm. "The oatmeal stuff helped. Thank you for everything. I'm going to slather this all over me and go to bed."

I blinked a few times quickly.

"Do you have something in your eye?"

"I'm blinking away all the inappropriate thoughts that the word *slather* ignited."

She stared at me.

"Look, I can't help it if I still think you're sexy even if I have a throbbing pain in my leg and your face is as puffy as a ski jacket."

She shook her head. "Men are weird." But I could tell from the expression in her eye that she sort of liked it.

I made a circling motion with my hand, indicating that she should turn around. "Let me do your back."

She hesitated. I knew what she was thinking. That this was a little awkward. I didn't care. "Say one little word. *O...kay.*" I said it slowly as I reached over and moved her jaw as if to sound out the word. "*O...kay.* Got it?"

"*Okay*," she said. I must've worn her down, because she surrendered the tube without a fight.

She took off her robe and lay belly-down on the couch. I lifted up her T-shirt and whistled.

"How bad is it?" Her voice was muffled from the pillow.

"Nasty bad," I said. Her back was loaded with raised, red, weepy bumps that were starting to blister. I snapped a photo and handed her the phone, then began rubbing ointment all over the inflamed rash.

It took a while. While I was focused on the task, I couldn't help noticing what a pretty back she had—elegant, beautiful lines. She sighed once, probably from exhaustion and from the fact that she was falling asleep.

I, however, was definitely not getting more relaxed. I was having the opposite problem, and I was having thoughts that had zero to do with poison ivy.

So I finished up quick and washed off my hands. By the time I came back, Sam was fast asleep, the towel off her head, her damp hair tucked over to the side. I grabbed a blanket from her bed and covered her up.

I took a few seconds to take in all her features without fear that she'd catch me. She had pretty arched brows, long lashes. Her full lips were parted in sleep, her breathing calm and even.

A flood of emotions washed over me—mainly, the strong desire to protect her. To stand guard over her, even though she'd proved time and again that she didn't need anyone to do that. These tender feelings—I didn't know where they came from. I didn't want them—they seemed reckless so soon after Lilly, but I couldn't stop them from coming. Before I could think, I bent to kiss her forehead and let myself out the door.

～

Samantha

When I woke up, it was dark, and I was hot and itchy all over. I had a room air conditioner, but it was in my bedroom, and I'd fallen asleep on the couch. I was parched, my throat so sandpapery that I could barely swallow. Through my grogginess, I heard rapping at my door.

"Sam? You okay in there? Open up!"

Caleb. Caleb in a panic. "Coming!" I managed. As I got up, my feet tangled inside a light blanket that I didn't remember putting on myself.

It all came back to me. The bag of medicines and the other, extra things Caleb had DoorDashed to my door. The way he'd drawn my bath and waited for me and rubbed medicine into my back. I didn't remember anything after that, but he must've covered me up too.

I dragged myself to the door and opened it to a worried-looking man in gym shorts, a gray T-shirt, and a bright green cast. His hair was mussed like he'd just gotten up from a nap too.

He looked relieved. And he was holding a pizza box. "You scared me."

"I was dead asleep."

"Well, it's nine o'clock. Time to eat."

He handed me the box and hobbled straight past me into my apartment with the confidence of someone used to moving around in the world with ease.

"Come on in," I said as if that made any difference, running a hand through my hair and realizing that it was sticking up all over the place. I didn't ever worry about how I looked to men, but right now I found myself in a mild panic. The swollen eye, the ugly red rash, the hair every which way—I was scarier than a creature on Halloween. "Make yourself at home."

"Thanks." He said it like I hadn't been sarcastic, as he plowed through the medicines, coasters, books, and other things on my coffee table, clearing room for the pizza.

The smell got to me. Cheese and warm baked dough, and I swear I could smell the pungent pepperoni before he even opened the box. I ran and got plates, napkins, glasses, and a two-liter bottle half full of fizzless Diet Coke and set everything in front of us.

"Half pepperoni, half veggie," Caleb cracked open the lid. "Okay?"

"More than okay. Thanks for this," I said awkwardly.

He flopped two pieces onto plates and handed one to me. "You're welcome." He took a bite of pizza. "If it makes you feel any better, I'm going to need some favors these next few weeks, so you might want to stop feeling bad pretty quickly."

I nodded, but I was worried about—well, everything. How was I going to get him out of here? Could I ask him to put more ointment on my back without it sounding like a come-on? Now that he'd seen me like this, would he still—want me? I mean, not now, but after I could open both eyes again?

Did I want him to? The honest, naked answer was yes.

And then I did something unusual for me. I let it all go. He was here, not with Lilly. He'd brought pizza, which I love. And he had this look in his eyes whenever he looked at me that made me want to smile. I decided right then and there to do my best to try to get over myself. "When you're ready to go back to work, I can drive you," I offered.

"Thanks. I'll take you up on that. But I'm not going in for two days, doctor's orders. Then I'm relegated to floor duty only. No surgery." He sounded disappointed.

"No surgery?"

"No weight-bearing for six weeks." He was staring intently at his pizza. Tapping his good foot. Looking a little upset. "Six weeks of purgatory."

"Six weeks of sleeping in," I said in my most cheery voice.

He shrugged. "I come from a family of farmers. I love getting up early."

I opened my mouth to say something, but he stopped me. "And don't tell me I can exercise more or read more books or watch my favorite shows. It's going to be torture, period."

"Okay, fine. If you don't try to cheer me up, I won't try to cheer you up."

"Deal. Have you called your chief resident?"

I set down the pizza and wiped my mouth with a napkin, careful not to touch any part of my face. I was learning that even accidentally touching my skin set off a torrent of insane itching.

"Why would I do that?" I asked.

"Because she needs to know that you're not coming in for a few days either."

"I *have* to go to work tomorrow."

"You work with kids."

"If I don't show, people will have to cover for me, and everyone's already overloaded with cases. I can wear a mask when I'm doing pre-ops. No one will notice."

"Sam, forget that you'll scare patients, which you will. You can only see out of one eye." He ran a hand lightly along my forehead. It felt cool and wonderful. "You might even have a little fever."

I frowned. I did feel very warm, but around him, my body seemed to forget how to regulate temperature. "Is that a thing?"

He nodded. "From all the inflammation."

I got up and paced. I hadn't missed a day of work or med school since the day I started. As residents, when one of us calls off, everyone gets burdened. Everyone suffers.

I walked to my bathroom and looked in the mirror, getting up close and tilting my head. My eye was still mostly shut. And he was right. I looked like an extra in a slasher film. "I am scary," I said, close to tears.

I saw his reflection in the mirror, his brows lifted. Then I felt his hands on my shoulders. "Even the hideous parts can't hide the fact that you're beautiful," he said, giving my shoulders a squeeze before he let go and disappeared down the hall. "Got any ice cream? The movie's starting."

"What movie?" Did he just call me beautiful? And was I actually about to sit down and watch a movie with him?

"The one I'm going to pick myself unless you get in here and help me. It'll probably have a lot of bloodshed and violence too. Swords, Vikings, gladiators, that kind of thing."

"Maybe we should just watch a game."

"I'll take a look at what's on." We sat together while he channel flipped with my remote, looking more at home on my couch than I did.

"Which one of us is more miserable?" I asked. "That person should pick."

"Ha. I think we're tied. I love rom-coms," he said.

"Stop." He was joking, right? "You do not."

"Classic ones. You call your chief, and I'll put on Harry and Sally."

I froze for a moment. Because New Years. But then I realized that I'd been given an opportunity to rewrite our story. I hadn't expected a chapter with poison ivy and broken bones, but all that aside, it felt like a new beginning.

I forced myself to make the call. And you know what? It wasn't as bad as I thought. My chief, Priya, told me to take all the time I needed. Of course, I left out the part where I picked up the poison ivy while skidding on my ass down a cliff, chasing after a guy that I was crazy about.

When I hung up, I found Caleb in the kitchen. "You have chocolate raspberry chip or strawberry." His voice was muffled because he was talking with his head inside my freezer. "Oh, and a little vanilla. And a little chocolate." He turned around. "I didn't know you were an ice-cream hoarder."

Of course I was. "Surprise me," I said, grabbing the remote from where he left it on the counter. He dished out the ice cream and I carried it in front of the TV while he got himself settled. Then I unceremoniously—but gently—stuffed my pillow under his cast. And passed him more Tylenol.

So we sat together on the couch and ate ice cream and watched Harry and Sally fall in love. And I forgot all about—everything: poor Ani's ruined weekend; missing work; the fact that I swore I could feel the rash bursting through my skin in clusters of tiny blisters that were now breaking open and oozing. Terrific.

Caleb didn't try to hold my hand. Or do anything remotely romantic. Even if I wanted to make out, my mouth was pretty much out of commission anyway. But sometimes he'd laugh at something on the TV and then turn to see if I was laughing too. Or he'd smile at me and glance at the TV and then I'd smile too.

I was at my absolute worst, and yet he looked at me like—well, like I wasn't. He seemed, despite everything, happy to be here. And also despite everything, my heart was full. I didn't want to be anywhere else but next to him.

Once I looked over and he was wincing a bit. And he shifted around a lot, trying to get comfortable and adjust his leg. But he never complained once.

After the ice cream, I took an anti-itch pill and then I never got to New Year's Eve in the movie. When I woke up, it was pitch-black. The TV was off, and the only light was moonlight, streaming across the floor from my bay window. I was leaning against Caleb, resting against his chest, my hands tucked under my face. He was leaning back against the couch, his head tipped back on the pillow in a position that would probably lead to neck strain in the morning.

I carefully propped myself up enough that I could look at him. Resting, at peace, his strong features appeared softened. That intense gaze of his was shuttered, and he seemed more serious, not ready to crack a joke at a moment's notice.

I thought about how easy it was for some people to give their hearts away. Like scooping up a bunch of fall leaves or dandelion seeds and releasing them off into the wind to land where they may. I, however, had learned to fix a vise grip on my heart. I'd safe-guarded it to the point where I'd forgotten why there might be any good reason to let it go.

I took in the light lines creasing Caleb's forehead, the soft ones around his eyes—from laughing too much, no doubt—his full, soft lips, his unreasonably stubborn jaw. He was never afraid to disagree with me, to push me, to see everything I hid from the world and pull it all back, to make me question everything I believed.

He was fun. And surprising. And kind. And he cracked me up. Most of all, he made me wonder what it would be like to be the kind of person who could take all that from someone, accept it, and then fling it all back with vibrance into the world.

Chapter Nineteen

Caleb

A week and a half later, at the end of a long Wednesday, I hobbled to the door of the old house, eager to reach my apartment, fall straight onto my couch, and rest my throbbing leg and aching hands, wrists, and underarms. I had about enough energy in me to ask DoorDash to bring me takeout—again.

I have to say that I'm a decent cook. And I'm cheap, so I don't order out often. But this week had kicked my butt. Even though I wasn't in surgery, I still had to get to work early because it took me twice as long to get around anywhere.

Sam was back at work too, her rashy misery improved enough to reenter society, at least with a decent application of makeup. A good thing, too, because Ani and Tyler's wedding was coming right up this Saturday, and we were planning on leaving tomorrow after work.

At the end of each day, we'd gotten into the habit of eating dinner together. Told each other about our days. Hung out. Sometimes we read, studying up on cases, flipping through journals, and preparing for weekly academic conferences in our programs.

Our evenings together were the highlight of my day. That and rubbing cortisone on Sam's back, but her rash was looking better and better. Looking forward to seeing her made me focus less on the misery of hobbling around on my broken foot and more on what was to come between us. It was an understatement to say that I was *really* looking forward to the weekend.

Every single night for the past week and a half, I'd asked her out. She'd laughed each time and said, *When I don't look like Frankenstein.*

I couldn't wait to go on a real date. I couldn't wait to kiss her again—at a time when I wasn't a minute away from being transported to the hospital. And I couldn't wait to spend time with her when we weren't debilitated from our injuries and acting like two nonagenarians on the couch holding hands. Not that there was anything wrong with that, but we were thirty-two, not ninety-two.

With those thoughts in mind, I took the stairs face-forward, my book bag hiked onto my back, then trekked down the hall to my door. Just ahead of me, there was a dark lump. Specifically, a lump in the shape of a tall, skinny girl propped up against Sam's door, scrolling her phone.

She resembled Sam in some familiar ways—she had Sam's thick hair, but hers was brown and wavy, not as dark, and she wore it piled up in some kind of bun thing on her head. She wore an oversized UW sweatshirt and leggings. Whereas Sam was curvy, this young woman was long and thin as a reed. But when she looked up at me, she had the same soulful brown eyes, the same arched brows, the same even skin tone.

"You waiting for Sam?" I asked.

I immediately noticed that her eyes were red. She wore no makeup, and she looked like she'd been crying. Her lips were dry. And she bit her lower lip in the same way that Sam tended to do when she was worried.

"Are you her neighbor?" the girl asked.

"Caleb," I said, cranking my thumb behind me to indicate my door. "Are you Wynn?"

She gave me a frown so like her sister's that I almost laughed. Great. Another skeptic. "I'm Mia's brother." That was a good lead-in, I thought, to establish trust right away.

"Hi," she said in a flat tone, not offering a smile or a hand or... anything. "Is it okay if I wait here for her?"

"Yeah, sure." I thought longingly about my giant DoorDash order, the game about to start, my evening of lying down with my foot up in the air. "She won't be back tonight until around eight. Want to come in? I was about to order some food."

She hesitated. Shifted the navy duffel at her side. Judging by the look on her face, her lack of put-togetherness, and what might've been a hasty flight, I guessed that this was some kind of crisis.

"Does Sam know you're here?"

She shook her head—half a shake, the barest kind. Which I took to mean *No. Absolutely not.*

"If you text her," I said cordially, "tell her that I'm ordering some dinner, and she can join us when she's finished with work."

That was met with more silence. When she spoke, it was with great patience. "I'm not going to text her because it will upset her that I'm here. Then she won't be able to concentrate at work, and her patients will suffer or die or something. And then she'll call me and bombard me with questions that I don't want to answer right now."

Okaay. I rubbed my neck. I hadn't dealt with a teenage girl since... well, since I was a teenage guy. I had no GPS here. She was upset and wanting Sam but not wanting to call her to upset her. "Well, how about this. I'm ordering some food, and you can come in and eat it or bring some out here while you wait."

Another way she seemed like a carbon copy of Sam—clearly

needing her but deciding to stick it out. What was with these Bashar sisters, not possessing the genes that enabled them to ask for help?

She looked up at me with reluctance. But just then her stomach growled about as loudly as a car revving it up on the street. "I don't know you, and I'm not going inside your apartment. I'll wait here, thanks."

Like sister, like sister, I thought, forcing back a smile. "All righty then." I unlocked my door and left her in the hall.

A half hour later, when I went out to collect the delivered food, she was fast asleep, her head leaning against the doorjamb.

I waved a bag of Thai food under her nose. "Hey, Wynifred," I said.

She cracked open an eye. I saw evidence of tear streaks on her cheeks. Uh-oh. I thought about calling Sam ASAP but decided to try and get more info.

"I've got egg rolls, pad thai, vegetable curry, and rice." I pulled out my phone and showed her the selfie of Sam and me from that morning at the farm, smiling into the camera, the sun peeking up from the rail fence behind us.

Sam's beauty was fully captured in that moment. She'd humored me, but she'd given the camera a wide, full smile. I confess I looked at it often, setting it as my phone screen saver.

"See?" I said. "Friends. We're in the same wedding together this weekend. And we work together at the hospital."

"Are you the annoying one?"

I grinned. "You bet. And you're my next victim. I'd help you up, but I've only got one hand. Come on in and eat something."

~

Caleb

. . .

"Hi there," I said, intercepting Sam in the hall a little while later.

"Oh hi." She smiled widely. Our gazes caught in that electrifying way that made me want so badly to pull her into my arms and kiss her. But I didn't want her to think I was a caricature of the romantic guy she'd first thought I was, a person who fell in love on a dime or switched objects of my affection from week to week. I wanted to take her out on a real date. I wanted to make sure she knew what had become crystal clear to me—that she was the only one for me.

"It's so nice to see both of your eyes blinking back at me," I said. She laughed and pushed me away playfully. The swelling was gone, the rash faded down to a smooth pink color and covered mostly by her makeup. Also, I was relieved that she seemed to be in a good mood for what I had to tell her.

"Hey," she said while I planned what to say, "I had an idea. What do you think about going out for some Thai food at that little place on the lake? The weather's perfect to sit and outside and watch the sun set. What do you think?"

Honestly, I wanted nothing better than to eat and watch a sunset with her. From my bed, preferably. But obviously, that wasn't going to happen tonight. I steered her down the hall and lowered my voice. "I love Thai food, and I can't think of anything better than spending time together, but I've got something important to tell you. It's all fine, and it's not a crisis, okay?"

She slowly lowered her book bag to the ground. "What is it?"

I held on to one of her arms as I was able. To anchor her. To subtly let her know that she could lean on me. "Wynifred is in my apartment."

The joy vanished from her face. "My *sister*?"

"She didn't text you because she didn't want to worry you while you were at work. She was planning to wait outside your door until you got home, but I got her to come in and eat something."

She frowned and instantly teared up. "What's wrong? Oh my God, she's pregnant. Is she pregnant?" She rubbed her temples. "I knew this boyfriend was bad news. I should have—"

"Whatever's wrong has something to do with breaking up with someone named Miles. She hasn't shared details." I increased the pressure on her arm a little so she'd look at me. I somehow wanted her to know that she wasn't alone without *telling* her that, which I knew she wouldn't take well. "At first she wouldn't even come in, but I think the hunger finally wore her down."

"She went into your *apartment*?"

I couldn't help cracking a smile. "Not until I showed her a photo of us."

"You have a photo of us?" Sam's eyes were brimming with tears. It amazed me—even though I'd seen it before—that worry over her sister could turn her calm, competent demeanor into a hurricane of emotion.

"A really nice one. I'll show you later."

She rolled her eyes.

"Sam?"

"Yes?"

"Whatever it is, it's going to be fine."

That seemed to be the right thing to say, because she released a big breath and gave my hand a squeeze. "I don't know why I believe you when you say that, but strangely, I do."

I thought of something else. "Also, Miles might not be terrible," I said. "He appears to be texting her every other minute."

One brow lifted. She was thinking—and she seemed to be struggling. Maybe with trying to not kill anyone who would dare hurt her sister. I had the feeling that she was used to that role—protecting. Fiercely. She loved her sister fiercely. That gave *me* hope.

She turned to me and did something surprising—she touched my cheek. I felt the soft graze, the coolness of her fingertips as she cradled my jaw for a brief instant, giving me a wistful smile. "Thank you." Her voice was practically a whisper. "For taking her in. And for slowing me down a little. Sometimes I need reminded to not come in hot."

I locked my gaze with hers. I thought of saying that she'd do the exact same for me, call me out on something, as she'd done with Lilly. But I left it at "You're welcome." Then added under my breath, "And also, you're always hot."

Her tiny smile broadened, and I felt my heart expanding. Ever since the cliff, things between us had shifted. We'd always had a give and take, a push and pull, except now we were using our wills to help each other instead of argue, to listen to each other and to give back. It felt like nothing I'd ever experienced before.

With a definitive nod, Sam headed into my apartment. As she passed, she gave me a little tap on my butt.

It happened so fast I blinked and wondered if it really happened.

~

Samantha

If that little punk Miles hurt my sister, I swear he would soon have deep regrets. Caleb had helped me calm down, but I was still a muddle of emotions as I walked into his apartment and found Wynn sitting at a retro sixties red-topped aluminum table before a carton of Chinese rice and a half-eaten egg roll.

As she glanced up, my heart contracted with a painful pang. Because instead of a hoodie-wearing teenager, I saw the eight-year-old version of her sitting at Oma's scarred oak table in her pink flannel mermaid jammies—eyes wide and tear-filled. Sad that our mother hadn't shown. Again.

I'd been furious. It had been her birthday.

"Maybe she's just late. Call her, Sammy," she begged me. "Tell her it doesn't matter how late she is. We'll stay up and wait, won't we?"

"Mom's not coming," I said. I did not want to say that. I hated saying it. But I had no choice.

I felt Oma's hand on my shoulder. She passed me and went to sit next to Wynn, wrapping an arm around her.

"Tell her, Oma," Wynn insisted, her little-girl voice high pitched with desperation. "Tell Sam she's just late."

I went and sat on the other side. I had no idea how to tell an eight-year-old that our mother was hopelessly and chronically unreliable. I wished, guiltily at times, that she would just leave for good. It would've been so much better than this constant rebleeding of wounds.

Our mother was already dead to me, and my anger at our impossible situation was making me cynical and bitter. But to kill all the joy and hope of an innocent eight-year-old? I couldn't do it.

But I owed her the truth.

"Mom's not coming because she's sick, Wynn," I said. Thinking back, I was only twenty-one with the forced maturity of a forty-year-old. "So sick that she can't really be our mom. She—she tries but she's got problems. In her head."

Would she understand what a mental problem was? I didn't have the words. I didn't have a way to make anything right.

Then Oma stepped in. "Samantha is right," she said firmly. "Your mother isn't coming. But we have each other." She gathered us up. "My sweet, sweet girls. I love you both so much. And I'll never let anyone hurt you."

Here in Caleb's apartment, I felt just as desperate. Just as worried that I'd never say the things Wynn needed to hear. But I reminded myself that she'd come here, to me, and I could somehow handle this. With Oma's loving memory guiding me, I closed the distance between us and pulled my sister into the biggest hug I could muster.

"I'm so glad you're here," I said. She immediately gave a sob. I squeezed harder, vowing to give her all the love I had and then some. "I really wanted you back for the summer but not exactly like this." For a second, I dared to dream that she would stay. That we could somehow get back the closeness we used to have before Oma died. If only I could win back her trust.

She took a paper towel that was folded in half and placed under her fork as a napkin and blew her nose. "Miles and I had a huge fight. I left and—I didn't know where else to go."

"Did he—did he hurt you?" I could barely force out the words.

She shook her head. "He wouldn't take my rent money. Like I'm some kind of sad sack or something. I told him that I work two jobs to make the stupid payment, and he needed to take it or else."

Caleb cleared his throat. I'd forgotten he was there, lingering in the background. "Um—excuse me, ladies." He pointed a crutch in the direction of the hall. "Sam, I'm going to go hang out over at your place."

"Thanks, Caleb." He'd done so much. And he just kept doing. For Wynn. For *me*.

"Is he your boyfriend? I'm just trying to figure out what's going on here." Wynn watched Caleb clomp along through the door.

"No," I said quickly. "Nothing's going on."

"Yet," Caleb called over his shoulder on his way out.

I immediately knew that I should've been more honest. I was beginning to see that I spent a lot of time covering my own feelings —and struggles—to try to act like an adult around my sister. Being around Caleb had made me understand how closed off I'd become. And that if I didn't make an effort to change, I was going to have a very lonely life—and not just romantically. "Actually," I said, "I think he might be my boyfriend. Except last weekend, he broke his foot, and I got poison ivy all over my body, so I can't really say what we are right now."

"You *are* his screen saver," Wynn noted.

"I'm his *screen saver*?" burst out of my mouth. Wynn looked at me with curiosity. I moved quickly on to what was bothering her. "So your boyf—Miles—refused to take your rent payment?"

"He like, knows I'm trying to save all the money I can. But that was so insulting. I can take care of myself."

I heard the metallic click of crutches in the hall. Suddenly Caleb was back in the doorway. "Not to interrupt, but was he being... nice?"

"He was being *misogynistic*," Wynn said. "He said he wanted to *take care* of me." She inflected "take care" like it was "murder." Then she threw her hands up in the air. "I mean, I thought we were equals. Partners. But it turns out that he's part of the patriarchy like everyone else!" She burst into tears. I held her. Above her mass of dark curls, Caleb stood in the doorway, shaking his head and pointing to her and me in turn.

I was torn between applauding the notorious Miles for being a nice guy and being proud of my sister for wanting to do things on her own. "We're strong, independent women," I said. "But Wynn, you don't have to work two jobs. I sent money to your account. I don't want you to struggle like this. How can you do well in school when you're stressed all the time?"

She looked up, her tear-streaked eyes and her wild, curly hair, making her a sight.

"I wanted to show you that I could do it," she said with passion, "that I could do what you did. I wanted to take responsibility for wasting the money on that class I failed. I wanted to find my own solution. But I-I thought Miles and I were on the same page. He's probably the kind of guy who wants the 'little woman' to stay home and cook his dinner after work and do all the laundry and put the kids to bed while he drinks beer and burps in front of the TV."

I forced myself to keep a serious face. I didn't know Miles. I had already decided that I didn't like him because since when is it ever a good idea for two broke nineteen-year-olds to move in together? But what if this rent thing was really the issue? I'd been imagining things that were much, much darker and far, far worse.

Caleb gave up the pretense of leaving entirely, clomping across the wood floor and dropping down into his La-Z-Boy chair. "Okay, as a male, I'd like to say something."

"Why is he here?" Wynn asked.

"To be fair," I said, "he does live here." I turned to Caleb. "But we are in the middle of a private discussion."

"Hold on a second." He held up a determined hand. "Maybe Miles is trying to alleviate your suffering. Maybe he's just trying to help you through a tough time. I mean, you Bashar sisters are independent to a fricking *fault*."

I threw up my hands. "There shouldn't *be* a tough time. The bank account has money in it."

Wynn pinched her nose. This was typical when we were at an impasse. "You don't understand."

Was she talking to me or Caleb?

"Look, honey, whatever happened, I'm so glad you're here. I'm glad you came ho—here." I reminded myself that home to her was still Oma's house. Which I'd ripped from her forever.

She was angry with me now. I could tell. I shouldn't have mentioned the money. But what was I supposed to do? Communicating with her was walking on eggshells, fractured pond ice, and a net fifty-feet high with holes in it. Impossible.

"There is no home, Sam," Wynn said with deadly seriousness, making my stomach plunge. "Not anymore."

I felt tears gather painfully in my nose. "Wynn, I *had* to sell Oma's house. I didn't have a choice. But that doesn't mean there's not a place for you with me. I love you. All I want is for you to be happy." I stopped short of saying *I'm your home*. Because to a nineteen-year-old, that didn't matter. She wanted the cute brick-and-mortar house with the ruffle curtains and the yellow kitchen cabinets and the smell of brownies baking, Oma sitting in front of the TV crocheting.

"We both just want Oma," I said.

Caleb got up and judiciously left us alone. Finally.

"I want to go back to before," Wynn said tearfully. "Jobs, bills, classes, the future... it's all so much."

Caleb hobbled back—so soon?—and dropped something into my lap. But it bounced onto the floor with a *chink*. Car keys. With a beer glass key chain filled up with foam that said *Brewers*. Not my keys. His.

Wynn bent to pick them up. "What are these for?"

"Somebody drive," Caleb said in a commanding voice. "We're getting out of here."

"What?" I asked, sounding kind of snippy, a little outraged, and not exactly nice.

"Where are we going?" Wynn asked. She didn't sound nice either.

"To get ice cream." Both of us stared at him like he'd just walked out of a spaceship. Those two words sucked all the steam out of my anger. Even worse, something in my heart split wide-open—that thick, unbreachable barricade I'd steeled tightly around it. Caleb had somehow managed to do exactly the right thing at exactly the right time—again.

What man would dare to interject himself between two very emotional women having it out with each other?

I stared at him, my eyes already filling up.

The answer was, a very remarkable man.

I loved him.

The thought didn't dawn on me so much as roll through me in a massive, gathering wave.

This man supported me at my worst and most challenging. Who was right there, when before it had always been just me.

He smiled a little. Gave me a little nod that might have meant

You're welcome. Then he said, "You two love each other. That's terrific." He made a shooing motion. "So head to the door. Ice cream makes everything better. Now move it."

As we both headed out, Wynn handed him one of his crutches that he'd propped against the door and shook her head. "He's bossy."

"I *know*." But we were both somehow smiling.

Chapter Twenty

Samantha

It was nearly eleven that night when I knocked on Caleb's door, very softly at first. Both of us started our days early enough that going to bed this late was a luxury we couldn't afford. But then I tossed caution to the wind and rapped more firmly. I had something I had to say, regardless of the time.

He answered wearing navy boxers and a gray T-shirt, the kind that might've said something at one time—a band name, a concert, a funny saying—but was now soft and old and worn. His hair was damp from a shower that he must've managed to take with a garbage bag over his cast.

His mouth lifted in that mischievous grin that told me a joke was coming. "If you're looking to borrow a cup of sugar or an egg, I'm out. Sorry." He began to shut the door. I put my foot out to stop it.

"Actually," I said, "I was wondering if there was any food left? The ice cream was great, but I skipped dinner. Didn't even realize it until now."

He eyed me up and down, taking in my bare feet, my pink nightshirt. "Enter at your own risk." That secret smile again. It made me flush.

"You're flirting with me."

"Damn right I am." Then he stepped aside, gesturing me in.

I was so, so glad he was.

He walked over to his kitchen counter and sat down on a backless stool, propping himself with his crutch. "Food's in there, if you don't mind grabbing what you want. Everything all right?"

I took the cartons out of the fridge, opened them, and set them down between us. "For the moment. Wynn's fast asleep." I spooned out some pad thai on a plate and licked the spoon. So good. And a little spicy, just the way I liked it.

"I have sparkling water in the fridge." He leaned over. "That smells good. Maybe I'll join you."

I grabbed another plate and ended up nuking food for both of us. For a few minutes, all we did was eat, but it wasn't awkward. I mean, I was a little nervous, a little buzzed from all the adrenaline pumping through me, from Wynn's crisis to what I'd done just now—strolling right over here in my nightshirt and helping myself to his food.

But he didn't seem to mind one bit.

Not to mention the flirting—a promise of more to come—was making me giddy.

I grabbed seconds, and he did too. Finally we finished, both of us tossing our napkins on our plates.

Caleb leaned back in his chair, his damp hair curling over his forehead, looking relaxed but expectant. It seemed like he was patiently waiting for me to say what I came to say.

I took up his hand. It was warm, his fingers long and beautiful, the hands of a surgeon. He entwined his fingers with mine, which sent my pulse soaring. If I were hooked up to a cardiac monitor, the beeps would be practically continuous.

Now I just had to get the words out before I chickened out. I cleared my throat, suddenly flustered. "Thank you," I said, my voice cracking, "for taking my sister in, for feeding her, for listening, for defusing the tension between us. I... It was very kind."

"You're welcome," he said, his lips lifting in a smile.

I added my other hand and then he did too. So now both our hands were joined, like we were going to cast a spell over the empty Thai food cartons. For an eternal supply maybe. He rubbed my palm with his thumb, which didn't help me get out what more I had to say.

Something on that cliffside had been set in action, like a match that had been struck, a fuse lit, and the only way was forward. I could no longer stay in my safe, insulated box. He'd smoked me out.

"I've been worried for months about Wynn," I said. "About our relationship. About how it hasn't been the same since our grandmother died. I felt so lost. I still have no idea what I'm doing."

He was stroking both my palms now but still listening intently, his gaze locked on mine. Did he not know he was stirring feelings that were making me barely able to concentrate?

"You helped me—us—through this difficult day. But really, you've been doing that all along. On the trail after you fell, you were worried more about me than yourself. And with my poison ivy and... again tonight. I was so wrong about you. Really wrong. And I've never—" My voice cracked. I had to stop. "I've never met anyone who was kind just to be kind. Who didn't want anything back. But you've done it time after time and, well—thank you."

He pulled me closer, until we were inches away. I felt transfixed by his gaze, so warm, so full of humor, and now so full of heat. "You did the same for me. Even when you hated me, you wanted to help me with Lilly."

"I didn't hate—"

"But you don't hate me now."

"No." I was trembling. And I knew he could tell because he

was holding my hands. So securely, so tightly, that I could see the muscles of his forearms flex. I knew he wasn't going to let me go.

"There's more," I said, looking deeply into his eyes.

"Oh, for heaven's sake, woman. More?"

"This is the first time I haven't felt like—" I choked on the emotion. "Like I was alone. Handling everything alone. Because of you."

"I'll never leave you alone," he said matter-of-factly. He could well have said, "I'll stop and get the milk."

"No, no. Don't—don't say that. I just—I just—"

"Yeah, yeah." He waved his hands in the air. "You don't do serious. Whatever."

I swallowed. I was completely overcome.

"So, okay?"

"Okay, what?" I whispered.

"Okay to kiss you?"

"I-I can't stay long. I have to get back." My hands fluttered some weak semblance of a gesture toward my apartment. But I couldn't stop myself from nodding.

"I get it. Sisters before misters."

Before I could even get a laugh out, his lips were on mine, warm and soft and determined. And oh, that kiss took me by storm. He wrapped his arms securely around me and moved his lips over mine, slowly, gently, feeling his way step by step, so carefully and thoroughly, as if he were memorizing every part of my lips, my mouth.

So different from that kiss before getting hauled up in the makeshift harness, which was gutsy and intentional and quick.

I grasped his beautiful face with both my hands, feeling the scratchy softness of his stubble, and I kissed him back, losing myself in the feel of his mouth, his tongue, the heat of his body next to mine.

He tasted so wonderful. And oh, he knew how to kiss. Around us, the apartment was silent and dark, save for the muted, flickering TV and two pendant lights hanging over the tiny island.

He was the one to slowly draw back. I felt it rather than saw it. My eyes flew open to find him solemnly regarding me.

"I know you have to go," he said, "but I'm going to take that as a yes."

"A yes?"

"That you'll go out with me."

"Okay. After the wedding."

"No, before."

"That's impossible. We leave tomorrow, remember?"

"Nothing's impossible when you feel this way."

I tilted my head and gave myself a harsh reminder that this was Caleb-the-romantic, wasn't it? Getting swept away? I warned myself to not put too much stock in his words.

He swept my hair back and gave me an adoring look. "I've dated around some. And yes, I was stuck on Lilly. But you've got to understand, I've never felt like this. I'm completely bowled over by you."

Oh, my heart. What I was hearing could not be real. I shook my head. "Listen to me. I only know reality. I'm not used to believing such pretty words."

He regarded me quietly, steadily. "They have substance behind them. You understand who I am. You're not afraid to call me out. You say things that are in my mind before I say them. You're kind and honest and beautiful." He paused. "And hey, we even go for the same french fries." His mouth quirked up in a fetching smile. "This isn't a passing fancy, Sam. I'll prove it to you."

"How can you be so sure? We haven't even had sex yet."

"That's going to be great too."

His confidence was, well, overwhelming. "How do you know that?"

"Because it's going to be making real love. Not just sex."

My head was spinning. My heart was pounding in my chest. I

wanted him so badly I could barely think of anything else. But there was no way that was going to happen with all of this other stuff going on—meaning, my sister asleep on my futon next door.

"I have an idea," he announced.

Full of surprises. "Okaay."

"Your sister needs you. Let's take her with us tomorrow. She's invited to the wedding, right?"

"Yes, but that's ridiculous. The wedding's not until—"

"She can stay with my parents. She knows them, right? She'll love the farm. My mom and dad will keep her busy, give her some TLC, and bring her to the wedding with them."

He was suggesting dropping my very upset sister off with his parents? "Shouldn't you check with them first?"

"I will. But Beth loves to adopt people. It's her superpower."

He had a point. "I've experienced that firsthand."

"Let me check with them, and then you can ask Wynn what she thinks. A weekend away might do her some good. Sound okay?"

It was only for a day, and maybe he was right. I gave a nod. "A change of scenery might be just the thing. Thanks for the idea."

He sat back and patted his legs. "So come here."

In his lap? "Over there?"

"I want to hold you before you go."

"That's not a casual thing to say."

He leveled his gaze directly at me. "Samantha, do you think this is casual?"

"No," I admitted to him—and to myself. I looked him right back in the eye. "But I want you to know that this is the scariest thing I've ever done."

He reached out his hand. I walked around the island and sat on his lap, and he immediately surrounded me with his arms. He looked up at me and smiled—a tender smile that took my breath away. He pushed back a strand of hair from my face. Studied me so intently that I felt safe and terrified all at once.

He kissed me on the mouth and then on the nose. "Don't be afraid. I got you."

I didn't know if he was talking about all my uncertainty about Wynn or my deep-seated fear of trusting someone—anyone. Of letting myself go with someone who actually meant something to me.

I couldn't even be angry with him for saying *Don't be afraid*, because he'd literally read my mind—I was terrified. But also the happiest I'd ever felt. So there was really only one thing to do. I bent my head toward his and touched his lips again.

Chapter Twenty-One

Samantha

Turned out that Wynn was up for a weekend with the D'Angelos. Caleb and I worked on Thursday before we all made the drive back to the farm. Then we spent the late afternoon in the fresh outdoors touring the farm, walking the fields, and checking out the spring crops—asparagus, kale, spring peas, radishes, and spinach—so of course our grilled-out chicken dinner included a giant fresh salad. The D'Angelos, with their easy friendliness, had been really welcoming to Wynn, who seemed to be feeling a little better.

That night, I'd taken a shower and was trying to unwind, propped up on the pretty pillows in the D'Angelos' guest bedroom. I attempted to read a book on my phone, but I couldn't concentrate, thinking of Caleb. It seemed that the universe was conspiring against us getting together, but what could I do? Go knocking on his bedroom door in his parents' house—ugh, no. I'd taken to deleting old emails and resolving to spend another restless night dreaming about him when there was a knock on my door.

I thought that Wynn, exhausted from all the physical activity, would've crashed hard, but I grabbed her fuzzy gray slippers that she'd forgotten earlier from a cute antique bench and threw open the door, thrusting them out to her.

Except it wasn't her. It was Caleb. He'd showered too, judging by his damp hair, that soft gray T-shirt I loved, and the familiar soapy scent that suddenly filled my senses.

"Um, thanks, but I actually prefer pink." He flicked an appreciative glance at my floral pj shorts, then looked me in the eye with a heat and an intensity that gave me goose bumps.

I tossed the slippers aside. "You again?" I said, trying to frown through the absolute pleasure and surprise of seeing him. "It's ten o'clock."

I said it with the outrage of getting a page in the hospital at around two a.m., but I wasn't outraged at all. I was excited, thrilled, and troubled. Troubled because I wanted him so badly, but I didn't want to tackily drag him through my door and rip his shirt off. Or maybe I should?

He leaned casually against the doorframe. "The night is young. And I want to show you something." That took me by surprise. "You'll love it."

"Just a sec." I couldn't run fast enough into the bathroom to throw on a T-shirt and shorts.

"Maybe grab a sweatshirt," he called through the door. "It's always a little chilly in the country at night no matter how warm the day is." I reached into my duffel and pulled out his old UW one.

"I'm ready," I said as I caught up to him at the door.

"Perfect." He smiled and took my hand. "I'm ready too." He reached down and kissed me quickly on the lips. "Just for the record, I never got lucky with that shirt. Until maybe now I might."

Oh hurray, at last. "Hmm," I said, unable to suppress a giant grin. "Just where are we going?" Honestly, I couldn't have cared less. I would've gone with him anywhere.

"Shh, woman," he said, grabbing my hand. "Trust me."

As we ran down the stairs to the front door, Beth and Steven, who were sitting on the couch in the family room, glanced up. I tried to release my hand, but Caleb held on tightly. "Hey, Ma, Dad," he said casually. "We're going for a little ride. I have a key, so don't wait up."

"Have fun," Beth said.

"See you tomorrow," Steven said.

"Did you see that?" I heard Beth ask in a not-whisper. "They were holding hands!"

"'Don't wait up?'" I asked. "Where exactly are you taking me?"

"Not far," he said in a mysterious tone as he handed me the keys to his truck. "We're going a little off road."

I swallowed. Driving his giant truck—well, to me it seemed giant—on regular roads in broad daylight was challenging enough. But off road? In the dark?

"Don't worry," he said. "The four-wheel drive almost always kicks in before it slides too far down the hill."

That was too much. "Please don't say 'slide down the hill' even if you're kidding."

"I'm sorry. Really sorry." But then he howled with laughter. "I'm teasing you. Come on."

I drove us a ways down the main road that ran in front of the farm until it turned onto a dirt road that ran alongside a field and then plunged into a thick line of trees. In the woods, the road narrowed. "Okay, now I'm scared."

"It's just a little farther." Caleb craned his neck to see the sky out the truck window. "No moon tonight—it's really dark. Just what I wanted." He put a hand on my arm. The road led straight into a clearing. "Now stop and cut the lights."

We were in the middle of a giant grassy field rimmed with trees. The air was cool and earthy-scented, and the sky surrounded us with an endless canopy of stars. "It's beautiful," I said as I glanced around everywhere. "It feels like there's no one around for miles."

"Just us and the crickets." As he grinned. I could see the flash of his white teeth in the darkness. He was right about that—the crickets were singing their summer soundtrack all around us. He grabbed his crutches and opened the door. "Come on. I want to show you the stars."

He sounded excited, full of that same exuberance he always had over the simplest things, and I was giddy with anticipation. I caught up to him about ten feet in front of the truck, where he stood, balanced on his crutches, looking up, transfixed by the thousands of pinpoints of light dotting the inky dark sky. He glanced over at me, I think to point something out, but caught me staring at him, not the stars. "What do you think?"

"I think you have all the excitement of a little kid."

"Well," he said quietly, "if I have that, then I want to give it all to you."

My hand flew up to my chest, pressing over my rapidly beating heart. He had no idea how much it meant that he wanted to share with me all the joy and thrills of this special night.

He kept his hand on my shoulder to steady himself as he pointed out all the planets and constellations I'd learned about in school, in Greek mythology, in science class. I loved the quiet cadence of his voice, but I could barely focus.

"Sam?" I suddenly heard my name. "What are you thinking?"

I wrapped my arms around him, making him turn to face me. "My grandmother was wonderful, but there was no time or money for spontaneous outings. This is... something I've never experienced." There was tenderness in his eyes. "Don't feel sorry for me. I'm just trying to say that you've opened my eyes to..."

"Fun. I want to show you so much fun. I want to *amaze* you." He sounded so intense, so sure, so full of emotion that I believed him. I believed every word. He lightly touched the space between my brows. "I want to show you things that make those little lines appear between your eyes when you're concentrating really deeply. I want to show you things that will make you full of wonder at what you're seeing."

"I *am* full of wonder at what I'm seeing," I said as I looked into his eyes.

He pulled me in and softly kissed my forehead. The summer night was quiet except for the low and steady song of crickets, the damp, dewy smell of growing things surrounding us. In the darkness, there was only the sensation of his nearness, of feeling his warm, solid body, hearing his quiet breathing. We stood together like that for a minute, my whole body seeming to hold its breath in anticipation. I was filled with a dizzy rush, my pulse pounding, every muscle poised and tense.

"I thought we could enjoy the stars from the back of my truck," he said. "I blew up an air mattress."

"Nice move." I couldn't resist that.

"Hey, give me a break. I've got a bum leg."

I was already halfway to the truck, beating him there. Giving a nod, he opened the tailgate and handed me his crutches, then braced and lifted himself up to the bed of the truck. Then he reached out a hand and helped me up.

We lay there together, side by side, enjoying being together at last. Caleb took my hand, bringing it slowly to his lips. "No streetlights, no farmhouse lights, no people. It's like we're the only ones on earth. Us and millions of stars."

As he turned to me, I yielded to his lips, felt the taste of him on my tongue, ran my hands through the thick silk of his hair, felt his back tense and arch as he pulled me to him. We spoke no more words. For once I forgot to protest, to warn myself, to pull away.

I'd had sex but I'd never made love. Or been made love to. And as we shattered into pieces, he was there, kissing me, holding me, murmuring softly how beautiful I was, how lucky he was to be here with me. I was completely overwhelmed. As a tear escaped from the corner of my eye, he caught it with the tip of his finger.

I traced his forehead, the ridge of his brow, the curve of his cheek, the strength of his jaw, memorizing every bit of him. "Are you real?" escaped from my lips. Silly words, but they were a reflection of what I was feeling—that this was a brief blip of time, too pure, too magical to ever last. Things in my world simply didn't.

He took my hand and kissed it. Looked deeply into my eyes. "Don't be afraid," he said as if he could read my mind. "I got you."

He pulled me to him, reached over for the blanket, and tucked it in around us. We fell asleep holding each other, under a sky full of stars.

Chapter Twenty-Two

Samantha

The wedding hotel was a renovated brick Victorian building about ten minutes from the venue in a sweet little town, and it was also where the rehearsal dinner was to take place. The next day, Caleb and I drove there, leaving Wynn behind to work the farm, so to speak. Or really, to have the farm, i.e., Beth and Steven, work their magic on her.

I dropped off my dress and suitcase in my room and went up to the sixth and top floor, where Ani occupied a large corner suite where all the bridesmaids were coming to congregate before the rehearsal. I walked in carrying two ice buckets, champagne chilling in each.

"Hey." I stuck my head into the room, seeing lots of long, double-hung windows and a big bay window in front of which Ani sat by herself on a green velvet-covered settee. I set the buckets on a counter. "I brought the champagne, but I need to go back and get the glasses—"

"Oh Sam, wait," she said. "Come in." She wore faded, ripped jeans and a white T-shirt and was barefoot. I immediately sensed a nervous energy as she stared at her newly manicured nails, her hands stretched out on her legs. She stared so long that I immediately sensed that something was wrong. Suddenly she stood and ran toward me, gripping me by my arms with a panicked intensity. "I'm so glad you're here."

"Me too," I said carefully, assessing the situation. "I'm glad to be here for your special day." I took a glance around the room—sitting area, coffee area and fridge, and a lovely view of the cute downtown, where an art festival was setting up for the weekend. My heart sank as I realized that she was clearly upset, and I was the only one here. Of course I'd heard of wedding jitters, but I, who typically ran from relationships faster than 6G wireless, was the last person on earth who should be on the front lines dealing with them.

Ani immediately dissolved into tears. Wrung her hands. Paced back and forth in the beautiful sunlit room. She was always so calm and often outright joyful—I'd never seen her like this. I put my arm around her, walked her to the sofa, and made her sit down. Then I grabbed a bottle of water from the fridge and made her drink some.

Scenarios rushed through my brain. Did Tyler cheat? Was there an accident? Those were justifiable crises. But another, in some ways even more ominous thought occurred—what if Ani had simply decided that she couldn't go through with this wedding?

Somewhere in the middle of all this, Mia walked in. She immediately sat down on the couch and wrapped her arm around Ani's shoulder. "Honey, what's wrong? What happened?"

"First of all, Tyler's perfect," Ani said between sobs. "He loves me. He's uncomplicated, and I'm complicated. He puts up with me. I couldn't hope for a better match."

"Yes," I said. "Tyler loves you." She sounded like... her mother convincing her of all that. Was this to be expected of someone on the brink of a lifetime commitment? I had no idea, but love wasn't merely being grateful that someone put up with you, was it? Unless it was both of you admitting that you put up with each other equally.

Maybe I shouldn't have agreed with the fact that Tyler loved her. Maybe Ani didn't need people to reassure her of that. What if Ani needed someone to let her be free to make her own choice? What if Tyler, awkward, sometimes rude, short-tempered, and condescending, wasn't right for her, as we, Ani's friends, suspected but tended to suppress?

I was always ready to fight for my friend, but I reminded myself that people express themselves differently. Some people who weren't great in a crowd were much better one-on-one. At least, that's how I'd managed all this time to give Tyler the benefit of the doubt. That and the fact that Ani loved him.

"My mom thinks that I'm just having typical wedding weekend jitters." She got up and walked to the bay window. "I mean, look at this. This is my dream wedding—a cozy, quiet, lovely little town, out in nature, with everyone I love. I'm so blessed. And the weather's going to be perfect! It's a perfect start for a perfect life!"

She over-smiled. Like, the kind of smile you give when you're trying hard not to cry.

"I finally got my life straightened out," Ani said. "Everything's on the path to perfection! My mom says that I'm the only person who could ruin my own happiness now, and I'd never do that, right?"

That was way too many *perfects* in a row.

Mia and I looked at each other. We both believed Ani's parents were part of the reason that she couldn't forgive herself for her youthful mistake. And that sense of shame had made her even more determined to get it right this time.

I walked over to the counter and was about to grab another water when Mia pulled a bottle of champagne out of a bucket and popped it, pouring us all full glasses in some cardboard coffee cups she found. We each sat on either side of Ani on the couch. I checked her pulse. Skyrocketing. "You're hyperventilating," I said. "Take some long, deep breaths and drink this."

"Hey," came a voice from the doorway. In walked Lilly, late as usual, dressed to perfection in yet another beautiful sundress, this one red, with red-and-white-polka-dotted pumps.

"Oh my God, what's happening? Ani, are you okay?"

"Ani's having some reservations," Mia said calmly, passing the champagne. "Have a seat." *And calm the eff down*, was the unspoken message.

"I'm so sorry, honey." Lilly patted Ani's knee and took a seat on a chair across from the couch.

"It's okay," Ani said, blowing her nose. "Thanks for being here."

"You and Tyler are perfect together," Lilly said. "I'm sure you're just having a big case of pre-wedding nerves."

Mia ignored that. "When you're ready, tell us what started all this."

Ani drained half the glass before she spoke. "I told Tyler that I really wanted us to have a little bit of quiet time before all the commotion. I thought we could take a drive through the pretty countryside, but he said he was tired, so we went down to the hotel bar to have a drink. I asked him to imagine one perfect evening far into the future. And you know what he said?" She started to cry, this time silent tears that ran down her face. "He said dinner, drinks, and a night at an all-inclusive resort."

I think we all looked at her like, *That wasn't so bad, was it?*

"Ani," Mia said in a firm but gentle tone, "tell us what you wanted him to say."

"He didn't say anything like tucking the kids in, letting the dog out one last time, and making love by the fire. And you know why?

Tyler hates chaos. He's made it clear to Marin that he doesn't want that cute little dog or her son anywhere near the ceremony. And granted, Tater almost caused a serious accident, but he's just a kid. Besides, the Browns are covering all of Caleb's uncovered medical expenses *and* giving us a huge discount on everything because of what happened."

We thought she was done, but then she added, "Tyler wants live-in nannies to take our kids off our hands. And he hates yard work!" She began to cry again in earnest.

I was concerned about everything but the last. I mean, who *liked* yard work? Although, I got what Ani was saying. She grew up in Oak Bluff, where she, like Caleb, loved the outdoor life. She grew more vegetables on her four-foot balcony than I have in my fridge. And she owned more potted plants than anyone I knew.

"Not everyone wants kids or pets at a wedding," Mia said judiciously.

"I think an exclusive resort getaway is romantic," Lilly said. "Tyler's probably just thinking of the two of you for right now. I mean, you're going to be newlyweds. Kids will be down the line... right? I mean, you've discussed this, obviously."

"Of course. I'd want four or five, but he said more than two would stress him out. I think he just needs to have an orderly plan in place."

Mia was telegraphing me dark looks. I knew she was thinking what I was thinking. That *any* number of children brought a certain degree of chaos to a marriage even if the ratios of parents' hands to children was 2:1. And if he couldn't handle chaos, they were in big trouble.

After everything Ani had just expressed, I worried about more than personality differences between Tyler and her. I worried about Ani being happy. About her settling. About her insecurities over being divorced and how not wanting to make another mistake could have led her to this very frightening moment. It was all adding up to a feeling of doom that I felt deep in the pit of my stomach.

"It's okay to have doubts," Mia said firmly. "But you really need to have a talk with Tyler."

"Yes, Tyler will make all this better," Lilly said. "I mean, he's such a sweetheart. I'm sure everything will be fine." She paused, and I thought—make that hoped—that she was done. But then she added, "Besides, the wedding's paid for. Too late for doubts now, right?"

Mia and I glared at her. I sat on my hands to stop myself from lunging for her.

"Kidding," she said in a singsong voice. "Just trying to make light."

Ani didn't get the joke. Frankly, none of us did. "I'm just panicking because of my big mistake the first time." Ani said, not very convincingly. Suddenly she grabbed my arm. "Sam, I just had an idea. Your matchmaker thing—you have to do it at dinner. Tonight. It will reassure me that everything's going to be fine. Okay?" She white-knuckled me. "Promise you'll do it."

No no no. That was absolutely not the right thing to do. Unlike Lilly, I wasn't going to say anything to falsely reassure Ani. "That matchmaking thing is, you know, just something my grandma did. I don't put any faith in it. Mia is right. Talking to Tyler is what's going to make you feel better."

Ani checked her phone. "He's golfing with the guys. I'll have to wait until before the rehearsal dinner to get him alone."

Mia and I reinforced what a great idea we thought that was. We gave her another drink and more water. Then the three of us took her for a walk. We meandered through the little downtown art show and tried to divert her attention. Finally, she begged to go back to the room and rest, and we all headed to our own rooms to change for dinner.

Lilly and I said goodbye to Mia on the first floor. As the two of us walked to the elevator, Lilly asked if I had a few minutes to talk, and suggested grabbing a couple of Cokes in a little outdoor café off the lobby.

I felt a strange foreboding in my gut that even the colorful bursts of red geraniums scattered around in hanging baskets couldn't quell. After all, Lilly was Ani's friend. Our only connection was Caleb, which come to think of, was a little scary, because she'd acted very possessive of him on the last day of farm weekend. But Caleb had sorted things out with her, right? I shrugged my worry off as me still being upset by Ani's troubles. But I *really* didn't want to sit down with her and talk.

"I'm a little nervous about something too." As we sat on the pleasant patio, Lilly tapped her nails on the wrought iron table. It was covered by a sunny yellow umbrella. Cheery, except I wasn't at all feeling it. "Do you mind if I run it by you?"

"Of course. Sure." Which was totally a lie. She'd somehow singled *me* out, and that made me concerned that this might be about Caleb. But that was ridiculous, right?

"I know this is crazy," she began, "but ever since our weekend at the farm, I can't stop thinking about Caleb." *Oh no.* My heart gave a painful squeeze as she met my gaze straight on with her wide blue one. It felt like all my blood was suddenly draining out of my body, from my head down. I fought lightheadedness by grabbing my drink and taking a huge gulp of Diet Coke.

She took a sip of hers, then flicked her gaze back at me. "When he said he wanted us to use being in this wedding to repair our friendship, I was afraid to trust him. I held back, and I didn't encourage him. But now I just keep thinking about how he saved that little boy. He was so selfless, jumping right after him without a thought. That made me rethink everything. And now that he's going to be working in Oak Bluff, all our stars might align. Maybe it's a sign that we're meant to be. It can be a true second chance for us." As she spoke, I could see how tightly set her mouth was, how intense the expression in her eyes.

My brain flooded with panic. Caleb was going to work in Oak Bluff? He'd been offered the job? I broke out in a cold sweat. Shaking, I put my straw to my lips. I could barely swallow the icy cold drink, much less concentrate on the rest of her words.

It occurred to me that she could be setting me up. That she knew or suspected that Caleb and I were together, and she was saying this to get me out of her way. But that sounded like something out of *Mean Girls*, too conniving to be true.

A sense of doom bloomed all through me as she continued. "I just—I just wondered what you thought about me talking with him? If he'd be receptive? If it's too late? I mean—I know you two are good friends." She sucked in an audible breath, and her deep blue eyes brimmed with tears. "I'm in love with him, Sam. I can't help myself."

I was choked with panic. And a strange sense of disbelief. I looked around the patio—people were laughing, chatting, sipping drinks. The bright day was warm with a light breeze. Had I fallen into a dream state, caused by Ani's distress and too much champagne, where my worst nightmare was playing out in real time before me?

With a clumsy jerk of my arm, I tipped over my drink, the icy liquid dripping onto my hand and through the table onto my legs. This was definitely not a dream. "You... you're in love with him?"

She nodded solemnly. Then she gave a nervous little laugh. "Strange, isn't it? How it can just hit you like a giant sledgehammer." She tapped her hand against the table so hard I started. "Caleb was right. We were so young when we were together, and we didn't have the tools to make it. But we're mature people now. I want to tell him that I'm ready. I want another chance, but I'm terrified. So, what do you think?"

It felt like she'd just driven a stake into my heart. And yet I breathed and lived, and my heart kept beating with a strange, slow pulse. The small, brief burst of happiness that I'd experienced with Caleb seemed precious and rare, like a visit from my mother that would be longed for, ached for, for ages, but never repeated. Clearly the universe was laughing at me, telling me that I'd been right all along—that love wasn't for me. Because I'd just been put into an impossible bind.

What would Oma say? This was proof that her matchmaking test was a sham. A silly game. Wishful thinking that I'd been desperate to believe because I'd needed to believe in some kind of magic.

My mind was whirling. Unlike in the OR when someone's oxygenation falls or their heart rhythm goes awry, and I was always clearheaded and ready, my brain was slow and sludgy. This time I could not think on my feet.

I thought of my options. I could tell Lilly right now that I was dating Caleb even though we literally hadn't had even been on one normal date. Yet I could step up and stamp him as mine. *Sorry, Lilly, too late. He's taken.*

But I couldn't do it. How could I rob Caleb of that choice? Something that he'd dreamed of for years.

What if *I* was just a passing infatuation, and *Lilly* was the one he was meant to be with? Lilly had said herself that initially she didn't trust his sincerity—how could she, after the rumors? Rumors I'd had a part in.

Caleb had sworn he was over her. But if I made his choice for him now, would there always be a tiny little *what-if* in the corner of his mind?

I'd always stood up for myself, been able to speak out, but now I found that I couldn't shut her down. Not because of any kindness I felt I owed her because of my mistakes or because of any sympathy I might have for her sudden affection for Caleb— because I had little of either. But because Caleb deserved to have the choice that he'd wanted desperately—until very recently. A *real* choice. A choice I found that I couldn't interfere with even if it meant ditching my own happiness.

How could I speak for him when he'd loved her for years?

He would always wonder. Or if I shut her down, I would always wonder if he'd choose her if given the chance. Either scenario was terrible.

I'd always told myself that I didn't want love. But I *did* want it. I'd been holding it, right in my hands. But this wasn't my choice to make. It was his.

When I did finally speak, I was amazed at how calm I sounded. Even-keeled. Surprisingly steady. "You should tell him everything."

Just then, my phone vibrated with a call. It was him, of course. I let it roll to voicemail. A few seconds later, a text came up. *Golf was fun. Miss you already. See you at dinner.* Followed by three emojis—heart eyes, double hearts, kiss.

The silly nonsense of lovers.

I turned my phone over on the table and closed my eyes. My breathing came in jerky breaths. The patio around me spun. The Coke kept dripping on my legs, as if gallons had spilled instead of a few ounces.

"Are you all right?" Lilly asked.

"Of course. Sure. Just clumsy." I withdrew my hands and placed them in my lap, where I shredded, shredded, shredded. Except I was just wringing my hands because there was nothing there to shred.

I felt that for a brief moment, my world had been lit up, wonderful and bright, full of hope that I'd finally found what I'd never dared to dream I would find.

But then, I thought bitterly, I never belonged in that world anyway.

～

Caleb

. . .

"Hey, beautiful." That evening, I walked up to Sam at the rehearsal dinner and whispered in her ear as she stood on the edge of a stone patio, overlooking manicured gardens. She wore an elegant black dress and heels, her hair up, and my heart flooded with joy at seeing her. It had only been a few hours, but I missed being with her, talking with her, touching her. I wanted to shout out to the world that we were together. I wanted to sit with her, hold her hand, and whisper words in her ear that would make her laugh or blush as we celebrated Ani and Tyler's love.

Tables filled with candles and flowers surrounded us. Strings of fairy lights were strung on trees and overhead. The sun was still golden in the sky, slanting across green hills and fields. It was a beautiful, warm evening without a cloud in the sky. I was happy to be with my friends at such a happy time. Hell, I was happy like I'd never been before.

Sam started from deep in thought. She was holding a drink, and her hand shook as she set it down on a side table meant for discarded dishes.

When she turned, I could see the tightness in her face, the rigidity of her posture.

"Hey," I said, reaching in for a kiss. She turned her head at the last second, and I ended up kissing her cheek instead.

"Hey, hi." Her gaze swept anxiously over me. "Nice suit," she said, noticing my jacket and tie.

"Thanks. You okay?" I thought of something to say to make her less worried. "I checked in with my folks. Wynn's had a busy day, but they've got everything ready for the farmers' market tomorrow. They're thrilled to have the company—and the help."

"I spoke to her too. She's having a great time."

"You don't look relieved."

"No, I just—"

I took her hands in mine. They seemed cold, despite the warm evening. "I've been thinking about you all day," I said in a quiet voice. "I wanted to ask you if it's okay with you if we go public." I did air quotes with my fingers.

"Go public?" she asked absently.

"You know." I moved my hand back and forth between us. "As a couple. I mean, I've been grinning all day, so I think the guys might suspect something. And I know you didn't mind my folks knowing. But I wanted to make sure you were okay with it."

Out of the corner of my eye, I saw Lilly enter the patio. She wore a formfitting silky, flowery dress in dramatic colors—reds, pinks, greens. Even from here, I could see that her bright pink lipstick, matching, was picture perfect as usual. She saw us and waved. It struck me at that moment that she looked intent, hovering at the periphery, edging in.

Sam cleared her throat. "Caleb, I don't think that—"

Just then, Brax walked up. "Hey, you two. Sam, this guy can't stop smiling all day." He placed his arm good-naturedly around my shoulder. "But no one will tell me whether you two are officially together. What's the scoop?"

Ordinarily, I'd laugh this whole thing off. But something was different. Sam was on edge, stiff and nervous. Suddenly the warm evening felt humid and hot. I yanked viciously on my tie.

"Oh, we're just friends." Sam waved a dismissive hand. "But at least we're not enemies anymore."

Brax looked surprised—but not as surprised as I was. "Just friends, eh?" he asked.

"Sorry, but just friends," she repeated firmly.

My jaw dropped because I was flabbergasted. Completely thrown. As soon as Brax moved on, I waited for Sam to say something to explain. But she was silent, her gaze cast into the distance.

"What was that about?" I finally asked, surprised and hurt. "It's one thing to keep our relationship quiet but another to completely deny it."

She opened her mouth to speak, but no words came out. I touched her shoulder, begging her to turn and look at me.

"Samantha, what is going on? Did something happen? Because it's like you've done a one-eighty on me."

"I just—I'm sorry, Caleb. I just need some space this weekend. To—think about things."

"*What* things?" Then it dawned. "To think about *us*?"

She bit down on her lip. She refused to meet my eyes. I began to pace. Out of the corner of my eye, I caught a glimpse of Lilly, oddly still staring at us.

"Tell me what's happening." I was practically begging now. "What's upset you?"

She winced beneath my touch. "Nothing's happened. I-I just —I can't talk about this now. Ani's really stressed. I'm sorry. I just can't—"

I dropped my hands. "What do you mean, Ani's stressed? Did something happen?"

"She needs to talk with Tyler. She's having a lot of nerves."

"Okay, I get it. But what about us? Tell me what you're feeling."

Had whatever was happening with Ani spooked her? A cold shiver went through me when it occurred to me that Sam was being... Sam. Running from a commitment. Because that's what Sam did. She'd said so herself.

Just then, Tyler's father made an announcement over the mic for everyone to please take their seats. I finally captured Sam's gaze and mentally begged her to say something, anything. In complete frustration, I yanked harder at my tie until it finally loosened up. I felt like I was suffocating.

She rubbed her forehead. "Look, Caleb, everything is so new with us, and there's so much going on, that I don't think now is the time to announce anything to anyone. Okay?"

That's when I finally caught on. "This isn't about Ani or wedding stress. *You're* having doubts." Anger bubbled up from deep within me. I'd been so naive to think that I'd be the one to change her. You can't ever change anybody, can you? How many times had my mom said that going into a relationship trying to change someone simply never worked. "You just can't take the leap, can you?"

She closed her eyes. Just for a few seconds, but it reminded me of what my patients looked like when I was about to stick them with a big old needle. "You're running away. From me. From us."

"I'm taking a step back," she said curtly. "For now. I'm sorry." Without another word, she turned and walked to her seat.

Chapter Twenty-Three

Samantha

Ani's parents played a slideshow on a fifty-seven-inch television set to Taylor Swift's "Invisible String" that featured photos of Ani and Tyler at *many* different ages and stages, side by side, as they grew up. It was probably adorable; I could barely focus on it. They had so many photos that the song played twice, and frankly, in the horrible mood I was in, once would've been plenty.

I had no idea what I was doing. I was numb—blind and deaf, barely aware of people around me dressed in colorful, bright outfits laughing and talking and eating, candles flickering, music and speeches droning on and on as the rehearsal dinner played itself out. Outwardly, I think I managed to smile—perhaps maniacally—but inside, I was in agony.

What had I just done?

I thought I'd done the wrong thing. But I didn't know how to fix it. I didn't know how to tell Caleb that Lilly still cared—that was Lilly's job. I couldn't warn him, and I couldn't call her a sneaky, conniving bitch because I wasn't sure if she was one—even though singling me out to announce her feelings just at the time when Caleb and I were finally together was ironically perfect timing. Running over to Caleb and shoving Lilly out of the way and telling him pick me, pick me! didn't seem right. Somehow I felt that I had to let this play out. But I was a wreck.

I tried different scenarios in my head: "Caleb, Lilly loves you and wants a chance with you," sounded like I should let Lilly speak for herself.

"Caleb, I wanted to warn you that Lilly's still after you," sounded insecure and ominous.

"Caleb, I told Lilly to back the eff off." Maybe I should've taken option three.

And what was the deal about Caleb working in Oak Bluff?

I took a sip of my drink, a gin and tonic, which I hated but was all I could think of to order. Caleb, sitting across and down the long table from me, next to Lilly of all people, wouldn't even glance in my direction.

Ani, at the table's other end, looked pale and panicked. Once I saw her clutch onto Tyler's arm and whisper something. He shook his head and looked puzzled. Their body language seemed out of sync and was telling. Ani also kept looking over at me, lifting her brows and gesturing for me to come over.

Oh. The matchmaking test. I'd forgotten all about it. That was the last thing on earth I wanted to do now—in the grand scheme of things, it would rank right after attending a malpractice deposition. I couldn't force myself to move.

Then Lilly stood up, her bold flowery dress directly in my line of sight. To make things even worse, Caleb scraped back his chair and left with her.

That was the final dagger to my heart. I thought I might throw up right then and there.

Ani gestured furiously to me to come up *now*. I managed to move my leaden legs up to the end of the table near the front of the patio.

"Do it now," she whispered insistently when I got there. "The test. Please."

I grabbed a vacated seat and sat down next to her. Took her hand and looked directly into her stricken, hollowed-out eyes. "Ani, listen to me. The matchmaking test is a fake. It was something I wanted to believe to feel closer to my grandma. It's not magic."

"I don't care." Her voice cracked. "I'm desperate. Please, please do it."

I thought about how I'd lied to Caleb about his and Lilly's test to prove that I wasn't interested. I was coming to realize that the question *Are we compatible?* had no good answers from anyone who wasn't in the relationship themselves. It was like a girlfriend asking her boyfriend, *Does this outfit make me look ten pounds heavier?*

Ani sounded so desperate, so on edge, that I felt like I was distressing her more by refusing. "Okay, fine," I said.

But now what was I going to do?

I walked behind Ani and Tyler and put my hands on their shoulders.

Everyone, seeing me with the bride and groom, immediately began yelling for me to make a toast.

"Okay, okay," I said when they wouldn't let up. I'd never been good at extemporaneous speaking, but now, all my grief spoke for me, for better or for worse. "How does anyone know if a person is right for them? Well, I think you know because this person just gets you." I closed my eyes for a second, not certain I could get through this, but feeling strangely compelled to continue, the words pouring out. "They are the best for you and sometimes the worst for you when they tell you the truths you need to hear. This person is the kindest, most wonderful person you've ever met, and every day they make you want to be the best person you could be. They believe in you, they cherish you, and they love you for exactly who you are. And they make you feel safe in their love."

My voice was shaking. All of me was. I lifted my glass and looked straight at Ani. This was the only gift I could give her, far better than a fake compatibility test that I should never have hyped as a piece of magic to replace the hard work of relationships. "To true love. The only thing that matters."

Apparently, that was quite a speech, because everyone clapped. Gabe even walked by and told me I should've been the officiant. But I ignored everything going on around me. Tyler rose to chat with some guests, so I sat down in his vacated seat and squeezed Ani's shoulder. Then I turned to her, sucked in a big breath, and took both her hands in mine. They felt colder than Antarctica.

"There's only one thing that's real, and it's right here." I patted my chest. "In your heart. You don't need me or anyone else telling you what you know deep inside you." The bride got teary. They weren't tears of joy. Basically, she was a miserable, unhappy bride. Why deny it? Why soothe her and tell her to marry Tyler, who probably wasn't ever going to make her happy? I didn't need a dead zero matchmaker test to know that. I knew it because I saw how Ani and Tyler acted when they were together. And it wasn't good.

And I knew that because I knew what was in my own heart. Caleb was everything I'd just said and more. And I'd lost him.

"Ani, you're a gem. But you shouldn't marry someone just because you desperately want this marriage to work. If it's not right, then you have to be brave and admit that to yourself and to Tyler. Mia and I will do anything to help and support you no matter what you decide. You deserve everything, the very best. Nothing less." I bent down and kissed her cheek. "I love you."

She squeezed my hand hard. "I love you too," she managed.

As I went to take my seat, I knew I would never tell Ani that I felt only a dead battery between her and Tyler. I also knew that I'd never do that matchmaking test again. People had to figure out their own love lives. And I sure had messed up mine.

I'd rolled over and given up my own chance at love. I'd taken some kind of matchmaking moral high ground, and it had hurt Caleb and driven him straight into Lilly's arms.

~

Caleb

"Ani's having second thoughts," Lilly said as we stood on an extension of the patio, watching the sun set spectacularly past the rolling hills of farmland. The brilliant oranges and pinks faded into indigo, which reflected my mood. *Black.* "We could barely calm her down. We told her to talk to Tyler."

"Second thoughts?" Looking back at our golf afternoon, Tyler had been Tyler, relaxed and joking. There'd been no signs of trouble. Was that why she'd called me urgently from the rehearsal dinner, to tell me this?

Lilly gave a little shrug. "They might want different things out of life. Or she might just be panicked because she's afraid of making a mistake again. I don't know."

To me, Lilly sounded like she was reporting a news story instead of relating a would-be tragedy. But then, I wasn't in the best frame of mind. I put my hands in my pockets and walked over to where a low stone wall held a flower bed that ran the entire circular length of the patio.

Something was tugging on my brain. Why was Sam so insistent that we not come out as a couple? It seemed abrupt and also very unlike her. I couldn't help feeling that something was really off. My anger had flared, and I'd been quick to accuse her of running away. Granted, I was hurt, but something didn't feel right.

We were always good about talking things out—one might call that arguing, because from the get-go, neither of us had been afraid of confronting the other. But she'd avoided discussion completely. Why?

On the far part of the patio, I could see Sam sitting next to Ani. Holding her hand, talking intently with her. Again I wondered why the hell she'd backed away from the idea of us so abruptly. What scared her off? Was going public so frightening that she couldn't handle it?

I was so distracted I forgot that Lilly was standing in front of me, her back to the stone wall, hands leaned against it, watching me carefully.

"Is that what you wanted to tell me?" I asked. "That Ani is struggling?"

She smiled—a little sadly, I thought. "No, I—I have to tell you something else completely." She tapped her chest, as if she were choking up. Then she cleared her throat. "Sorry, I'm nervous, and this is difficult for me."

It was unlike Lilly to be nervous. I instantly thought about how she'd jumped right in and taken over after I'd been hurt, almost like we were still a couple. My Spidey sense told me that whatever she had to say, it wasn't going to be what I wanted to hear.

"When we first met up again, I was really wary of you. But during that weekend on the farm, I got to see who you are, and I was reminded of so many wonderful things."

Oh no. I wondered if I should stop her now, because I didn't want to hear what was coming. I glanced over at the rehearsal dinner in the distance and saw Sam headed back to her seat. I balled my fists, trying to prevent myself from going to her.

I missed some of what Lilly was saying, so I forced myself to pay attention.

"Anyway, the bottom line is, I saw what you did for that little boy. I couldn't believe how brave you were. And I realized that I'd been letting the bad memories of that awful time we had cloud my judgment. We were kids, and we both had so much growing up to do. But I've finally figured out that I'm in love with you, Caleb. I —I've decided that I want another chance."

I felt my body go rigid, my heart thudding ominously as I took that all in. Life is so funny. It slaps you on the ass when you least expect it. I'd kept Lilly in my mind for years, holding up her memory as my ideal woman. But after spending less than a day with her, I knew beyond a doubt that she wasn't. I should've done that long before to save myself the headache.

Samantha called me a romantic, but I didn't really like that word. Hopeful? Optimistic? In this case, *totally ridiculous* was more like it.

To get into med school, you have to persevere over and over again. You're taught to excel, because if you don't, you are eaten for breakfast. And so you pick yourself up again and again and redirect your determination into better grades, bigger accomplishments, greater achievements. Hopefully you end up sincerely wanting to make the world a better place and not becoming some jaded person always looking for the next proverbial "A."

I think I'd put Lilly in that same kind of box as any of my so-called accomplishments. If I'd only tried harder, paid her more attention, been more attentive to her needs, we wouldn't have crashed and burned. That failure was a persistent scar that I kept trying to erase. My mind hadn't been able to wrap itself around the fact that I'd been unable to turn our relationship into a win.

I looked at the woman in front of me. She shifted her weight from one high heel to the other, staring at me expectantly.

I was pretty sure that regardless of what she'd just said, Lilly wasn't in love with me. She always glommed on to the newest, shiniest thing—that's what I became when I'd saved Tater. The hero of the day.

It was like when I was valedictorian. And again when I got into med school. She'd always admired success. I mean, she became successful herself, which was admirable.

But during the hard times, the times of struggle—like, when I could barely keep my head above water that first year—she hadn't been so impressed. And while she suffered too, it seemed to be all about her.

All this time, I'd tended to blame myself. But love was a two-way street.

Oh, I was past blaming. I just knew who I loved. Really loved. And it wasn't her.

I turned to her. "Lilly," I said, taking up her hands. "I love our memories together. I love our history. You were a wonderful first love. But—"

Tears welled. "Caleb, we have a long history. Did one weekend with her erase everything? I knew I shouldn't have left that square dance so early."

One weekend with *her*. It was the way she said it. One weekend with *her*. Not vindictive, but somehow... spiteful? Or at least, envious.

How did she know about Sam and me if we hadn't even told anyone yet?

Maybe it was simply obvious to everyone. Maybe we just couldn't hide it. If only Sam would believe it too.

"Lilly, look." I took hold of her hands. "We shared so many great times. I'm really glad this wedding got us back on better terms with each other."

"Stop." She paused, appearing to collect herself. "You're in love with Samantha."

"Yes." The plain, simple truth. "I love her."

"I thought so." She gave me a sad smile. "I just had to take the chance."

She was crying. "I'll always treasure the good times." And I planned to forget all the bad ones as soon as possible, I thought as I hugged her goodbye for good.

I did love Sam. This time, I knew that what I felt was real, mature love. It hurt too damn bad not to be.

Sam

At around ten-thirty, the rehearsal dinner finally over, Mia found me sitting on a bench by myself in a pretty solar-light lit garden that at the moment, I could not appreciate.

"There you are," she said, taking a seat beside me. "How was the test between Ani and Tyler? I saw you doing it."

I shook my head. "Only because Ani begged me to. I told her the truth—that the result didn't matter. That she already knew the answer in her heart, and we'd support her no matter what she decided."

Mia nodded. "This wedding is sort of turning into a real shit show. Pardon my language."

"Ha. Tell me about it."

"I'm glad you didn't appease Ani—you know, tell her everything was going to be all right. Because I'm not sure it is."

I turned to my friend, full of different torments of my own. "Could we have prevented this?"

"I've been thinking about that." Mia looked off into the shadowed gardens. "I don't know for sure. I think I passed off a lot of sketchy behavior by rationalizing. *Oh well, Ani loves him.* That was probably a mistake."

"We'll help her through this."

Mia hiked a thumb over her shoulder. "Ani's with her mom now. I'm afraid her mom's going to talk her into going through with it."

"We'll see her in the morning and do our best to be there for her."

We fell into silence. Ani and Tyler. Lilly. Caleb. My mind flitted from one disaster to the next. And to other things. "I've been a terrible best friend. I don't share things with you."

Mia gave a soft chuckle. "You share everything with me." She counted off on her fingers. "Your lunch, your car—when you had one that worked, that is, and your favorite lipstick when I forgot mine. Most importantly, you share your time. You not only listen to me when things are going well but especially when they're not." She took a glance over at me, clearly trying to figure out what was going on. I didn't even know where to begin.

I felt a deep-seated need to—change. To be more honest. More open. Because this staunch independent thing I had going on wasn't working all that well for me. "I'm a bad friend because I don't open myself up to you in the same way you do to me. Even though I know you wouldn't judge me if I told you more."

"You can change that at any time, you know." She paused. "Did Caleb do something dumb?"

"I slept with your brother," I blurted.

"Oh, okay," she said with a wry smile. "*You both* did something dumb."

I knew that she was trying to get me to laugh, but it didn't work.

"I *did* do something dumb. Like, really dumb."

"Well," she said, shrugging, "now's your chance to spill."

I turned to my dearest friend. I felt gutted like I'd never been gutted before. And for the first time in my life, I was desperate to tell her everything. "Lilly told me that she's in love with Caleb. Ironically, right before he asked me if it was okay to go public with our relationship."

"Wait," Mia said, trying to absorb it all. "You two got together, right? Caleb doesn't care about Lilly."

"No, you don't understand. Yes, we got together, and yes, it was amazing, but then I ruined it all by saying nothing when he wanted to tell everyone and then letting Lilly tell him everything he's been wanting to hear for four years."

Mia rubbed her forehead. "Are you saying that you let Lilly make a play for him? Why did you do that!"

"I told him I had to think about things because I—" I got choked up. I started to cry, and my nose began running, and I had to wipe it on my arm. I felt certain my makeup was running too. "Because I thought he needed to have a choice. I didn't want him to look back and think that after all those years wanting her, he could've had a chance to get her back." And I'd basically effed myself in the process.

"Oh, Sam," Mia said, which made me cry more.

I tried to wipe my eyes, but the tears kept coming. "But the truth is, I don't have to think about anything. I love him. But it got in my head that he's loved Lilly forever and he should have a choice. I couldn't tell him, 'Guess what, surprise! Lilly loves you! And so do I. Now pick!'"

"Wow." Mia was stunned into silence. "So what happened?"

"I don't know." I gave a sad shrug. "He walked out of the dinner with Lilly. And that's where we are."

Mia patted my shoulder. "I understand why you did what you did. But you can't just let Lilly do what she wants. You've got to tell him how you feel."

Suddenly, someone called my name in the semi-darkness. A figure stepped into the light. "There you two are." Wynn was busy looking around at the lighted gardens, the pretty winding paths. "This is a cool place."

"Wynn!" I exclaimed, shocked to see her. I knew that she would be coming with the D'Angelos, but I didn't expect her until tomorrow.

I turned my head and tried to wipe the watery streaks of makeup around my eyes, but it was no use. She would see me as I was, a complete and total mess. "What are you doing here?" I asked as I kept furiously swiping. "I thought you had the farmers' market tomorrow morning?"

She was still checking out the scenery and hadn't really focused on me yet. "The D'Angelos gave all the vegetables and stuff to their neighbors to sell for them. They thought it would be fun to stay over tonight and not have to rush to get to the wedding. I'm staying on the pullout bed in their suite."

That was when she saw my face. And all the pain I couldn't disguise. "Oh my God," Wynn said. "What's wrong?"

I'd never expected to open myself up to everyone all at once. And the struggle was oh, so painful. I realized then how little I told —well, anyone, but especially her. How I kept all my troubles to myself so that she could have this perfect life. Only I hadn't made it perfect. My silence had just pulled us apart.

Mia stepped in because she knew I couldn't. "Sam loves Caleb, but Lilly told Sam tonight that *she's* in love with him. And long story short, because I don't know if you know this, but your sister used to hate my brother until she started helping him get Lilly back a few weeks ago."

"I sort of get that," Wynn said, sitting down on the other side of me and resting a hand on my back. That simple gesture of comfort from my little sister undid me even more. "Caleb loves you too," she said simply, as if it weren't complicated at all. "I could tell. Plus I did Oma's matchmaking test on you two."

I sat up. "Wynn, no! Oma's test is a bunch of—of *malarky*. It's a fake. It's gotten me into so much trouble. Doing it will only get you into trouble too."

"No, it won't," she said very calmly. "It works."

"When did you do that?" I thought of that night in Caleb's apartment, when we were fighting. And driving her to the D'Angelos. I couldn't recall her ever stopping to touch both of us at the same time.

"I did it on the way out the door to get ice cream the other night. I handed Caleb his crutch, and I touched you at the same time."

I'd had no idea. "The fact that you did that for me is—really sweet. And clever. But it doesn't change the fact that the test isn't real."

Wynn opened her mouth to protest, but before she could, Mia spoke. "Okay, forget about Oma's test for now, ladies." She was all business. "We have other problems."

I looked at my sister. So young. So worried-looking on my behalf. "I'm sorry, Wynn." I grabbed her hand. "I'm sorry for not sharing more of my life with you. I thought that I was protecting you from pain. But I was only preventing us from being closer."

"I know you do everything for me," she said. "I was a brat about Oma's house. I knew you did what you had to." She paused, seeming to be thinking of what to say. "It is kind of nice to see that you're not perfect either. And you shouldn't have been so nice to Lilly."

My sister had just bowled me over with maturity and compassion. I should have breakdowns more often if this is what they led to.

"Okay, I'm glad you two have resolved things," Mia said. "But focus, people. A few weeks ago at the farm, we all saw how you and Caleb were laughing, joking, and eyeballing each other—it didn't take a rocket scientist for Lilly to see what was happening."

"Are you saying that Lilly *planned* this?" That had crossed my mind, but Mia saying it confirmed my deepest worry.

"I don't know," Mia said. "But telling you she's in love with Caleb is a great way to get you out of her way."

"That's devious," Wynn said.

"This is the same woman who used to feign headaches to get out of having dinner with us when we'd go to see Caleb in Milwaukee."

Nice.

"What are you going to do now?" Wynn asked.

"I mean, he left with Lilly," I said. "I haven't seen him since."

"Caleb wouldn't go off with her to like, to be with her," Wynn said.

As I sat there thinking of the mess I'd created, my own words that I'd said to Ani came back to me, paraphrased of course. *You don't need anyone to tell you what's in your heart.*

If I loved Caleb, that meant that I also trusted him. He'd already chosen me over Lilly. Why hadn't I believed that? If I had, I never would have given him a straight path back into Lilly's arms. This bitter truth left me cold.

"What are you going to do?" Wynn asked.

This was exactly why I'd vowed not to fall in love—it made your life an absolute mess. But it was my mess, and I would do anything to fix it. "I need to find him and tell him that I love him and that I messed up."

Mia's phone rang. "Hi. Yes, of course," she said. "Sure. We'll be right there."

I could tell from the solemn expression on her face that something was wrong. "What is it?"

"It's Ani. She needs us."

Before I got up, I grabbed my phone. *I'm sorry,* I texted Caleb. *Please forgive me.* That was all I had time for.

I prayed that would be enough.

∾

Caleb

The rehearsal dinner ended, but Sam and Mia had gathered around Ani and then left with her. I took out my phone and hovered my fingers over a blank message box. The thing was, Sam had said in no uncertain terms that she was taking a step back. She didn't want us to be public. Was she running scared, or had she simply decided that she didn't care enough?

Needing to get my own head on straight, I pocketed my phone, yanked my tie off for good and shoved that in my pocket too, shrugged off my stifling coat, and started walking. I ended up outside a nineteenth-century glass greenhouse not far from the gardens. Twinkle lights lit up small trees that were inside. Nearby, there was a grassy knoll and a bench. I sat down, bending over, tenting my fingers, thinking. How had things gotten so messed up?

A little while later, I heard footsteps behind me. I turned to find my mother. How she found me there, I had no idea.

"Hi, Ma," I said, but my heart wasn't in it. "I thought you weren't coming until tomorrow."

"We came early. I just ran into Mia and Wynn, and Mia asked me to find you. How are you doing?" she asked, patting my knee.

That was the thing with Beth. She should've been a therapist, because she was so nonthreatening that she made nearly everyone she came into contact with want to spill their deepest secrets. She'd definitely had my number—from birth. The woman could tell when something wasn't right with me from miles away. I blew out a big breath. "Why did Mia send you to find me?"

"Ani's not doing well."

"Oh. How serious?"

"She's having second thoughts. The girls are all with her."

"I'd better go check on Tyler."

She held me back with her hand. "Yes, but first talk to me about Sam."

"I have a feeling you might already know what happened." If Mia had gotten to her, I was sure of it, and her shrug confirmed it. "Lilly somehow thinks she's in love with me. But Sam told me she wanted to step back—from us. I guess she needs some time. Or maybe she's run scared. Or just done with me. So... I'm not really sure how I'm doing."

"There is *a lot* going on at this wedding."

"Yes." My voice sounded deadpan. Which was what I was inside.

"Can I tell you my thoughts?"

I gave my mother a wry smile. "Was there ever a time when you didn't?"

She patted my knee again. "And I hope there's never a time when I can't. There's something I've held back from saying all these years."

"You? Hold back? How unusual."

"The thing about Lilly is that she never supported you. Instead, she demanded support from you at a time when you were fighting for your life, so to speak. I'm exaggerating, but you understand what I mean about your first year of med school."

"I guess I thought that by having her at my side, we could weather anything."

"I always thought it was a dumb idea for you two to move in together as new college grads but whatever."

She wasn't wrong.

"No matter what happened between you two, you never faulted Lilly. You always said that *you* led her to Milwaukee, that *you* didn't have enough time for her, et cetera. Your impulse is always to protect. To see the best in everyone. To be positive and optimistic. I think you learned that from protecting Gracie. And of course Mia afterward."

"I think you might be right on that. But Sam doesn't need my protection. And she doesn't believe in fairy tales."

"Sam's called your bluff," she said softly. "Maybe she doesn't need things in the way that Lilly was needy. Maybe she's more your equal. But that doesn't mean she doesn't want someone to be there for her and show her that things can work out occasionally."

"She was pretty unreasonable when I asked her to act like a couple. Why didn't she stand up for us?"

"I look at it a little differently. Letting you figure all this out for yourself is not running away."

"What do you mean, 'letting me figure this all out'?" I couldn't have been more confused.

"Lilly made sure to tell Sam that she was in love with you *before* she spoke to you."

Lilly told Sam..."Wait. Are you saying that Sam pulled away because of Lilly?" I'd sensed some jealousy—that *her* comment—and I remembered seeing her hovering around while Sam and I were talking, but *this*?

"Sam didn't rant about Lilly or run to tell you about Lilly's feelings for you. She let Lilly do that. I believe it was her way of giving you a choice."

"Lilly set things up to get Sam out of the way?" I was incredulous.

"I don't think that was an accident."

"Mom, you're essentially saying something here. Something big."

My mom shrugged. "I'm usually like you in that I like to give people the benefit of the doubt. I'm just not so sure I can in this case."

I raked a hand through my hair, trying to wrap my head around everything.

She said, starting to get up, "Hope you can get a hold of Sam." She gave me a kiss on the cheek.

I gave my mom a giant hug. "You're the best, Ma," I said. "Thank you for being you."

"I love you too," she said as she hugged me back. "Good luck."

Chapter Twenty-Five

Samantha

The wedding morning dawned sunny, clear, and gorgeous. Only the bridesmaids all seemed to be exhausted wrecks when we showed up for makeup at a little cottage near the entrance to the venue at eight a.m. Beyond the cottage, men were setting up rows of white chairs on a grassy lawn, and florists were working their magic.

I'd missed four calls from Caleb, but I'd been with Ani until four a.m. She'd talked to Tyler again and they seemed to have settled things, and then we'd all tried to get a few hours of sleep.

Talk in the morning, okay? I read Caleb's last text, which I read over and over again, clinging onto those words as a tiny shred of hope.

I was shocked to see that even Lilly's eyes were puffy and her skin blotchy. Part of me wanted to grab her and force her to tell me what had happened between Caleb and her, but to be honest, I already knew exactly just by looking. But a huge flood of relief didn't bowl me over. I didn't know if Caleb would forgive me for publicly denying him. And for having so little faith in us that I'd allowed Lilly to enact whatever drama she'd managed to with him.

I would've tried to talk with her, but I felt certain that would make me want to kill her, and there was enough going on. Right now things were about Ani. I needed to push aside all my own sorrows and focus on helping her.

Ironically, this morning, only Ani seemed strangely calm. Also, both Ani's and Tyler's moms had joined us in the small cottage not far from where the final touches were being put on the straight rows of white chairs, a magnificent floral arbor, and the gorgeous arrangements of salmon and white flowers that lined the aisles. Around us, curling irons were plugged in and giant professional kits of makeup unfolded as we got to work getting ready.

Mia and I secretly wondered if this was a hostage situation—if whatever Ani's mom had told her after we'd left had caused her to squash down all her doubts. And so we kept trying to find an opportunity to get her alone, but it was impossible with all the commotion.

"Ani, how are you?" Mia and I finally cornered her near the brunch buffet the moms had delivered and set up on the kitchen island. A makeup artist was working on Tyler's mom in the corner, and a stylist was curling Lilly's hair at a table. The scent of hairspray was thick in the air, which didn't exactly mesh with the food —or the stomachs of the rest of us.

"How did the talk with Tyler go, honey?" Mia whispered.

"Now, girls," Ani's mom, who was petite like Ani and elegantly dressed in a beige silk dress, said. "Nerves are to be expected before such a big decision like marriage. But everything's fine." Then she gave Mia and me a studied look just short of a glare. A clear warning not to upset the bride.

Ani's mom got called over to consult on Tyler's mom's hair. Ani stood in her cute white satin pj top and shorts, her hair in an elegant updo, holding a paper bowl in front of a large fruit salad. I moved closer and started to say something, but she cut me off with a tight smile. "I love you both, and I'm okay," she said firmly. But the only thing she put on her plate was a piece of watermelon, and I don't even think she even ate it.

Ani set down her plate. "Tyler told me he loves me," she said in a quiet voice. "We talked out our future again. He said once the kids come, I can work part-time if I want. We could have a nanny or even one for day and a separate one for night. He'll come home in the evenings and we can have drinks while our personal chef prepares our dinner and the nanny plays with our kids. We can see them once they're all clean and in their jammies right before bed. Isn't that a tidy plan?"

I swallowed. I thought for some reason about Beth, who had this uncanny way of not telling anyone what to do but somehow letting them figure it out for themselves. How did she do that? Because the inside of me was screaming, "Put on the brakes!"

"Ani, did you take a Valium?" Mia asked, still whispering.

"My mom gave me one, but I flushed it."

"Oh, thank God," I said.

"I really wanted a man with a tidy plan. Maybe because I felt like a mess. I depended on him to organize me."

A glance over my shoulder showed that her mom was on the way back.

"Ani, what are you saying?" I asked. "You know, you don't have to—"

"All morning long, I've been trying to figure out what the problem is," she said in that deadly calm voice. "I had a messy divorce. I left my nursing job at a time when all my friends were making good money and buying things and settling down, and I had to start all over again from scratch. At that time, I needed someone to make my life—me—feel more in control. Tyler did that for me. He's organized and he always has a plan. There's only one problem."

"What's that, honey?" Mia stroked her arm.

She gave a sad shrug. "Tyler's version of our life isn't messy enough."

"Excuse me?" This from Mia, who looked like she was struggling to follow.

"His view of our life. It's so... tidy and neat. Life isn't neat. It's messy."

"You can say that again," I said. "Really messy." Didn't I know it.

"I mean, I want chaos," Ani continued. "I want kids and puppies and all the happy commotion that comes with having a family. I don't want to be removed from chaos. I *want* to be in the thick of it."

I nodded. "Those are all good things." I thought I understood. She didn't want to be an observer in her own life. She didn't want to be removed from the good stuff. That appeared to be exactly what I'd done to myself, sheltering myself from relationships, protecting Wynn from my messes.

"Honey, it's almost time to put on your dress," her mom called. "Are you ready?"

Ani had a vise grip on my hand. "What would you like to do?" I asked. Honestly, all she had to do was say the word and I was ready to call this game. I can be loud too.

"Ready, sweetie?" her mom asked. "The photographer just went into the bedroom to take photos of us helping you into your dress."

Ani looked at her mom. "I need to speak with Tyler," she said slowly and calmly.

Oh, thank God. I didn't have to do the Armageddon call. Ani had done it all by herself.

"Well, we can't do that now," her mom said, reminding me of a parent talking to a school-aged child. "Come get dressed, and maybe then..."

"No, Mom," Ani said.

A hush came over the room. The curling irons paused. The hair spray stopped spraying.

"Now," Ani said, very much in charge. "I need to speak to Tyler right now." She got up, ready to hunt him down herself in her little satin pj's and fuzzy white slippers.

I held her back. "I'll get him." Then I lifted my skirt and ran out the door and into the entrance to the grassy knoll, where the perfect rows of chairs were now beginning to fill with people. The groomsmen were lined up before an arbor covered with fragrant roses. Caleb saw me running from the cottage and immediately ran to meet me.

Seeing him dressed in a gray tux, looking so handsome, stole my breath and nearly broke my heart. "What is it?" he asked urgently. "Are you okay?"

Are you okay? Oh, my heart. He was concerned about *me.* "Yes, I... Things aren't good. Ani needs to speak with Tyler." I had so much I wanted to say. *I got your calls. I want to talk. I'm so, so sorry.*

But in medicine you triage, and Ani was my only concern now.

"Have Ani walk out by that hedge." He pointed right behind the cottage, out of view of the guests. It would be the perfect place for privacy. "I'll go get Tyler."

He gave a nod and ran off. I did everything I could to not dissolve into tears. Miraculously, he turned around. "We'll talk soon," he said. "Okay?"

I nodded, but I couldn't read him. His tone offered no reassurances. Maybe I didn't deserve any. I swallowed and straightened out and walked back into the cottage, but Ani had already come out, still in her pj's.

"Ani, do you want us to stay nearby?" I asked.

"I want you and Mia here," she said, her voice a little deadpan. But to her credit, she was holding it all together. "Not far away."

Tyler came jogging out to meet her, dressed in a dark suit. "That animal is running rampant through the flowers," he said, flustered. "It's pulled some out of the aisle arrangements and dragged some of the garland down. Honestly, that woman Marin has no control over her son *or* her dog." I got the feeling that he saw the writing on the wall. Maybe by complaining, he was simply trying to distract himself from the truth.

Ani met him halfway, grasping his hands. "Tyler, I can't marry you," she said, her voice soft but steady. "I'm sorry."

To his credit, he looked devastated. And completely unsurprised.

Ani stayed firm. "I don't want to work part-time. Because I *bled* to get to where I am, and *I* want to be the one to decide how much I work. I know we can balance childcare, except you seem to want me to negotiate dinner and dropping off the dry cleaning and chauffeuring the kids while you play tennis and go to the club. And the live-in nanny will absolve you even further of not doing anything with our kids. I can't live like that. I want a hands-on life. I love you, but not enough to marry you."

The wedding party gathered nearby collectively gasped. By now, everyone had come out of the cottage, including Ani's mother. Her dad had walked up beside her mom, and the groomsmen stood awkwardly at Tyler's side. My gaze strayed over to Caleb, who happened to be staring at me. "I'm sorry," I mouthed, but I had no clue if he understood.

"Well, that's a slap in the face." Tyler rubbed his neck. "You're making a scene."

She frowned. "Tyler, this is our life. I should have made a scene a long time ago." She paused and took a breath. "I have a few more things to say. One, how can you yell at that little sweetheart of a dog?" She turned to Tyler's parents. "Look, your *mother* is petting her." Sure enough, the puppy was now quietly hanging out at his mom's feet. "And lastly, if you really loved me, you would've remembered your damn allergy medications."

Ani turned away from Tyler walked over to Mia and me. I'd like to have said that Lilly was with us but I honestly had no idea where she'd gone. Ani stood in front of us and faced her parents too. "Mom and Dad, I'm sorry. Really sorry that I didn't figure this out a long time ago. But I'm not getting married today. If you truly want my happiness, you'll understand that this isn't the right thing for me."

To their credit, they didn't say anything, but they nodded. And then they walked up and stood beside her. Ani's mom wrapped her arm around her shoulders. *Thank goodness.*

Ani bit back a sob. "I'm not sure where I'm going tonight."

"We got you," Mia immediately said.

Ani's mom stepped forward. "You should take your honeymoon."

"No, Mom," she said. "There will be a lot of things to do, a lot of phone calls and presents to return—"

"Mom's right," her dad said. "Catch the plane and get away for a while."

"By myself?"

"Why not?" Her mom's tone was full of concern. "By the time you get back, things will have calmed down."

"I'm so sorry," Ani said.

"No," her mom said firmly, "we're sorry. If you were that miserable but held it in because of us, that's a problem." She stepped forward and hugged her daughter, and Ani started to cry. "But for now, let's get you dressed."

While Mia and I walked back with them to the cottage, Caleb went to talk to the minister and make the announcement that the wedding was not taking place.

Samantha

A half hour later, after we helped Ani gather her things and saw her off as her dad drove her away—maybe to the airport, maybe not—I ran out to the lovely grassy hillside full of empty, perfectly placed chairs and sat down in the last row. *I'm here*, I texted. *Please come.*

But no one came. Only a handful of guys who began stacking chairs on dollies, starting at the front. The wedding that wasn't was now being disassembled.

The exhaustion and stress made my eyes close, listening to the soft clatter of the chairs being folded and loaded, and I nearly fell asleep.

"Hey," someone said, my eyes flying open. Caleb? No. I blinked awake to see Quinn standing in front of me, shuffling his feet. "Mind if I sit a minute?"

He took a seat next to me. Cleared his throat. Tapped his fingers together. Then he spoke. "I owe you an apology."

I almost said *Oh, no, forget it, don't worry about it, whatever.* But instead, I just listened.

"My breakup has made me insane."

"I get that." Totally. "Breakups can do that."

"And this wedding has compounded my PTSD." He laughed a little before he leaned over and tented his fingers together nervously. "I wanted to throw myself into dating again, sort of force myself to get over my ex, but I realized things don't work like that. I'm sorry for not getting the hint. I think you're a really cool person. And I wish you all the best."

"You're a nice person too," I said. "Thanks for saying that. Hang in there."

After he left and I was checking my phone again, I heard a bark and some dog tags jingling. The notorious little Labrador wedding crasher came bounding down the aisle. With, of all things, a rose in her mouth.

The dog bounded right up to my chair, sat, and looked up at me adoringly.

"You're precious," I said, bending down to take the rose. I looked around, but no one was in sight. So I petted the dog—

without hesitation this time. She nuzzled my fingers and jumped up on my dress, licking my face. Okay, so she didn't have the best manners. Yet.

I confess that at that moment, I really needed every bit of the love and affection that she lavished upon me.

"You need a name," I said. "You need a person. I think you're really special. Not every dog can help stop a wedding that never should've happened in the first place."

"I think you're really special too."

I jerked up my head to find Caleb standing there, looking unbelievably handsome in his suit, his cast mostly hidden by some seamstress magic.

I tripped on my dress as I tried to stand up. Which got the hem grassy, but it didn't really matter, did it? As I straightened out, I was close enough to see that his hair was a little out of place, and that he had gray circles under his eyes. We could all use a few more hours of sleep. "You don't love Lilly," I blurted.

"I do not."

Tears rose to my eyes. I felt relief, but really—I'd known that all along. "Did you take a job in Oak Bluff?"

"I'm still waiting to hear back. Why?"

"Lilly told me you did."

"I think we both realize now that the truth for Lilly is what she wants it to be." He moved his crutches to sit, and I sat down beside him. "Why did you give her a free pass to tell me she loved me?"

"At first, I thought I did it because I wanted you to have the free will to choose. But now I think I did it because part of me didn't believe you could really love me—my problem."

"Samantha, what's not to love about you?" He took my hands. Held them so tightly that I teared up with relief. "You're the whole package. Everything that I ever could want in a partner. Beside you, Lilly is just... Lilly was my temps."

"Your...what?"

He shot me a handsome grin. "My permit. Now I have my driver's license."

That was so cornball. But they were words I didn't know I'd been waiting my whole life to hear. And I couldn't stop smiling.

"I'm sorry that I was so quick to believe that you'd run away," he said. "My problem. I kept thinking something wasn't right, but I had no idea Lilly would do something like that. I'm sorry she put you in that position."

"I didn't know what to do. But I was afraid to make the choice for you."

"My mom helped me see that Lilly put you in an impossible position—and that you were giving me a full, free choice." He looked deeply into my eyes. "But Sam, I already had it figured out long before that. I love you."

"I love you too." And just like that, the awful weight on my heart lifted. Caleb looked at me with love in his eyes and gently cradled my face, stroking my cheek with his thumb. "It's been you ever since you stomped up to me with your pink clogs that day in the OR and called me a handsome meathead ortho guy. Handsome being the key, of course. That made me fall in love with you right then and there."

I looked into those beautiful, familiar pale green eyes and smiled. "I think I fell in love with you when you offered me a ride to the farm even though you couldn't stand me."

He gave a little shrug. "There's a fine line between love and hate."

I was crying, and the dog was too, so I picked her up and put her in my lap. "She's special. And I've got the perfect name for her."

"Uh-oh," Caleb said, rubbing her head. "You know what that means. If you name her, she's yours."

"What do you think of Dora?"

He lifted a brow in inquisition. "Like the Explorer?"

"No. Like *Adorable*." I scratched behind her ears. "Which she is. In spades."

"I do believe you've fallen in love, Dr. Gas."

I nodded. "A double fall. Except I'm not so sure about the guy —he fed me some line about looking at stars or something, and turns out he had a blow-up mattress in his truck bed."

Caleb chuckled. "It worked though, didn't it? That plus my get-lucky sweatshirt. You might be a magical matchmaker, but I've got a few tricks up my sleeve too."

"No more magic. No more tricks. No more matchmaking," I said.

"No more denying we're a couple." He wiggled his toes. "With a giant heart on my foot, guess I definitely can't do that."

I giggled. "I love you, Caleb."

"Samantha, I love you."

Then he kissed me, long and sweet and wonderful. The first of a lifetime of kisses. That lifetime starting right now.

And wouldn't you know, the pup wedged herself between us, her propeller of a tail rotating a mile a minute.

I petted her, and she nudged my hand with her wet little nose.

"I thought you didn't like dogs," Caleb said, scratching her behind the ears.

"Well, I didn't like you much either at first, and look what happened."

"Magic happens," he said. And then we kissed again.

Epilogue

Caleb

"Look!" Sam said, pointing to the baseball field in front of us. "Joseph grew." It was a sweltering Saturday in August, the sun casting golden rays across the slightly burnt-out grass just as it should on a hot summer evening, the bleachers around us were filled with the sounds of happy parents and grandparents and kids. The Little League team on the field was dressed in blue and bright, clean white that was undoubtedly going to be grass stained and dusty really soon. Joseph stood behind the fence laughing and clowning around with his teammates, his skinny legs in white pants with blue-and-white baseball socks. Notably not limping.

Just like me. I'd gotten my cast off. *Finally.*

"An inch since winter," his mom Terry called up from the bleacher below us.

Joseph looked up, grinning and waving at us, giving giant thumbs up. We did the same right back.

"He's so excited to have his doctors here today," his mom said. "Thanks for coming."

"Thanks for inviting us," I said. "We wouldn't miss it."

Next to me on the bleachers, Samantha squeezed my hand. She wore white shorts and sunglasses, her hair high up in a ball cap with her ponytail sticking out the back. I touched her lightly on her leg, still in awe that she was mine. "Hey," I said, unable to stop smiling.

"Hey back," she said with a giant smile.

That made my heart expand to bursting—it felt like that a lot lately—making me utter a silent prayer of thanks. I shook my head in disbelief. *Was she really mine?*

"You okay? Anything wrong?" she asked. She knew I'd been excitedly anticipating this day. Now that it was here, I was a little anxious.

"I just want Joseph to smack it out of the ballpark." I made a big arc with my hand.

She shook her head, but she was still smiling. "Would you settle for a little less?"

"No." That made her laugh.

"Remind me not to sign our kids up for Little League. You might be one of those super aggressive parents." She looked me over, noting my tapping foot, my inability to sit still. "He's going to be fine," she said. "You know that, right?"

She looked so beautiful I wanted to kiss her right then and there. In fact, I did, good and quick. In my mind, I was half-tugging her down to the bleachers, kissing her everywhere.

I whispered something in her ear that made her blush.

"Why are you grinning like that?" she asked.

"It's so easy to get you flustered."

"It's so easy to get *you* flustered," she said right back.

True. "Honey, you can get me flustered any time you want." Nothing to argue about there. She was one hundred percent right. "I'm glad we're here for this together."

She squeezed my hand. "Me too."

"I'm a little nervous," I confessed. "Hope he does well." My gaze drifted to the bottom row of bleachers. "Well, I'll be," I said, sort of speechless. "Look who's here." I nodded my head to where Lilly sat, dressed all in white with big designer sunglasses propped up on her head.

"Why on earth is Lilly at a Little League game in suburban Milwaukee?" Sam asked.

Just then, she looked up and waved. So did the guy next to her.

"No," Sam said, her mouth dropping open. "She's dating *Tyler*?"

I shrugged. Guess she'd learned zero. But you know what? Lilly wasn't our concern anymore. I only wished her well.

"Glad Ani's not here," Sam added.

Ani was doing okay. Working a lot of extra shifts lately to keep busy, but we made her get out and try to have some fun. She was tough, and I knew she'd be okay.

I waved back. So did Sam.

"You're pretty amazing," I said.

"Why's that?"

I looked into her warm brown eyes. "You don't hold grudges."

"What for?" she said. "I got you. The rest doesn't matter."

She was right about that—that we had each other. I snuck a kiss and squeezed her hand, and was going in for another kiss when someone said, "Which one's your little patient?"

Wynn grinned and waved, taking the seat beside Sam, who gave her a big squeeze.

"Hey, Docs," Miles said, sitting in front of Wynn, hauling a canvas bag on his shoulder that he set down on the bleachers beside him.

"Hey, Miles," Sam and I both said in unison.

"I was hoping you'd bring Dora," Wynn said. "Who's dog sitting?"

"Mrs. Von Gulag," I said. Turned out she couldn't resist our dog. Who knew she was a dog lover? Even though she'd raised our rent too, according to her dog clause, which she'd promptly made up on the spot. So a win-win for her. At least until we found a less restrictive place, which hopefully would be soon.

"What's in the beach bag?" I asked.

"Wynn's sun block." Miles beamed at Wynn. "Want some?"

She rolled her eyes. "You're so protective."

"I just like taking care of you." He beamed up at her. I knew that look.

She pushed his shoulder, and he fake-doubled over. Wynn laughed and gave him a look. The same one that he'd just given her.

"Can I borrow some?" Sam asked. "My nose is burning." She reached over and took the tube from Miles. She just so happened to have her hand on Wynn's arm. Not so accidentally, I'd bet.

I lifted a brow. "I thought you stopped doing that," I said in a low voice.

She answered with a shrug. I'd bet it was highly positive. It was hard to hate Miles. And he did tend to take care of Wynn, even if she didn't need it. He was surprisingly mature for his age.

"What'd you get?" I whispered after a while.

"Mr. Right-for-Now. I mean, come on. They're in college."

I laughed. What did I know about young love? Anything could happen.

Turns out Wynn was taking care of herself too. She'd passed summer semester calculus. And quit the perfume job. She was all signed up for organic chemistry in the fall. And the MCAT, too, next spring. Guess another Bashar sister was going to join the medical profession.

"Here goes," Joseph's dad, Henry, said, and we all turned with anticipation to the field.

Sam grabbed my hand. I could tell she was holding her breath. She glanced at me and smiled. "No limp so far," she said. "Good job there, Doc."

I nodded. "We'll see how he runs." That was the true test.

Strike one. Then strike two. I found myself leaning forward, gripping the bleacher hard, wanting to mentally help him strike the ball. Suddenly he smacked it good and hard, sending it skittering out into left field, past the first and third basemen, leaving the outfielders to scramble.

I rose to a stand—we all did—Sam, Wynn, Miles, Joseph's parents—and I cupped my hands around my mouth. "Run, Joe, run!"

We all screamed. And cheered. And kept cheering because Joseph kept running. With perfect strides indistinguishable from any of the other boys.

That to me was a success right there.

But the kid overachieved—he ran through all the bases and even dove into home base, rifling up the dust.

The crowd went wild. His mom shed tears. So did I. Sam hugged me into oblivion.

"He did it," she said, beaming.

"He sure did." I was so proud.

"You did it too. Your surgery gave him a normal life."

I shrugged, but I was overwhelmed. Medicine really could work miracles. And when it did, there was no better feeling. "It was just a bunch of power tools."

"Look, Dr. Caleb," Joseph yelled from the field, now dusty and out of breath. "I got a home run! I got a home run!"

"You sure did, buddy," I yelled right back.

As I headed out with Sam after the game, I said, "Maybe I'll coach Little League one day. In Oak Bluff. What do you think?"

"I like that idea," she said. "I like it a lot."

I hadn't asked her to marry me yet. But we both had one foot in Oak Bluff, with the potential for both feet someday. We were both working one day a week out there—Fridays—Sam in the new surgery center run by Children's, and me with Dr. Blumenthal's group. For now, that was a good plan. And we often stayed over on Friday nights with my folks, so win-win.

"Maybe we can take the truck out later and watch the sunset. What do you think?"

She squinted at me as the late-afternoon sun got in our eyes. "Is that a pickup line?"

"I've got a better one too." I held her hand as we walked.

"What is it?"

"That home run was amazing. But I hit a home run too. By finding you."

We stopped on the field. She looked at me, her pretty brown eyes full of light and love. "Aw. You are such a romantic. I love your pickup lines. But I love one thing more."

"What's that?"

"You."

She kissed me as the sun was setting past the backstop on this fine summer evening. Maybe tonight we'd hang out and watch the stars. Or scour the internet for new apartments. Or just hang out and read or watch TV. The possibilities were endless, because our future together was just beginning.

∼

Samantha
Four months later

"Wanna dance?" Caleb smiled at me as he tossed his napkin onto the elegant white-tablecloth-covered table.

"Of course." It was New Year's Eve—our last one in Milwaukee. This spring, I was going to start working full time in Oak Bluff, after having gotten Wynn's blessing, of course. After all, she loved it there too—Beth and Steven had essentially adopted both of us.

Besides, Caleb and I were going to start house hunting soon, and I was already planning on finding one with a cute bedroom just for Wynn. Just so that she knew beyond a doubt—and I felt certain that she did—that she would always be welcome, no matter where she was or how old or in what stage of life.

Caleb led me onto the dance floor, which was crowded with couples of all ages dressed up in their New Year's Eve finery.

As we danced a couples' dance, he checked his watch, seeming a little nervous. It was sweet to bring me here, to this fancy place that cost a fortune, so that he could redeem himself at midnight, he'd said. I would've been happy with a pizza and a movie, but he'd insisted. I knew he wanted to make certain that we didn't miss that midnight kiss.

I think it was on his bucket list for us to have a fun New Year's Eve.

He'd been anxious all through dinner, repeatedly checking his watch, tapping his fingers on the table, tugging on his tie. Granted, he didn't often wear a tie, so putting one on was a big deal.

It had crossed my mind that he might have something bigger in mind than a kiss at midnight, but that started making me *really* nervous, and I didn't want to lose the enjoyment of this moment. So I tried not to think of it, even as my heart started a heavy, rapid thud in my chest.

Then "It Had to Be You" started playing. The Harry Connick Jr. version, just like in *When Harry Met Sally*.

"Let's dance," he said, his voice full of anticipation.

"It's nearly midnight," I noted. When we were finally on the dance floor, I said, "I think Harry and Sally danced to this song."

"They didn't dance. They fought to this song. And then the countdown was over, so they missed the midnight kiss too."

"Well, we're definitely not going to." I smiled, half because I couldn't have been happier and half because I wanted to reassure him of that. I decided that even if he was planning to ask me The Question, he probably wouldn't do it during the dance at midnight.

Would he?

For a little while, we danced cheek to cheek. My heart was overwhelmed with joy. I didn't care about fancy dinners, and I had no stress about missing a midnight kiss. After all, I could have kisses from him whenever I wanted them. I had Caleb. And he was all I wanted.

He pulled back a little to look at me. He looked so broad-shouldered, so intensely handsome, that I would've gladly skipped midnight and gone home with him right then. "Do you remember that once you asked me how a person knows someone's the right person?"

Uh oh. "I think at the time I was asking how you knew *Lilly* was the One."

Things were starting to add up in my mind. The fancy evening out, his insistence that we dance right then and there, and now this sketchy attempt at reminding me of relationships. Something big felt about to happen.

As I pressed my cheek against his, he said, "Okay, forget the Lilly part, but I remember how I answered. I said that your true love is someone who gets you. Who has your back no matter what. Who you miss when you're not with them, because you find yourself wanting to tell them all the little things that happen throughout your day. Who's kind and smart and fun."

It had taken zero time for tears to gather. When I drew back, I found that Caleb was looking directly into my eyes. His expression was hopeful. Expectant. And full of love. "That about says it all," I said, my voice cracking.

"Not all," he said.

The music stopped. "Ten, nine," began a loud chanting chorus around us.

"That's you, Samantha. You're the One."

My vision blurred as the tears leaked down my cheeks. The noise around us muted, and suddenly Caleb was slipping out of my hands.

"Six, five..."

He dropped to one knee, right there on the crowded dance

floor with everyone counting down all around us. "I'll have your back in life no matter what. Every day, I want to tell you all the things that amuse me, or worry me, or interest me. I want you to be the last person I talk to every night. Forever. Will you marry me?"

"Yes." Easiest answer *evah*.

"Happy New Year!" crescendoed loudly all around us. The band began playing "Auld Lang Syne."

Someone handed us something. Glasses of champagne. The someone turned out to be Caleb's dad. He gave us a little wave. I looked around to find everyone surrounding us—Beth, Mia and Brax, Ani, Gabe and Jason, and Wynn and Miles.

I locked gazes with Mia—a grateful gaze meaning *thank you*—after all, she was the one who'd run and told Beth everything that awful night when Ani was so upset. Everyone needs a friend like that, who is a sister in every way except for the shared genes.

I clinked glasses with Caleb and went to take a sip.

"Wait," he said, his expression a little panicked.

"What is it?"

"Better look down first."

At the bottom of the flute there was an object. Shiny and twinkling. Some kind of giant honker of a ring that I couldn't even see very well because of the bubbles, but I knew it was gorgeous.

"Oh my gosh."

The rest was a blur. Our families cheered and clapped. We kissed until I was weak-kneed and dizzy and felt as if I was made of champagne bubbles as all the noise and cheering continued happily all around us.

Wynn came up behind me and roped an arm around me and Caleb. She closed her eyes for a few seconds. "Wynn," I said in a warning voice.

"You people are smokin', you know that?" She took her hands off of us and shook them out, as if her hands were hot to the touch.

"I thought we agreed not to do that anymore." I still had PTSD from doing it with Lilly, so it was fine with me that Wynn take over the matchmaking. But once in a while, I confess, I did sneak in a quick one, just in emergency cases where I just *had* to know.

I mean, Oma would have wanted me too, right? When it was absolutely necessary. Or thereabouts.

"I can't help it," Wynn said. "I can feel the energy. Congrats, new brother." She kissed Caleb on the cheek. "Oma would love Caleb," she whispered to me, and then planted a kiss on my cheek too. "Love you."

"Love you too. So much." My heart was full. Somehow a person who didn't believe in love had gotten myself a family *and* a much better relationship with my sister *and* someone to love. Oh, and not to mention an adorable little dog.

Our family and friends left us to dance one alone. Caleb kissed me, then put his cheek once again next to mine. I felt his warmth, his big arms surrounding me. "I still believe that unicorns poop rainbows."

I pulled back fast. "What?"

"Magic. I believe that love is magic. Maybe we create it between us, but it's definitely there. I think you and Wynn pick up on that energy."

"You're a hopeless romantic."

"Probably always will be."

"That's okay. As long as you keep loving me." And then I kissed him again, longer and less PG since our whole family wasn't watching this time. To ring in the new year and our new life.

Acknowledgments

This story came about because I'm three for three—all of my kids will have gotten married a year apart from each other, with the last wedding coming up right around the corner in 2026. So I have weddings on the brain! And I am endlessly fascinated by the question, what makes someone the right match for another person? I hope you enjoyed this story about a fiercely independent woman who had no reason to believe in love and a hopelessly romantic man who might have just changed her mind.

I have never met more selfless people than those who work in children's hospitals. I honor you with this series, and I thank you from the bottom of my heart.

Thanks so much to my readers for buying my books, leaving reviews, and writing to me about them. I really appreciate your support!

xo
Miranda

About the Author

I am a former pediatrician and an Amazon Top-Five best-selling author who writes about the important relationships in women's lives. My heartwarming and humorous romances have won numerous accolades and have been praised by *Entertainment Weekly* for the way they "deal with so much of what makes life hard... without ever losing the warmth and heart that characterize her writing." I *always* believe that we can handle whatever life throws at us just a little bit better with a laugh—it's the best medicine, after all!

A proud native of Northeast Ohio, I live in a neighborhood of old homes that serves as inspiration for my books. I'm very proud of my three now-adult children. When I'm not writing or enjoying books, I can be found biking along the old Ohio and Erie Canal Towpath trails in the beautiful Ohio Metro Parks.

I love to hear from readers! (See next page for where to find me.)

Learn more at:

MirandaLiasson.com

Facebook.com/MirandaLiassonAuthor
    (my Author Page where I hang out daily 🤍)

Instagram @mirandaliasson

X @MirandaLiasson

🤍Find all my books and sign up for my newsletter on my website.

🤍Coming next: *Take Me Home to You* (Ani's Story).